# THE DEBUTANTE

Kathleen Tessaro is the author of three previous works of fiction, *The Flirt*, *Innocence*, and her debut novel, *Elegance*, which became a bestseller in both hardback and paperback. She lives in Pittsburgh with her son.

Praise for *The Debutante*:

'The latest from the author of bestseller Elegance. New Yorker Cate immerses herself in the mystery of the Mitford-esque 1920's London debutante.'

*Red Magazine*

'A shoebox filled with mementos sets artist Cate on a hunt for the truth behind the disappearance of a dazzling 1920's 'it' girl in Kathleen Tessaro's The Debutante.'

*Good Housekeeping*

'Tessaro gets her story-weaving wand out with a gloriously rich story of past and present love'

*InStyle*

## Also by Kathleen Tessaro

*Elegance*
*Innocence*
*The Flirt*

# KATHLEEN TESSARO

# *The Debutante*

Harper  **Weekend**

Harper Weekend

*The Debutante*
Copyright © 2010 by Kathleen Tessaro.
All rights reserved.

Published by Harper Weekend, an imprint of HarperCollins Publishers Ltd.

First published in Canada by HarperCollins Publishers Ltd in an original
trade paperback edition: 2010
This Harper Weekend trade paperback edition: 2011

HarperCollins books may be purchased for educational, business, or sales
promotional use through our Special Markets Department.

HarperCollins Publishers Ltd
2 Bloor Street East, 20th Floor
Toronto, Ontario, Canada
M4W 1A8

*www.harpercollins.ca*

Library and Archives Canada Cataloguing in Publication

Tessaro, Kathleen, 1965–
The debutante / Kathleen Tessaro.

ISBN 978-1-55468-589-9

I. Title.
PS3620.E87D42 2011    813'.6    C2011-902319-9

Printed and bound in the United States
RRD 9 8 7 6 5 4 3 2 1

For Annabel

# Acknowledgements

I'm enormously grateful for the support and guidance of both Lynne Drew and Claire Bord at Harper Collins. They have worked closely with me on this novel from its inception and have played a crucial role in shaping its tone and content. I'm extremely lucky to work with such talented editors who are still willing to invest in the long term vision of a novel (and an author) very much in progress. Equally, both Carrie Feron of William Morrow and Jonny Geller of Curtis Brown deserve huge thanks for their faith, enthusiasm and invaluable notes. A special mention goes to Victoria Hughes-Williams whose patience, insight and quick intervention has saved my skin on more than one occasion. I also wish to thank Gillian Greenwood, Debra Susman, Kate Morris and Jill Robinson for providing extra doses of courage and infallible sounding boards.

I would be remiss if I didn't mention the tremendous love and kindness of my parents, Anne and Edward Tessaro, who have never failed to provide both practical and emotional support, as needed.

And of course to Annabel Giles, who showed me, through example, the way forward and whose generosity of spirit has never failed to inspire me.

There is a dangerous silence in that hour
A stillness, which leaves room for the full soul
To open all itself, without the power
Of calling wholly back its self-control:
The silver light which, hallowing tree and tower,
Sheds beauty and deep softness o'er the whole,
Breathes also to the heart, and o'er it throws
A loving languor, which is not repose.

LORD BYRON, *Don Juan*

# Part One

In the heart of the City of London, tucked into one of the winding streets behind Gray's Inn Square and Holborn Station, there's a narrow passage known as Jockey's Fields. It's a meandering, uneven thread of a street that's been there, largely unchanged, since the Great Fire. Regency carriages gave way to Victorian hackney cabs and now courier bikes speed down its sloping, cobbled way, diving between pedestrians.

It was early May; unseasonably hot – only nine in the morning and already seventy-six degrees. A cloudless blue sky set off the white dome of St Paul's Cathedral in the distance. The pavement swelled with armies of workers, streaming from the nearby Tube station; girls in sorbet-coloured summer dresses, men in shirtsleeves, jackets over their arms, carrying strong coffee and newspapers, the rhythm of their heels a constant tattoo on the pavement.

Number 13 Jockey's Fields was a lopsided, double-fronted Georgian building, painted black many years previously, and in need of a fresh coat, sandwiched between a betting office and a law practice. The door of Deveraux and Diplock, Valuers and Auctioneers of Quality, was propped open by a Chinese ebony figure of a small pug dog, most likely eighteenth century but in very bad repair, in the hopes of encouraging a gust of fresh morning air into the premises. Golden shafts of sunlight filtered in through the leaded glass windows, dust floating, suspended in its beams, settling in thick layers on the once illustrious, now slightly shabby interior of one of London's lesser known auction houses. The oriental carpet, a fine specimen of the silk hand-knotted variety of Northern Pakistan during the last century, was threadbare. The delft china planters which graced the mantelpiece, brimming with richly scented white hyacinth, were just that bit too chipped to be sold at any real profit; and the seats of the 1930s leather club chairs by the fireplace sagged almost to the floor, their springs poking through the horsehair backing. Reproduction Canalettos hung next to the better watercolour dabblings of long-dead country-house hostesses; studies of landscapes, flowers and fond attempts at children's portraits. For Deveraux and Diplock was the natural choice of those once aristocratic families whose fortunes had lost pace with their breeding and who wished to have their heirlooms sold quickly and discreetly, rather than in the very public catalogues of Sotheby's and Christie's. They were known by word of mouth and reputation, having traded with the same European and American antique dealers for decades. Theirs was a dying art for a dying class; a kind of undertakers for antiquities, presided over by Rachel Deveraux, whose late husband Paul had inherited the business when they were first married thirty-six years ago.

Rachel, smoking a cigarette in a long, mother-of-pearl holder which she'd acquired clearing the estate of an impoverished 1920s film star, sat contemplating the mountain of paperwork on her huge, roll-top desk. At sixty-seven, she was still striking, with large brown eyes and a knowing, disarming smile. Her style was unorthodox; flowing layers of modern, asymmetrical Japanese-inspired tailoring. And she had a weakness for red shoes that had become a personal trademark over the years – today's pair were vintage Ferragamo pumps circa 1989. Pushing her thick silver hair away from her face, she looked up at the tall, well-dressed man prowling the floor in front of her.

'It will be fun, Jack.' She exhaled; a long, thin stream of smoke rising like a spectre, floating round her head. 'Think of her as a companion, someone to talk to.'

'I don't need help. I'm perfectly capable of doing it on my own.'

Jack Coates gave the impression of youth even though he was nearing his mid-forties. Slender, with elegant aquiline features, thick lashes framing indigo eyes, he moved with an animal grace. His dark hair was closely cropped, his linen suit well-tailored and pressed; yet underneath his polished exterior a raw, unpredictable energy flowed. He was a man straining at his own definition of himself. Frowning, he stopped, fingers drumming the top of the filing cabinet.

'I prefer to do it alone. There's nothing more tedious than talking to strangers.'

'It's a three-hour drive.' Rachel leaned back, watching him. 'She'll hardly be a stranger by the time you arrive.'

'I'd rather go on my own,' he said, again.

'That's the trouble with you; you rather do everything on your own. It's not good for you. Besides –' she flicked a bit of ash into an empty teacup – 'she's very pretty.'

He looked up.

She arched an eyebrow, the hint of a smile on her lips.

'What difference does that make?' Jamming his hands into pockets, he turned away. 'Perhaps I should point out that this isn't some small turn-of-the-century Russian village and you're not an ageing Jewish matchmaker eking a living out by tossing complete strangers together and adding a ring. We're in London, Rachel. The millennium dawns. And I'm perfectly capable of doing the job I've been doing for the past four years on my own – without the assistance of young nieces of yours, fresh from New York, trailing round after me.'

She tried a different tack.

'She's an artist. She'll be very helpful. She has an excellent eye.'

He snorted.

'She's had a difficult time of it lately.'

'Which what, roughly translates to "she's broken up with her boyfriend"? Like I said, I don't need a companion. And especially not some moody art student who'll spend the entire time on the phone, arguing with her lover.'

Stubbing out her cigarette, Rachel took out her reading glasses. 'I've already told her she can go.'

He swung round. 'Rachel!'

'It's a large house, Jack. Even with two of you, it will take you days to value and catalogue the whole thing. And whether you deign to acknowledge it or not, you need help. You don't have to talk to her at length or share the contents of your innermost heart. But if you can manage to be civil, you might just notice that it's actually nicer not doing everything on your own.'

He paced like a caged animal. 'I can't believe you've done this!'

'Done what?' She looked at him hard over the top of her glasses. 'Hired an assistant? I am your employer. Besides, she's smart. She studied at the Courtauld, Chelsea, Camberwell –'

'How many art colleges does a person need?'

'Well,' she grinned slyly, 'she was very good at getting *into* them.'

'This isn't helping.'

She laughed. 'It will be an adventure!'

'I don't want an adventure.'

'She's different now.'

'I work alone.'

'Well –' she rifled through the stacks of invoices and receipts, searching for something – 'now you have an assistant to help you.'

'This is nepotism, pure and simple!'

She looked up. 'Nothing about Katie is pure or simple. The sooner you understand that, the easier it will be.'

'What did she do in New York anyway?'

'I'm not sure.'

'I thought you two were close.'

'Her father had just died. He was young; an alcoholic. She wanted a new start and we had some connections there; Paul knew one or two dealers who might be willing to help her find her feet. Tim Bolles, Derek Constantine –'

'Constantine?' Jack stopped. 'I thought he only catered for the super-rich.'

'Yes, well. He took a shine to her.'

'I'll bet he did!'

She gave him a look. 'I don't believe he's that way inclined.'

'I'm sure he inclines himself to whoever's got the cash, which doesn't exactly add to his charms.'

'New York is not a city a young woman can just waltz into. You need contacts.' Opening the top drawer, she sifted through its contents. 'I'm just guessing, but I take it you don't like him.'

'My father had dealings with him. Years ago. So –' he changed the subject – 'she's staying with you, is she?'

'For the time being. Her mother lives in Spain.' She sighed; her face tensed. 'She's so different. So entirely, completely different. I'd heard nothing for months . . . not even a phone call . . . and then out of blue, there she was.'

Suddenly a courier bike, buzzing like a giant wasp, tore past the doorway at breakneck speed.

'Good God!' Jack turned, tracking it as it narrowly avoided a couple of girls, coming out of a coffee shop. 'They're a menace! One of these days someone's going to get hurt!'

'Jack.' Rachel pressed her hand over his and gave him her most winning smile. 'Do this for me, please? I think it will be good for her; a trip to the country, time with some-one closer to her own age.'

'Ha!' He squeezed her fingers lightly before moving his hand away. 'I'm not a babysitter, Rachel. Where is this house anyway?'

'On the coast in Devon. Endsleigh. Have you ever heard of it?'

He shook his head. 'Look, I'm not . . . you know, good with people.'

'Maybe. But you're a good man.'

'I'm an awkward man,' he corrected, wandering over to the fireplace.

'You don't need to worry. Katie won't be a problem, I promise. You might even enjoy it.' She caught his eye in the mirror hanging above the mantelpiece. Her voice soft-ened. 'You need to make an effort now.'

'Yeah, that's what they tell me.'

Rachel was quiet. A rare breeze rustled the papers in front of her.

'Well. There we go,' Jack concluded. He picked up his

briefcase from where he'd left it, on the seat of one of the sagging leather chairs, and headed for the door. 'I've got work to do.'

'Jack . . .'

'Tell your niece we leave at eight thirty tomorrow.' He turned. 'And I'm not wasting the whole morning waiting for her, so she'd better be ready. Oh –' he paused on the threshold – 'and we'll be listening to *Le Nozze di Figaro* on the way down, so no conversation necessary.'

She laughed. 'And if she doesn't like opera?'

'She doesn't need to come!' He waved, striding out, quickly lost in the stream of people on Jockey's Fields.

Rachel pulled off her glasses, rubbed her eyes. They hurt today; not enough sleep.

Digging through her handbag, she pulled out her cigarettes.

This job wasn't good for him. He needed to be somewhere he could be around people, back in the thick of life, not picking through the belongings of the dead. Perhaps she ought to hire a secretary. Some cheerful young woman to bring him out of himself. A redhead, perhaps?

Catching herself, she smiled. He was right; she wasn't a Jewish matchmaker.

Swivelling round in her chair, she flicked through the piles of paper, looking again for the phone number. Her late husband always claimed her very distinctive filing system would fail her one day. Today was not the day though; she needed more than anything to talk to her sister Anna. Especially now that Katie was back. The role of matriarch was Anna's forte. Rachel did Bohemia, Anna domesticity. That was the way it had always been. At least that was the way it had been until Anna's recent decampment to a small town outside Malaga left Rachel feeling unexpectedly abandoned and strangely affronted. Her shock was purely selfish, she knew that. Her sister had dared to change the well-worn script of their roles without consulting her, tossing off her old life as if it were nothing more than a garment, grown shapeless and ill-fitting from too much use.

'I'm tired of London,' Anna had declared, as Rachel helped her pack up the flat she'd owned in Highgate for twenty-two years. 'I want to start again, somewhere fresh, where nobody knows me.'

She'd had a child's optimism that day; a purpose and energy Rachel hadn't seen in her for years. And secretly she'd envied her courage and the audacity of her sureness. Anna's life hadn't been easy. The childhood sweetheart she'd married failed her, turning into a desperate, unreliable alcoholic. She'd struggled to raise Katie on her own, only to endure her silences and rebellion, followed by her sudden desertion to America. It was no wonder Anna decided to escape. And she deserved a new life in a country bathed in sun and warm Latin temperament. Still, when she'd rung last week, Rachel had been short with her; fractious. She'd scribbled her number down on some scrap, promising herself she'd transfer it to her address book later. Now it was later and she couldn't find the damn thing.

Hold on. What was this?

She tugged at the corner of something jutting out beneath a pile of overdue VAT forms.

It was a postcard.

At first glance it appeared to be of Ingres's famous painting *Odalisque*. But on closer examination the blue eyes of the reclining courtesan were painted pale green, the same clear celadon as Katie's. One half of her face was bathed in shadow, the other in light. Her unnerving gaze managed nevertheless to be elusive; her very directness a mask behind which she remained hidden. Turning it over, there was a message scrawled across the back in Katie's near-hieroglyphic hand.

'Portrait of the artist'
xx K

Across the bottom it read, '*The Real Fake: Original Reproductions by Cate Albion*'.

Cate. She'd changed everything she could about herself – her name, her hair colour, even her work. Reproductions of old masters were a far cry from the huge triptychs she produced in art school; full of rage and surprising power. But then again, part of her talent was always her ability to reinvent herself, ransacking wide-ranging styles and iconography with a ruthlessness and speed that was frightening.

Nothing was pure and simple about Katie. Even her career was layered with illusion and double entendre.

It wasn't what she was looking for, yet Rachel slipped it thoughtfully into the large leather handbag at her feet.

The real fake.

As a child Katie was shy, introverted; looked like she was made of glass. But if there was something broken, something missing, she was invariably behind it. Or, later on, if there was a party when someone's parents were out of town, it would turn out to have been Katie's idea. The girl caught not only smoking behind the bicycle sheds at school, but selling the cigarettes too? Katie. There was fire, a certain streak of will that burned slowly, deeply, beneath the surface; flaring when challenged. It was surprising, perverse; often funny and ironic.

Rachel thought again of the lost young woman, wandering around her flat in Marylebone. So quiet, so unsure.

When she'd asked Katie what had brought her back to London, she'd simply shrugged her shoulders. 'I need a break. Some perspective.' Then she'd turned to Rachel, suddenly wide-eyed, tense. 'You don't mind, do you?'

'No, no of course not.' Rachel had assured her. 'You must stay as long as you like.'

She'd dropped the subject after that. But the expression on Katie's face haunted her.

Lighting another cigarette, Rachel cradled her chin in her hand, taking a deep drag.

It wasn't like Katie to be frightened.

Secretive, yes.

But never afraid.

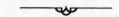

Jack drove up in front of number 1a Upper Wimpole Street the next morning in his pride and joy, an old Triumph, circa 1963. There on the doorstep was a young woman, slight, slender; hair in a sleek bob, white blonde in the early-morning sun. Her face was oval, with green eyes; her skin a light golden tan. She was wearing a pale linen dress, sandals and a cream cashmere cardigan. In one hand she had an overnight case and in the other a vintage Hermès Kelly bag in bright orange. Silver bangles dangled from her delicate wrists, a simple, slightly pink strand of pearls round her neck.

She was beautiful.

It was disturbing how attractive she was.

This was not the struggling artist he was expecting. This was a socialite; a starlet; a creature of style, grace and poise. Walking down the steps, she moved with a slow undercurrent of sexual possibility. When she slid into the seat next to him, Jack was aware of the soft scent of fresh-cut grass, mint and a hint of tuberose; a heady mix full of sharp edges and refined luxury. It had been a long time since an attractive woman had sat next to him in his car. It was an unsettling, sensuous feeling.

Turning, she extended her hand. 'I'm Cate.'

Her palm slipped into his; cool and smooth. He found himself not shaking it, but instead holding it, almost reverently, in his own. She smiled, lips parting slowly across a row of even white teeth, green eyes fixed on his. And before he knew it, he was smiling back, that slightly lopsided grin of his that creased his eyes and wrinkled his nose, at this golden creature whose hand fitted so nicely into the hollow of his own; who adorned so perfectly the front seat of his vintage convertible.

'You don't want to do this and neither do I.' Her voice was low, intimate. 'We needn't make conversation.'

And with that, she withdrew her hand, knotting a silk scarf round her head; slipping on a pair of tortoiseshell sunglasses.

And she was gone, removed from him already.

He blinked. 'Do you like . . . is opera all right? *Le Nozze di Figaro*?'

She nodded.

He pressed the play button, started the engine and pulled out into traffic. He'd been dreading the social strain of today so much that sleep was an impossibility. Earlier, while packing his bag, he'd cursed Rachel.

Now, as he drove into the wide avenue of Portland Place, the cool green of Regent's Park spread before them, he was baffled, bemused. He'd anticipated a nervous self-absorbed girl; someone whose inane questions would have to be fended off. It was his intention to create an unspoken boundary between them with the briskness of his tone and the curtness of his replies. But now his mind raced, trying to devise some clever way of hearing the sound of her voice again.

Of course, he could always ask a simple question. But there was something delicious about sitting next to her in silence. Their intimacy was, after all, inevitable; hours, even days, stretched before them. He sensed that she knew this. And it intrigued him.

Keenly conscious of every movement of his body next to hers, he downshifted, his hand almost brushing against her knee. The furious zeal of the overture of *Le Nozze di Figaro* filled the air around them with exquisite, frenetic intensity. They sped round the arc of the Outer Circle of the park. The engine roared as he accelerated, ducking around a long line of traffic in an uncharacteristically daredevil move.

And suddenly she was laughing, head back, clutching her seat; an unexpectedly low, earthy chuckle.

She's a woman who likes speed, he thought, childishly delighted with the success of his manoeuvre. And before he knew it, he was overtaking another three cars, zipping through a yellow light on the Marylebone Road and cutting off a lorry as they merged onto the motorway.

Horns blared behind them as they raced out of London.

And, for the first time in a long while, all was right with the world. It was a beautiful, sun-drenched morning – the entire summer spread out before them. He felt handsome, masculine and young.

And he was laughing too.

High on a cliff where the rolling countryside, dotted with cows and lambs, met the expanse of sea, Endsleigh stood alone. Part of an extensive farm, it commanded a view over the bay beneath and the surrounding hills that was breathtaking. Built in pale grey stone by a young, ambitious Robert Adam, it rose like a miniature Roman temple; its classical proportions blending harmoniously into the rich green fields that surrounded it, mirroring the Arcadian perfection of the landscape with its Palladian dome and restrained, slender columns. High stone walls extended for acres on either side of the house, protecting both the formal Italian rose gardens and the vegetable patches from the stormy winter winds, while the arched gravel drive and the central fountain, long out of use, lent the house an air of refined, easy symmetry.

It was impressive yet at the same time unruly, showing signs of recent neglect. The front lawns were overgrown; the fountain sprouted dry tufts of field grass, high enough almost to blot out the central figure of Artemis with her bow and arrow, balanced gracefully on one toe, mid-chase. There was no one to care if the guttering sagged or the roses grew wild. It was a house without a guardian;

its beautiful exterior yielding, slowly, to the inevitable anarchy of nature and time.

Just before the drive, a discreet sign pointed the way to a campsite on the grounds, nearly a mile down the hill, closer to the shore and out of sight of the occupants in the main house. Below, the bay curved gently like an embracing arm, and beyond, the ocean melted into the sky, a pale grey strip blending into a vast canopy of blue. It was cloudless, bright. Cool gusts tempered the heat of the midday sun.

Jack pulled up, wheels crunching on the gravel of the drive, and turned off the engine.

They sat a moment, taking in the house, its position; the view of the countryside and the sea beyond. Neither of them wanted to move. Silence, thick and heavy, pressed in around them, tangible, like the heat. It was disorientating. The internal compass of every city dweller – the constant noise of distant lives humming away in the background – was missing.

'It's much bigger than I thought it would be,' Cate said at last.

It was an odd observation. The beauty of the place was obvious, overwhelming. Could it be that she was calculating how long they would be alone here?

'Yes. I suppose it is.'

Swinging the car door open, she climbed out. After so much time driving, the ground felt unsteady beneath her feet.

Jack followed and together they walked past the line of rose bushes, full-blown and fragrant, alive with the buzzing of insects, to the front door.

He pressed the bell. After a moment, footsteps drew closer.

A tall, thin man in a dark suit opened the heavy oak door. He was in his late fifties, with a long, sallow face and thinning, grey hair. He had large, mournful eyes, heavily ringed with dark circles.

'You must be Mr Coates, from Deveraux and Diplock,' he surmised, unsmiling.

'Yes.'

'Welcome.' He shook Jack's hand.

'And this is Miss Albion, my . . . assistant,' Jack added.

'John Syms.' The man introduced himself, inclining his head slightly in Cate's direction, as if he'd only budgeted for one handshake and wasn't going to be duped into another. 'From the firm of Smith, Boothroy and Earl. We're handling the liquidation of assets on behalf of the family.' He stepped back, and they crossed the threshold into the entrance hall. 'Welcome to Endsleigh.'

The hall was sparse and formal with black-and-white marble tiles and two enormous mahogany cabinets with fine inlay, both filled with collections of china. Over the fireplace hung a large, unremarkable oil painting of the house and grounds. Four great doors led off the hall into different quarters.

'How was your journey?' Mr Syms asked crisply.

'Fine, thank you.' Cate turned, examining the delicate Dresden china figurines arranged together in one of the cabinets. Their heads were leaning coyly towards one another, all translucent porcelain faces and pouting pink rosebud mouths, poised in picturesque tableaux of seduction and assignation.

'Yes, traffic wasn't too bad,' Jack said, immediately wishing he'd thought of something less banal.

Mr Syms was a man of few words and even fewer social graces. 'Splendid.' Pleasantries dispensed with, he opened one of the doors. 'Allow me to show you around.'

They followed him into the main hall with its sweeping galleried staircase, lined with family portraits and landscapes. It was a collection of country-house clichés – a pair of stiff black Gothic chairs stood on either side of an equally ancient oak table, stag's heads and stuffed fish were mounted above the doorways; tucked under the stairwell there was even a bronze dinner gong.

Cate looked up. Above, in a spectacular dome, faded gods and goddesses romped in a slightly peeling blue sky. 'Oh, how lovely!'

'Yes. But in rather bad repair, like so much of the house. There are ten bedrooms.' Mr Syms indicated the upper floors with a brisk wave of his hand. 'I've had the master bedroom and Lady Avondale's suite made up for you.'

He marched on into the dining room, an echoing, conventional affair with a long dining table tucked into the bay-fronted window overlooking the fountain and front lawns. 'The dining room,' he announced, heading almost immediately through another door, into a drawing room with an elaborate vaulted ceiling, library bookcases, soft yellow walls and a grand piano. Marble busts adorned the plinths between shelves; two ancient Knole setees piled with cushions offered a comfortable refuge to curl up with a book and a cup of tea. A ginger cat basked contentedly in a square of sun on top of an ottoman, purring loudly.

'The drawing room.'

He swung another door open wide.

'The sitting room.'

And so the tour continued, at breakneck speed; through to the morning room, the study, gun room, the fishing-tackle room, the pantry, the silver room, the main kitchen with its long pine table and cool flagstone floors leading into the second, smaller kitchen and cellars. It was a winding maze of a house. No amount of cleaning could remove the faint smell of dust and damp, embedded into the soft furnishings from generations of use. And despite the heat, there was a permanent chill in the air, as if it were standing in an unseen shadow.

Mr Syms returned to the sitting room, unlocking the French windows. They stepped outside into a walled garden at the side of the house where a rolling lawn, bordered by well-established flower beds led to a small, Italian-style rose garden. It was arranged around a central sundial with carved stone benches in each corner. In the distance, the coastline jutted out over the bay; the water sparkling in the hazy afternoon sun.

Mr Syms guided them to the far end of the lawn where a table and chairs were set up under the cool shade of an ancient horse-chestnut tree. Tea things were laid out; a blue pottery teapot, two mugs, cheese sandwiches and a plate of Bourbon biscuits.

'How perfect!' Cate smiled. 'Thank you!'

Mr Syms didn't sit, but instead concentrated, going over some internal checklist.

'The housekeeper, Mrs Williams, thought you might need something. Her flat is there.' He indicated a low cottage at the back of the property. 'She's prepared a shepherd's pie for tonight. And apologises if either of you are vegetarians.' He checked his watch. 'I'm afraid, Mr Coates, that I have another appointment and must be going. It's my understanding that you and Miss Albion will be spending the night, possibly even two, while you value and catalogue the contents of the house. Is that correct?'

'Yes.'

'Here's a set of keys and my card. If you need anything while you're here, please don't hesitate to contact me. Otherwise, you may leave the keys with Mrs Williams upon your departure and I anticipate hearing from you in due course regarding the value and sale of the contents.'

Jack took the keys, frowning. 'And is everything to be sold? There are no pieces the family would like to keep?'

'There is no family left in this country, Mr Coates. The

entire estate has been purchased by developers who wish to turn it into a luxury hotel, the proceeds of which go to a number of charitable causes. So, sadly, no. Again, if I can be of any help –'

'Forgive me, but who were they?' Cate interrupted, settling into one of the chairs. 'Who lived in Endsleigh?'

'I thought it was common knowledge. The late Lady Avondale, more famously known by her maiden name, Irene Blythe, lived here, the widow of Colonel Sir Malcolm Avondale. She died two months ago, aged ninety-two. She was a wonderful woman; very loyal and generous. Lady Avondale was an extremely active campaigner for children's causes, especially of UNICEF. She received her OBE in 1976. Unfortunately, of course, it's her sister everyone knows about. But that's the way, isn't it?' he sighed. 'The good in this world are never as glamorous as the bad. I'm sorry but I really must go. I'm reading a will in Ottery St Mary in an hour.' He nodded to them. 'It was a pleasure to meet you both. Mrs Williams is always on hand if you need anything. I hope you enjoy your stay.' Then, with a small bow, he took his leave, cutting across the lawn with long strides.

'Is it just me or does it feel like he's running away?' Cate poured out two mugs of tea. 'Sugar?'

'No, thank you.' Jack picked up a sandwich. 'He wouldn't be the first. I have that effect on people.'

'I've never heard of the Blythes.' She passed him a mug. 'And who is this infamous sister?'

'Diana Blythe. The beautiful Blythe sisters. They were both debutantes; famous for being famous between the wars. Do you really not know who they are?'

Cate shook her head. 'Am I just a mass of ignorance? Tell me everything you know.'

'Well,' he admitted, 'to be honest, that's it. I know Diana went missing during the war and was never found. Some say she went to live in America. Others think she was murdered. I'm surprised you haven't heard of her.'

'Obviously my education is lacking.' Cate sipped her tea. 'How strange and romantic!'

'You have a very odd idea of romance.'

'I have odd ideas about a lot of things.' The wind blew across the lawn, gently ruffling her skirt. 'What an old relic!'

'The house?'

'Hmm.'

'You don't think it's charming?'

'Well, it may be. But it's sad too. And so staid; a great big cliché of a house.'

'All these houses have a sameness about them. I've seen dozens and dozens over the years. It's the position and the grounds that make this one special. I love looking out over the sea. And although it's only small –'

'Small!'

'Ten bedrooms is nothing.' He settled into the chair opposite. 'I mean, it must've been wonderful for entertaining but it's no size, really.'

'Now there's only you and me and Mrs Williams.' Cate closed her eyes. 'It's peaceful,' she sighed. 'And the name is so evocative. Endsleigh!'

The sea was too far off to be heard but the sound of the wind through the trees, the birds and the warm smell of freshly cut grass bathed in sunlight soothed her.

'It is peaceful,' Jack agreed.

The dull, persistent ring of a mobile phone buzzed, coming from her handbag.

Her eyes flicked open.

It continued to ring.

'Aren't you going to answer it?'

'I didn't think there'd be a signal here.'

Finally, it stopped.

'So,' Jack grinned, 'avoiding someone?'

The look on her face was cold, like being splashed by a bucket of iced water.

'I was only –'

'It doesn't matter.' She stood up. 'It's too hot out here. I'm going upstairs to unpack. Let me know when you'd like to begin.'

He tried again. 'Look, I'm sorry if I –'

'It's nothing,' she cut him off. 'It's of no importance at all.'

Taking her handbag, she walked across the lawn. Jack watched as she stepped between the layers of sheer fabric floating in the breeze by the French windows, disappearing into the house.

17, Rue de Monceau
Paris

13 June 1926

My dearest Wren,

Muv sent me a copy of the article in The Times
featuring your lovely photograph. Miss Irene Blythe –
one of the Debutantes of the Season! And rightly so!
How did they get your hair to look like that? Have you
had it shingled? Remember that I want to hear every tiny
detail, especially about anything that HAPPENS to
you – even a brief fumble in a corridor is thrilling for me,
as I am in EXILE till next year.

As for me, I am limp with boredom, despite the
romance of the Greatest City in Europe. That is
Madame Galliot's constant refrain. 'You girls are spoilt!
Here you are in Paris – the Greatest City in Europe –
your parents are spending a fortune on you . . .' on and
on and on . . . Of course she doesn't actually allow us
to go anywhere, which is too vexing. Apart from our
drawing classes and trips to Ladurée (the French
cannot make a decent cup of tea) and endless
expeditions to churches – you can see she is truly
exerting herself on behalf of my education – we are

rarely allowed to venture foot into Paris itself – a theatre or nightclub, let alone two Les Folies-Bergère. She also has perfected a sneer she reserves for me when she says things like, 'There are certain subtle refinements that simply cannot be taught,' (cue said sneer), referring of course to the fact that you and I were not born into our class so much as thrust upon it. To her we are and always will be counterfeits. Which is why it is so thrilling to leave cuttings of The Times around for her to see!

Under her tutelage I have learned precisely three things:

* How to eat oysters.
* How to wear my hat at a beguiling angle.
* How to engage in surreptitious eye contact with men in the street, who, being French, are only too glad to ogle you back.

She has two other English girls staying with her – Anne Cartwright, who is charming, great fun and not at all above herself (she has taught me how to smoke quite successfully and without the least bit of choking) and Eleanor Ogilvy-Smith, who is a great lump of wet clay. Eleanor lives in terror of any possible form of enjoyment and every time Anne and I campaign for some tiny inch of freedom, she immediately sides with Madame Galliot and suggests another outing of the religious variety. She

*also spends far too much time in the bathroom. Anne
and I have bets as to what she does in there – all of which
would offend your propriety.*

*So, please! More news of the Season and every
man you dance with and every single dress you wear
and what you have for supper (each course) and how
many marriage proposals you receive this week and
if they kneel and blush and stutter with nerves, etc.,
when faced with your overwhelming beauty or simply
faint. Also, please, please, please give me some small
commission here in Paris so that I may have a legitimate
reason to set forth into some of the Forbidden Zones –
for example, do you need any gloves from Pigalle?
Or stockings from the Lido?*

*I am too, too proud of you, darling! And I think
Fa would be too. How am I ever to live up to my
beautiful sister? J'ai malade de jalousie! (See how
my French improves!)*

*Send my love to Muv, who must be finding the fight to
keep you both chaste and marry you off at breakneck
speed quite an exhilarating moral dilemma. She does, as
always, write the most fantastically boring letters. They
read more like housekeeping accounts than anything
else. How did a woman so dull marry so well? (Anne
says she must have Hidden Longings, which is quite
revolting, especially when you consider what our stepfather probably looks like sans clothes. I told her surely*

*such things should be outlawed amongst the elderly and besides, ma chérie maman does a very good line in Virgin Queenism – her poor Consort has Jesus to contend with now. I wonder she hasn't invested in a life-sized crucifix to hang above the bed, now that we are so hideously rich.)*

*Oh! To Be In London!*

*I do so long to join you and be in the thick of life at last!*

*Yours, as always,*

*Diana xxxx*

*PS Have just tried to cut my own hair with a pair of sewing shears and now look like the boy who delivers for the butcher's. Anne has kindly lent me a cloche. Pray for me.*

Cate walked up the central staircase, to the large open landing of the first floor. It was galleried, furnished with plush red velvet sofas and end tables. She sat down, gathering herself. There was no need to snap at him, she thought, cradling her head in her hands. She was on edge, that was all.

The truth was she'd assumed Jack would be an older man, a contemporary of Rachel's; some sexless uncle type who needed a helping hand for a few days. Not a man speeding around in a convertible, staring at her with intense blue eyes, asking questions.

She was safe, she reminded herself. This was England, after all. And here, hidden in this remote house, immersed, like a reluctant time traveller, she was protected, surrounded by the beauty and opulence of another, more elegant age. Nothing could touch her. Least of all a man she hardly knew.

Taking a deep breath, she looked around. It was such a luxurious expanse of space to have at the top of a staircase. People must've congregated here, talking, laughing and smoking in their evening clothes before going down to supper. She tried to imagine their easy, urbane conversation; the air a cocktail of French perfume and thick, unfiltered cigarette smoke; flattery and flirtation. Running her hand along, she felt the lush, worn velvet, soft and inviting.

Still, she was tense, unsettled. Getting up, she turned down the hall, looking in each of the rooms until she found what was clearly the master bedroom, with its rich mahogany sleigh bed and dark, masculine furniture. She headed in the opposite direction. All the way at the other end of the long corridor was Lady Avondale's suite, decorated with lighter, more restrained feminine touches. Soft primrose walls were covered in watercolours, the bed was in the French Empire style and blue-and-white chintz curtains were pulled back across the bay window overlooking the front garden. There was a view of the sea. Someone had opened the windows. Fresh towels were placed neatly on the dresser.

She was expected.

Sitting down on the edge of the bed, she tried to still her racing thoughts. It was useless.

Why was it that no matter how far she travelled from New York, it was never far enough?

Opening her handbag, she took out her phone. The number was withheld. A red light flashed – a message. She threw it back into her handbag. Lying down across the bed she curled into a ball, arms wrapped round her knees.

The room was pretty, elegant, but it offered no comfort. She rolled over on to her back. There was the unfamiliar sound of birdsong. It should've been soothing but instead it felt insistent, nagging. She was used to car horns, the roar of traffic; too many people, too close together. Nature felt like a black hole into which she was falling, weightless.

Breathing deeply, she tried to relax, pressing her eyes shut.

But as soon as they were closed, the film began to play again. It always began the same way: with his touch on her skin, the musky scent of his cologne, the pressure of his lips, softly caressing against her bare shoulder . . .

'Go on.' He dipped his finger into the glass of cognac, tracing it along his lips. 'I dare you.' He leaned down, his breath warm against her cheek. 'Kiss me.'

How many times had she promised herself she wouldn't? She wouldn't answer his calls; wouldn't go to him; definitely wouldn't drink.

He was like an invading army; he didn't want to love her so much as to occupy her. And to her horror, she wanted to be annihilated; overwhelmed. It took so much for her to feel anything at all.

She flicked her eyes open. These dreams were dangerous.

There were other memories, less palatable; even terrifying. So why was this the one that haunted her? The glamour, seduction; the full force of his desire and attention.

Sitting up, she caught sight of herself in the dressing table mirror on the other side of the room. The slim, blonde woman who stared back was almost unrecognisable, even to her. When she'd first gone to New York, she'd been a brunette, hair halfway down her back, hanging like a veil, hiding her face. Her shoulders were hunched forward, rounding protectively over her solar plexus, which felt permanently tender and bruised.

She wanted to be someone else. Anyone else.

It was Derek Constantine who suggested she cut and dye her hair. 'Something timeless, classic.'

'But I can't afford it.'

'You can't afford not to be blonde,' he corrected her. 'And,' he sighed, his upper lip curling slightly as he looked down at her ankle-length skirt, 'we need to do something about all those black clothes. You're not an Italian widow. This is a city of very fine social distinctions. Everyone nowadays has money, what's important is pedigree, exclusivity. You're like a debutante, before the ball. With proper grooming and introductions to the right people, who knows how far you could go?'

She didn't understand; it all sounded so conservative and staid. 'You mean in art?'

His slate-grey eyes were remote, unreadable. 'In life,' he answered, pressing the tips of his long fingers together under his chin.

In life.

She blinked back at herself now, two sizes smaller, head to toe in crisp white linen. Clean, controlled, refined. In the hazy afternoon light, she looked golden; angelic.

If only you could remove the darkness of your character with the ease with which you could change your clothes.

He'd sounded so sure, taken such an interest in her. The idea of being guided by this successful, sophisticated man was too compelling to resist. So she hadn't. Instead she'd abdicated, bit by bit, her faltering, embryonic conception of herself, deferring to his clearer vision and experience.

But the debutante he had in mind wasn't staid. And the society he introduced her to even less so.

Digging through her bag, she pulled out a pack of cigarettes, and, lighting one, crossed to the open window. She'd given up. She'd given up a lot of things that hadn't stuck. And she had the feeling, all too familiar nowadays, of trying to stem the tide with a teacup.

I just want peace, she prayed silently, taking a deep drag. Here I am, thousands of miles away from New York, with some strange man, doing a job I know nothing about . . . I'm meant to be getting my head together. I'm meant to be figuring out what I want to do with my life.

She pushed her hair back from her face. It was so hot. And everything was baffling.

Suddenly she had an overwhelming desire to get high, to be out of her head, to seduce someone. Pornographic visions filled her brain – a tangle of naked limbs; someone licking her flesh, her mouth travelling across the contours of another body . . . Her heart seized.

Was it just a fantasy or a flashback?

Naked, she was on her knees in front of him. He was holding her head in his hands, pressing his hips forward . . .

She bit her lower lip, hard. So hard, it bled. And the desire built, to escape the present moment.

Stop.

She couldn't stop.

What did Jack look like without his clothes on? They were alone. He was attracted to her, she could feel it. And he was a stranger. Why was it easier to fuck a man you didn't know?

She exhaled.

Don't go there.

But a languid sensuality already coursed through her limbs, her imagination spinning like a mirrored top, casting images she couldn't control. The one thing she shouldn't think of was the only thing on her mind.

She turned. The bedclothes were torn away, two naked bodies, strangers, reached for one another . . . If only she could be obliterated, fucked, destroyed.

She closed her eyes. The fantasy dissolved. Taking a last drag, she stubbed out the cigarette and threw it away, into the drive below.

Wandering into the bathroom, she splashed her face with cool water and sat down on the toilet seat. She thought again of the telephone message waiting, with all the others.

It was only a matter of time before she answered one of them.

I am insane, she thought. I'm broken and bad and cannot be fixed.

Covering her face with her hands, she cried.

Jack finished his cup of tea and walked round to the front of the house, unpacking his bag and his equipment, the digital camera and notebooks, from the boot of the car. He caught the faint smell of cigarette smoke and looked up at the open window on the first floor. He smiled. She'd been sneaking a crafty fag!

So, she wasn't quite as well behaved as she appeared.

It amused him to think of her, only feet away, doing forbidden, clandestine things.

He walked into the house, his footsteps echoing across the cool marble floor, and up the stairs. As he reached the top, a door closed to the right of the landing. So he turned left, heading down the opposite end of the hall. In the master bedroom, he threw his things down on the bed and took off his jacket. Crossing to the open window, he looked out over the lawn.

There was a crackle of anticipation, a tension in the air that he hadn't felt in years. And it threw him off balance. It was wrong to be excited by this girl; to look forward to standing next to her, to seeing her. Already he was devising possible subjects for dinner conversation; questions and clever little observations that might impress her. He was wound up, he could feel it.

What an idiot!

But in truth, it was terrifying to feel anything again.

He was used to being on his own. It was safe. And he had a routine now. He sat at the same tables in the same cafes, ordered the same food. The waitress remembered how he took his coffee, the owner chatted about the book he was reading. (They knew how to treat a regular customer.) And there were things you could do, if not happily, at least peacefully, quietly – wander around galleries, listen to concerts, sit in the cinema on your own, in the dark. This was his life.

But now, for a moment at least, the seat next to him had been taken. He could still smell her perfume.

Don't be seduced by the romance of the setting, he reminded himself. It's about sex, pure and simple. It always was, always would be. It came dressed up as love, passion and romantic obsession, but sooner or later the gilding wore off and the coin underneath was always plain old sex.

Suddenly a memory seeped through his defences. He winced inwardly but couldn't stop it. He was reaching across to touch his wife, when he saw her face, her large, dark eyes. They were full of sadness and, worse, resignation. He pushed it away but the feeling lingered.

Sex had been unsatisfactory. That was the truth. Reduced to a kind of shorthand, pornographic role play. The act itself wasn't faked but the connection was, which was worse.

And he hadn't wanted to discuss it or fix it. That was the awful thing. There'd been a part of him that had found it easier; that wanted to let go. It was as if he'd wished her away.

He was guilty of the crime of withdrawing. She'd seen it and let him go.

That haunted him too.

Jack turned away from the bucolic view.

It was a massive bedroom, practically the size of his entire flat. That's what you got when you moved out of London – space, beauty, freedom.

He ought to move. He ought to start again somewhere new.

Sinking down on the bed, he yawned, rubbing his eyes.

He ought to do a lot of things.

It wasn't a long-distance car, his Triumph. His back was stiff from driving. Lying flat, he closed his eyes.

Still, those hours driving across the countryside with Cate by his side were the happiest he'd had in a long time. The sun, the speed, the exuberance of Mozart contrasting with her calm, cool presence. It was exhilarating. He'd felt the hope of happiness; its possibility glimmering on the horizon, like a destination. He hadn't realised how long he'd lived without the hope of anything, dragging himself mechanically through days, months, years. Now there was an aching in his chest, an animal desire to touch and be touched; to punch his way through the inertia of loss and grief.

He sat up, forced his fingers roughly through his hair.

It was insane to be so taken with this girl. He didn't even know her.

He was just tired, lonely. Bored.

Still, there were laws of physics, of nature; mysterious, inconvenient gravitational pulls which couldn't be denied.

At the opposite end of the house, a woman, a complete stranger, was drawing closer all the time.

17, Rue de Monceau
Paris

24 June 1926

My darling Bird,
You will be pleased to know that I have finally
perfected the art of pressing myself up alluringly
against a man while dancing and at the same time
maintaining an expression of complete and utter
indifference verging on contempt. Anne says it is
essential and we have been practising it all week.
Now all we need are some men.

How is that dashing Honourable of yours? I'm
certain his shyness only masks an ardour that will soon
make itself known to you (again, details of all carnal
encounters kindly requested).

You are probably right that this business of coming
out is more difficult and exhausting than I imagine
and perhaps, as you say, I would benefit from taking
a more serious view of the entire task. But as we both
well know, seriousness is not my strong suit. I am,
alas, not gifted with your natural good sense but rather
destined to be somewhat ridiculous by comparison.
I console myself that you have gone before me, made

*innumerable social contacts and charmed everyone so completely that when I arrive they will simply indulge me as an oddity before packing me off to a remote corner of the Empire with some ageing, palsy-ridden husband in tow.*

*And yes, I suppose my remarks about our mother are a little cruel. I should be more kind. Especially to Her Consort, the Benefactor of so much Good in our lives.*

*I know we are lucky, Irene. We certainly have a great deal more than we have ever had. And yet I miss Fa and, if truth be known, I hate Paris and all who sail in her. I am not like you, darling. I am not naturally good or calm or sensible. And I have the feeling of being a fake, everywhere I go — like an actress wandering around onstage in a play she hasn't read, who can't recall any of her lines. You seem to understand everything perfectly — why am I such a dolt?*

*Yours, as always,*
*The Idiot Child*

She tried to nap, but still Cate was restless. She sat up on the bed. It was a vast room, as big as most flats in New York. An entire wall of windows looked out onto a vista of rolling hills, curving dramatically down to the sea.

Who had lived here? Who had chosen these primrose walls, this chintz curtain fabric with its design of blue wisteria and green ivy? This elegant walnut Empire bed? She ran her fingers lightly across the cool linen pillowcase. Its edges were monogrammed, 'I A', in pearly silken thread. Was it a wedding gift?

She opened the drawer of the bedside table; it shuddered slightly in protest. Two neatly folded cotton handkerchiefs, a tube of E45 eczema cream, half empty, a few stray buttons, a receipt from Peter Jones in Sloane Square for wool, dated 1989.

Cate closed it and picked up a well-worn volume from the top of a pile of books, *The Poems of Thomas Moore*, and opened it. On the flyleaf, in a bold flamboyant hand, was written '*Benedict Blythe, Tír na nÓg, Ireland*'. It fell open to a page marked by a frayed crimson silk ribbon.

'*Sail On, Sail On*'

*Sail on, sail on, thou fearless bark –*
*Where'er blows the welcome wind,*
*It cannot lead to scenes more dark,*
*More sad than those we leave behind.*

*Each wave that passes seems to say,*
*'Though death beneath our smile may be,*
*Less cold we are, less false than they,*
*Whose smiling wreck'd thy hopes and thee.'*

*Sail on, sail on – through endless space –*
*Through calm – through tempest – stop no more.*
*The stormiest sea's a resting-place*
*To him who leaves such hearts on shore.*
*Or – if some desert land we meet,*
*Where never yet false-hearted men*
*Profaned a world, that else were sweet –*
*Then rest thee, bark, but not till then.'*

It was a strange, desolate poem – an unsettling choice for an elderly woman, living out her final days, alone, by the sea.

Putting the book back with the others, Cate peered into the wardrobe. A clutch of naked wire hangers swung in the draught. Apart from a few extra blankets piled on the shelves, it was empty. The same was true of the chest of drawers. Faded flowered lining paper and a few yellowed sachets of potpourri were all that was left.

She turned to the dressing table. A silver brush and comb, a porcelain dish of wiry brown hairpins, a dusty box of Yardley's lily of the valley talcum powder. And an old black-and-white photograph, presumably of Irene with her husband. She picked it up. They were both in their seventies, standing bolt upright, close but not touching.

Irene was thin to the point of physical frailty, wearing a trim straw hat and a dark, neatly tailored suit. Her husband was proudly wearing the full dress uniform of his regiment, a silver-headed walking stick in his right hand; hat tucked under his arm. She was smiling, chin slightly raised, her eyes a distinctive clear blue. It was a bright day, yet the photo was flawed. There was a dark patch, a shadow falling across the right-hand side of the Colonel's head. It must've been taken at a veterans' event. Irene was holding a plaque of some kind, but the writing on it was too small for Cate to make out.

She wondered where the plaque was now; where all the accolades were that marked Irene Avondale's lifetime of charitable service to the Empire.

It was a room of order, pleasant and curiously unrevealing, like a stage set. It had a numbing effect as if everything ambiguous had been smoothed over by a large, firm hand. Was Irene's existence really so tidy and presentable? Or had someone removed any intimate traces of its owner?

Walking out and down the hallway, Cate opened doors, exploring the upper regions of the house. There were equally large bedroom suites both with sea and garden views, bathrooms, dressing rooms, some with floral themes, others with nautical designs . . . She moved quietly, aware that Jack was resting. She wanted to get a sense of the place on her own, like an animal finding its bearings. Turning in the opposite direction on the landing, she headed down the long hallway that separated the two wings of the house. Dappled sunlight danced in patterns across the faded oriental runners, worn from decades of use. There were two more guest rooms, a large family bathroom and then, at the very end of the hall, a closed door. She turned the knob. It was locked. Jack must have the key.

Cate bent down and examined the old lock. It wasn't very sophisticated. In fact, it would be easy.

As she headed back to her room, digging out a nail file and credit card from her bag, she knew it would be simpler to wait for him – that it wasn't really normal to pick the lock. But there was a swell of perversity in her; a childish stubbornness to do what she wanted, when she wanted. The idea of asking for help was inhibiting. And she felt a thrill of defiance as she walked quickly back to the locked door and, in one swift movement, jemmied the latch open.

It was a skill she'd learned from her father when she was eleven – part of an ongoing education that he liked to refer to as 'life's little talents'. They included such gems as how to roll a cigarette, the construction of the perfect bacon sandwich, and how to charm virtually anyone with a view to establishing a running tab without any credit at all. After his divorce from her mother, he'd lived in a small Peabody flat near the back of Bond Street Station. A promising guitarist in his youth, his career as a session musician floundered, an unwelcome by-product of his drinking. His once striking good looks faded, worn away by years of self-neglect. His sandy hair and grey-green eyes seemed to lose colour each time she saw him, and his swaggering self-confidence and physical ease were eroded by countless hangovers. She would visit him, and when he was sober, he'd take her for an all-day breakfast and then on to a half-price matinee at the Odeon Cinema in Marble Arch. On a good day, he would seem genuinely pleased to see her; chain-smoking, talking ten to the dozen about the things they would do, the jobs he had in the pipeline, the trips they would take after he next got paid. Maybe Brighton, Europe, perhaps even Africa on safari. Each plan was more magical and ambitious than the next; each promise heartfelt and genuine. When he smiled, he was the most handsome man in the room. 'This job is different,' he'd say. 'This time it's all coming together.' And she would believe him.

Then around three o'clock, he would grow inexplicably agitated and irritable. No matter how hard she tried, no matter how many amusing stories she told, she couldn't keep his attention. And before she knew it, they'd be sitting in a pub. One drink would turn into five, then seven. His face would go hard, his speech began to slur and his whole character would change. He'd lose his keys, misplace his wallet; start a fight with a stranger about some insult only he could hear. And then 'life's little talents' would come in handy as she struggled to get him home without him falling over or getting punched or seducing some ridiculous old barmaid he'd been poking fun of only two hours earlier.

They never did go to Africa or even to Brighton. He spent his life making promises he never kept. Yet she loved him with that stubborn, painful, magical love that children have for their parents. A kind of willing suspension of disbelief that in spite of all of the years of evidence to the contrary, he would somehow, at the very final hour, manage to keep his word. When he died, she felt as if she'd spent her whole life on a train platform, checking her watch in anticipation, waiting for him to arrive. Only he'd been diverted; headed in a different direction entirely. And no one had bothered to tell her.

Perhaps if she'd been more interesting, prettier, smarter . . .

Now she seemed to have inherited his moral flexibility; his dark, moody restlessness – the same ever-widening discrepancy between her words and actions. Nowadays she too found herself making promises she couldn't keep, even to herself.

The latch clicked.

The locked door swung open.

Cate blinked, blinded by the brightness.

It was a large, square room with high ceilings and a wall of French windows leading to a balcony overlooking the rose garden. All around the room, the most delicate plasterwork and cornicing shone, covered in gilt; bright gold garlands twining against creamy white walls. The effect was dazzling.

Cate stepped out of the cool darkness of the hallway. The room was stifling, airless. She opened the French windows, their hinges creaking from lack of use. Wind rushed in and the vacuum of heat and stale air released like a sigh. It was as if the room were holding its breath. But for how long?

Above a marble fireplace hung an elaborate overmantel. The Aubusson carpet, sun-bleached and pale, was patterned with circlets of flowers and cherries. More garlands wove around the ceiling rose, filling the room with a soft burnished glow. It was easily the loveliest room in the house; beautifully porportioned, ornate, like a miniature ballroom.

So why was it locked?

There was a single bed against one wall and a dresser. A thick layer of dust covered everything. Cate opened a drawer and dust ballooned into the air, making her cough. There was nothing inside.

Bookshelves lined the wall opposite. She examined the faded spines. *The Wind in the Willows*, *The Water-Babies*, *The Faithless Parrot*, *The Children of the New Forest* as well as *Grimm's Fairy Tales* and works by Hans Christian Andersen and a large collection of Lewis Carroll. Pulling out *The Wind in the Willows*, she opened it. Its spine creaked stiffly. Apart from damage from dust and age, however, it was pristine.

Then, kneeling down, she noticed something. There was an anthology of Beatrix Potter books, small, taking up only half the width of the shelf. Behind them, an old shoebox was wedged into place, filling the gap, making all the rows look even. Cate carefully dislodged it. It was printed in soft brown ink to look as if it were made of alligator skin and tied together with a salmon pink ribbon. It was heavy.

On the side of the box there was a label. 'F. Pinet, Ladies' Footwear'. In pencil beneath, written in a florid, old-fashioned hand, there was the shoe size, 4.

Cate untied the frayed silk ribbon and lifted the lid. Wrapped between layers of crumpled newspaper was a pair of delicate silver dancing shoes. They were made from rows and rows of fine braided mesh, finished off with rhinestone clasps. The handiwork was remarkable; intricate patterns of silver thread glittered across the back heel and along the toe. Judging from the style, the roundness of toe, they must have been from the late 1920s or early 1930s. And they looked expensive. Did they belong to Lady Avondale?

Cate turned them over. They'd been worn only a few times; the leather was barely scuffed. She traced her finger along the smooth leather arch. They were so small! Someone, presumably the old lady, used the box to even out the rows of books. But why? Why would anyone bother with such a detail in a room that was locked, virtually empty of furniture?

Picking up the box, she felt something slide to one end. It wasn't empty. She lifted out the crumpled newspaper.

There, hidden underneath, was a collection of objects.

One by one, she took them out.

There was a worn, pale blue velvet jewellery box. Cate flicked it open.

'My God!'

It was a tiny bracelet, fashioned from pearls, diamonds and emeralds. 'Tiffany & Co, 221 Regent Street, W. London' was printed on the white satin cover of the lid. Cate undid the clasp and held it up to the light. The pattern was a delicate combination of pearl flowers with emerald centres, interspersed with slender pearl ovals augmented by rows of diamonds. The diamonds were dulled by dust and age but the emeralds glittered in the sunlight. She tried it round her own wrist. It only just fitted. Incredibly finely made, it was probably extremely valuable.

Closing the clasp, she laid it neatly back in its case.

Next was a slim silver box with an elaborately scripted 'B' in the centre decorated with diamonds. Here was a battered green badge with a picture of a candle on it. It bore the inscription 'The prize is a fair one and the hope great', and in the centre were the letters 'SSG'. A small tarnished brass key, too tiny for any door, had rolled into one corner. It fitted into the hollow of her palm like something from *Alice in Wonderland*. Perhaps it belonged to a desk or a locked drawer? And at the very bottom of the box, there was a photograph of a handsome, dark-haired young man in a sailor's uniform. He had even features and black, lively eyes. It was a formal photograph, taken in a photographer's studio. He was posed against a vague classical backdrop of a Greek column, one arm resting casually against a pedestal draped in heavy cloth, the other placed confidently on his hip. 'HMS *VIVID*' was embroidered on his hat. He couldn't be older than twenty. Underneath, on the black border, the photographer's name, 'J. Grey, 33 Union Street, Stonehouse, Plymouth', was written.

Cate felt a sense of building excitement. This was no random selection of objects but something personal. Each bit – the shoes, the bracelet, the photograph – were related somehow. Someone had gathered them, hidden them in the shoebox, and concealed them behind the books. But why?

A bee flew in through the open French windows. It buzzed wildly, looking for a way out.

She stared at the photograph of the handsome young man with the laughing, defiant gaze.

It was a chronicle, an archive – of something worth hiding – marked by diamonds from Tiffany's, silver dancing shoes, beautiful young men . . .

Her memory tripped. Suddenly she was back in time, walking down the long corridor, into the ballroom of the St Regis Hotel, all gilt mirrors and low lighting. People were turning, people she didn't know, smiling at her, staring. The soft green silk of her dress swirled around her legs. A jazz trio played 'Please Don't Talk About Me When I'm Gone'.

Something marked by diamonds, dancing shoes, handsome men . . .

He was there, in front of her. His hair smooth and glossy, sleek against his strong features; his eyes dark, almost black. He wasn't handsome but rather compelling; dominating.

'Some people are afraid of success. Afraid of really being alive.' His tone was challenging, his expression amused. 'Are you afraid?'

'Nothing frightens me,' she had answered coolly, turning away.

Cate closed her eyes.

In truth she had been afraid; afraid of everything, everyone. But she had lied. She had walked away and he had followed, through the crowds of men and women in evening dress, waltzing and turning, their reflections spinning in the mirrors lining the walls.

The bee veered out of the open window, into the vast freedom of the garden.

Cate watched it disappear.

If only she'd known then that soon he'd be the one walking away and she'd be the one following, stumbling behind.

There was a noise.

Cate tensed as she listened to Jack cross the landing at the end of the hallway.

He was looking for her.

Gathering the things together, she put them back in the box, hastily retying the lid with the ribbon.

It ought to go back where she found it. Or she should show it to Jack.

That was the right thing to do.

'Cate? Cate?' He was heading down the stairs. 'Cate!'

Instead she tucked the box under her arm, racing soundlessly along the corridor, heart pounding, back to her room.

They began their work at the front of the house, with the entrance hall, working fastidiously at what seemed like a painfully slow speed. Little stickers went on each item with a number. Each number corresponded to a description dictated to Cate by Jack and then they took a photograph, sometimes several from different angles. Every figurine, every painting, every detail of the lives that were once lived here were recorded and priced for quick sale.

Each piece had an estimated value. Cate filled in the figures next to the descriptions in uncharacteristically careful, neat handwriting, the total mounting by the minute. It was mind-numbing. How sad that all these objects, acquired and beloved through generations, were to be reduced to nothing but a few lines in a catalogue. Endsleigh had been a home once – a refuge against life and the world. Some of these things had been favourites; treasured. Now she and Jack were the last people ever to stay there in its incarnation as a private home. A couple of strangers; strangers to the house and its history, strangers even to each other. Soon bulldozers would be knocking down Mrs Williams's low-ceilinged cottage to make way for a luxury spa; the front hallway transformed into a reception area and bar. Already she could imagine the delight of tourists as they arrived for their country-house weekend.

Jack was good at his job, clever and concise, reeling off complicated accounts of styles and conditions of objects without pausing for breath. And Cate was grateful for the lack of demanding interaction between them. He dictated; she recorded. She was invisible and it soothed her to forget for a while who she was and how she'd ended up here. By the time they stopped at seven, her fingers ached from the effort of trying to write clearly and yet at speed.

'Shall we leave it here for tonight?' he suggested.

She nodded gratefully, filing away the forms in a folder.

'I think I can smell something cooking,' he added, yawning and stretching his arms above his head.

They wandered into the kitchen. Mrs Williams had been hard at work – the shepherd's pie was browning nicely in the oven and two place settings were laid out on the long pine table along with a green salad, a bowl of fruit and some cheese.

'Thank God for that!' He rubbed his hands together. 'I'm famished!'

'And yet where is the invisible Mrs Williams?' Cate wondered, leaning up against the worktop. 'This is like something out of a fairy tale; *Beauty and the Beast*.'

'Don't we all wish we had staff like that?'

'Hmm.'

'Oh, and here's just the thing!' Jack picked up a bottle of red wine airing on the worktop next to two glasses. 'Can I pour you one?'

'No, thank you.'

'Really? Are you sure?'

'I'm fine, thanks.'

Then he remembered his conversation with Rachel, some mention of her father being an alcoholic. Of course, he wasn't meant to know anything about her. He poured out a glass. 'I hope you don't mind.'

'Why would I mind?'

He shrugged, trying to appear nonchalant. 'No reason.'

Feeling self-conscious, he smiled and sipped, as if to prove that he was completely ignorant of her family history.

Cate frowned, unable to disguise her irritation. Rachel had obviously been talking. 'It's so hot in here!' She turned away, looking out of the window.

'You're right. Let's eat outside instead.'

'Fine.'

Once out in the garden, the tension relaxed. It was good to get away from the heat of the kitchen with its ancient Aga. They sat under the chestnut tree again at the same low table where they'd had their tea, carrying the food out on trays.

A cool breeze rustled through the foliage. And suddenly, after the pleasant anonymity of working together for hours, the strangeness of being alone was palpable again.

'So,' Cate pushed her food around on her plate, 'have you always been a valuer?'

It sounded dry and stupid.

Jack looked across at her. 'No. You're an artist, aren't you?'

'Yes.' She hadn't expected him to bat the conversation back at her quite so quickly.

'What kind of work do you do?'

'I paint. Reproductions.'

Up shot an eyebrow. 'Really? You mean *Whistler's Mother* and that sort of thing?'

She tore at a piece of bread. 'I specialise in French and Russian eighteenth-century Romantic painting.'

'The Enlightenment?'

'Yes.'

He chuckled.

'What?'

'Rachel didn't tell me you were a faker.' He looked at her sideways. 'Ever try to pass anything off?'

'It's all real,' she said, jabbing the bread into a pocket of gravy. 'It's just not original. And yes, pieces get "passed off" all the time. Most of the work I do is for insurance purposes. Very few people can afford to lose a masterpiece, even a minor one, to theft or fire.'

'I've offended you. I'm sorry. My mother always told me I had the social skills of a cabbage.'

'I'm sure she was just being kind.'

He laughed. 'Mothers are bound to be indulgent. So,' he tried again, 'why that period?'

'I sort of fell into it.'

'Into the Age of Reason?'

'Someone asked me to do some work for them. A *trompe l'oeil* in a quite amazing flat overlooking the park. I found I had a certain aptitude for it. Also, there's considerably more scope for economic success. After all,' she took a bite, 'if you hang a copy of *Sunflowers* on your wall, everyone knows you've got a fake. But if you choose something more elusive, unknown . . .'

'Very clever. Was that Constantine's idea?'

His astuteness caught her off guard. She shifted. 'Well, the commission did come through a client of his.'

'He's always been, shall we say . . . enterprising.' He took another sip. 'And what about your own work?'

'This *is* my work.'

'Of course. I just meant your own subject matter.'

Again, she felt wrong-footed. 'I get paid very well. And there's nothing particularly worthy about starving to death in a garret.'

He said nothing. But his expression was amused.

'This is more sustainable.'

'Well, yes. We must do what's sustainable.'

'Have you always been a valuer?' she asked again, crisply.

He looked up, grinning. 'No. My father had an antiques business in Islington. I trained as an auctioneer at Sotheby's one wayward year after university before I came up with the brilliant idea of becoming an architect. Then, unfortunately, my father became ill. Parkinson's. And

I took over the business.' He paused. 'I should've sold it and moved on; just been brutal and done it that same year. Instead, I got stuck.'

'In what way?'

'Pretending to be my dad, I suppose.'

'You don't like it?'

He shrugged his shoulders. 'A job's a job, right? And –' he flashed her a smile – 'at least it was sustainable. For a while, anyway. I was forced to sell a couple of years later.'

'How is your father now?'

'The truth is, it's hard to tell. One day he's quite bad and the next he seems like his old self. My mother is thinking of moving him to a nursing home. They live in Leicestershire now and I don't see them as often as I'd like.'

'And you never finished your training?'

He stabbed at a bit of salad. 'I was married by then. To a girl who came into the shop to buy a mirror.'

'I see. Did you sell her one?'

'No, she couldn't afford any. But I made her cups of tea and she used to stop in quite often on the pretext of finding one. In the end I gave her a really quite beautiful Edwardian overmantel.' He smiled to himself, remembering. 'I searched high and low for something decent I could afford to part with. I tried to act like I was going to give it away anyway. I don't think she was fooled.'

'But she married you. So it worked.'

'Yes, it worked. I got the girl.'

'But you sold the shop anyway.'

'Turns out you need quite a lot of ambition to run your own business. After my wife's death, I let it go.' His eyes met hers. 'She was killed in a car accident, two years ago.'

He said it simply; quickly. She wondered if he'd practised how to get it over with the least amount of emotion possible.

'I'm so sorry.'

Cool air rushed around them.

'Yes. Thank you.'

They ate in silence.

'It's strange, isn't it?' Jack put his fork down. 'That's what everyone says – "I'm so sorry." And I say "Thank you", like I was buying a pint of milk in a shop. It's somehow . . . wrong, inadequate, that it should be reduced to that. And in the end, the whole thing gets reduced down to a single sentence. "That was the year my wife died."'

She nodded. 'The whole thing's an absolute cunt.'

He looked at her in surprise. 'Yes, well . . . that's one way of putting it.'

'I didn't mean to offend you.'

'It makes a change from people apologising.'

'When my father died, I dreaded speaking to anyone I hadn't seen in a while; going through the whole dance of clichés. It made me angry. At them, which of course was stupid.'

'Were you close?'

'He wasn't exactly warm and fuzzy. But I don't think it makes a difference. Mostly what I missed was the idea that one day it might be different. When he died the relationship became written in stone. It was too late to change it, even if I wanted to. Or could. And I was left, wandering around saying "Thank you" to a bunch of people who didn't really want to talk about it and had no idea of what to say anyway.'

'Yes,' Jack conceded, taking another drink of wine, 'it is a cunt.'

They watched a flock of house martins swoop in and out of the high hedges on the south side of the garden.

'And what about you?' He leaned back. 'Married? Divorced? Widowed?'

She looked up sharply.

'Or shall we leave all that?'

She stared at him a long time. 'I'm . . . I was involved with someone.'

'You have a boyfriend?'

'It wasn't quite so clearly defined.'

He raised an eyebrow. 'You seem a little vague, Miss Albion.'

'That's my intention, Mr Coates.'

'Do you instinctively balk at being defined, or simply in matters of the heart?'

'Who said this was a matter of the heart?'

'Well,' he laughed, 'isn't it?'

'I'm not sure.' She ran her fingers lightly along the rim

of her glass. 'There are so many more territories in the heart than one expects.'

'Like what?'

'Possession, power.' She spoke slowly, softly, lifting her eyes to meet his. 'It's confusing sometimes, isn't it?'

He felt his pulse quickening, the surface of his skin alive with increased sensitivity. 'In what way?'

'To tell which is which. They are intimacies, not so polite as love, but compelling just the same. Not everyone longs for tenderness.'

'And you?'

'I long for all sorts of things. Some of which I understand and some which I don't.'

'Are you saying you don't know your own mind?'

'Do you?'

'I like to think I do.'

'You're deceived.'

'And you're presumptuous.'

'What does the mind have to do with it anyway?'

'I'm not referring to intellect but to intention,' he clarified, aware that he was overcompensating with a certain loftiness of tone. She was clever and provocative. But it was the speed of her that was most thrilling.

Her lips widened in a slow, teasing smile. 'And are all your intentions transparent and worthy?'

'Isn't that possible?'

'Possible, perhaps. But not natural.'

'And why not?' He shifted, recrossing his legs. 'Why

can't you be aware of your actions before you take them? Set your own course for your heart rather than blundering in blindly?'

'My, you really are a rare breed!'

The wind tossed the thick boughs above them, elongated black shapes stretching towards them across the lawn.

'That's not fair. You make me sound like a prude!'

'Well, let's see. A man whose motivations and desires are completely known to him at all times and absolutely under his control, who never stumbles into the murkier depths of human relations, whose affections only follow his pre-sanctioned plans . . . No, you're not a prude. You're a statue. Something Olympian. Definitely marble.'

'And what about you?' he countered. 'A woman who doesn't know her own mind, can't even tell if she's having a relationship or not, but is only certain it doesn't involve love. What does that make you?'

In the dimming light, a shadow fell across her, bathing her in darkness. 'I don't know. I don't know what it makes me.'

The air felt suddenly cooler.

He tried to think of a way to backtrack without losing face. 'Cate . . .'

But before he could, she pushed her chair back and stood up.

'I'm tired,' she said. 'It's been a long day. Do you mind if I . . . ?'

'Yes, go on.' He said it a bit too quickly; his mind

racing to figure out exactly how he'd offended her; certain that he was likely to do it again if he pursued the matter. 'I'll look after this.'

'Thank you.'

She crossed the lawn, retreating from him, into the house, through the open French windows where the wind gathered and released the gauzy white sheers with invisible fingers.

The old house changed with the encroaching darkness. Rooms that were open and inviting in the daylight took on an unfamiliar coldness; shadows loomed and uneven floorboards sent her stumbling along the hallway. Although they were too far away from the shoreline, she thought she could hear the sea; surf crashing into cliffs.

Suddenly, her body felt leaden with exhaustion; her mind numb. The stairs groaned as she climbed up to her room. Without turning on the lights, she slumped on the edge of the bed. The last pink embers of sunset faded into the west. A minute later they were gone.

She picked up her mobile phone, lying on the bedside table. Two more missed calls. She was unable not to check it. Unable to return the calls, yet unable to delete his number; unable to move forward in any way, trapped in an invisible cage of contradiction and obsession. She switched it off, tossing it across the room where it landed in a corner. Far away enough so that she couldn't reach across and grab it in the night; close enough to be retrievable. Self-loathing swelled and saturated, bleeding silently through her, like ink across a clean sheet of paper.

She could see Jack's blue eyes, narrowed, triumphant; hear the superiority of his voice.

What did that make her?

She knew all too well what that made her.

It still thrilled her. That was the most disgusting part. She dreaded the missed calls yet feared the day when there were no calls at all. Her motives were clouded, filthy. Nothing about her was clear or good or pure any more.

'We're bound, you and I.' The memory of his voice, low, just above a whisper, his breath hot against her cheek played again and again in her mind. Without thinking she rubbed her forearm; she could still feel the pressure of his fingers, digging into her flesh when she tried to move away.

Twilight reigned. A pale sliver of moon began to rise.

It was an unknown house; veiled yet alive in the darkness. It sighed and trembled. Things shifted, shapes, half seen, darted across the floor.

And without even bothering to wash her face, brush her teeth or take her clothes off, Cate curled up on the bed and closed her eyes.

17, *Rue de Monceau*
*Paris*

*20 July 1926*

*My darling Wren,*
*Well! Finally something interesting has happened*
*here! Eleanor's cousin has arrived in town – Frederick*
*Ogilvy-Smith or Pinky, as he's known, on account of his*
*permanently flushed cheeks (they really do look like a*
*freshly spanked bottom) – and he is the most fun, which*
*is surprising, considering how congenitally dull Eleanor*
*is. He's on his way to Nice to join the Hartingtons*
*at their villa near Eze but decided to stop a bit longer*
*to take us all out to supper and a show. Of course*
*Eleanor was mortified but he and Anne and I all got*
*on brilliantly. Perhaps a little too brilliantly – tell me*
*what you think. We are strolling out across the Place de*
*la Concorde after leaving the Ritz and he takes my arm.*

*'You're the bread girl, aren't you?'*

*'I beg your pardon?!' (I was trying to be serious and*
*aloof but really there's no point with Pinky – he just*
*carries on regardless.)*

*"Now don't be coy. Everyone knows your mother*
*married Lord Warburton of Warburton's Wholesome*

Wholegrain. And a fine loaf it is.' He looks at me sideways. 'I expect I best woo you, now that you're a famous heiress.'

'I'm not famous.'

'You will be.'

'And I'm not an heiress!'

'Yes, well, insanely well off then. Shall I do it now?'

I sigh. 'If you must.'

'Best get it over with.' He takes his hands out of his pockets and puts on a wobbly sort of voice. 'Your eyes are like two perfect blue –'

'Please stop.'

'Fair enough.'

'What about Anne?'

'What about her?'

'Well, oughtn't you woo her too?'

'It's not really how it's done. Not strictly speaking. You're meant to wait for one girl to go before you have a bash at another.'

'We're friends.'

'I see.' He turns to Anne. 'Your eyes are like two perfect blue –'

'Brown.'

'Ah.' He stops. 'This is too complicated! Shall we all have a cocktail? A cigarette?' He turns to me. 'A kiss?'

And I did, darling – that is, let him kiss me. And before you become too livid let me explain that the thing about Pinky is he's good fun and quite harmless. He's

more like a brother than a man and we were aching to
find out what it was like. Besides, he kissed Anne too.
There's really no point in him kissing just one of us as
we won't have anyone to discuss it with later. We both
agreed it was a bit wetter than we thought it would be
and probably would've been nicer if it hadn't been Pinky.
He asked if he could write to me and I said yes. Already
I've had a postcard of a goat and a rather suspect-looking
peasant girl. And instead of the bread girl he's taken
to calling me Toast. Do you think we're engaged?

Please don't tell the Holy or I shall be forced
to elope with a man I've only met once.

Piles of kisses from,

The Wayward (Libertine)

Jack took the plates into the kitchen, piling them into the sink. Mrs Williams would probably do them in the morning. He should leave them. Still, he turned on the water and squirted some sharply scented lemon washing-up liquid into the bowl, dunking his hands into the hot soapy water. Here at least he could make progress; change something. Doing the dishes was proof of a civilised world and a sure-fire remedy for existentialist angst.

Besides, he wanted to buy some time, put some space between them.

He'd intended to be witty, charming. Intelligent yet funny and unpretentious. But none of his carefully composed observations were required. The conversation had a life of its own that he hadn't been able to control.

He rinsed a glass clean under the tap.

He didn't agree with her. Found her thinking flawed; a curious combination of honesty and elusiveness.

And yet she was undeniably compelling. When she moved, his gaze followed. When she spoke, he found himself leaning forward not just to hear what she had to say, but to catch what she didn't; the spaces between her thoughts, which seemed to reveal even more. There was an unwilling transparency about her; a glassy fragility in spite of all her defences. His instinct was to protect it.

No wonder Derek Constantine was captivated. And he wondered again as to the exact nature of their friendship.

Some people were like viruses, infecting everyone they come into contact with. Derek Constantine was one of them. A fatal combination of glamorous tastes and plausibility, Constantine possessed a sleek moral dexterity masquerading as open-mindedness and sophistication that was almost impossible to resist. Why did he, of all people, have to be her connection in New York? Exactly what kind of clients did he introduce her to? Could he be the man she was referring to earlier? Jack tried to push the idea out of his mind, but it adhered itself to his imagination with unreasonable tenacity. He felt his jealousy twist into life, creating visions, scenes – Derek's permanently tanned, manicured hand reaching to unzip Cate's dress, his fingers travelling across her skin, his tongue darting, serpent-like, moistening his lips . . .

Jack reached into the soapy dishwater. 'Damn!'

The tip of a carving knife jabbed his palm.

He rubbed it angrily under the tap. It wasn't cut, just smarting.

He should be more careful – there was nearly always a blade beneath the water.

Jack stacked the last plate, folded the tea towel and hung it across the Aga.

Suddenly the weight of the day hit him; his resources not just depleted but gone.

He knew nothing, he reminded himself, yawning. Constantine could've been like a father figure to her for all he knew.

Then he spotted the wine bottle. Should he drain it down the sink?

He was thinking too much, as usual. Do nothing, leave it. Pushing the cork in, he turned out the lights.

Moving slowly through the hallways, he checked the doors, locking up. He imagined Cate upstairs, maybe sleeping already, and him below, going through the end-of-evening rituals. And for the second time that day he felt a pleasing swell of masculinity.

It was a beautiful house. Elegant, substantial; refined. A house that knew what it was and what it was doing. Once there'd been a whole Empire like that.

Jack tried to recall if he'd ever felt that way in his own life; that bright, hard sureness about who he was and where he was going. It existed. There was a time when he was first married that he felt in charge of his destiny; young, smart, capable of great things. He had only to conceive of a desire and he could achieve it. It was a wonderful, glorious feeling.

And then Fate intervened. This vast, self-determining power turned on him, without warning, and suddenly the godlike ability to steer his own course in life, free of any lasting obstacles or opposition, evaporated. Worst of all, he no longer possessed an inner compass. He was off, like a man suffering from vertigo. Instead he hesitated, floundered, fell. The tide that had pushed him so firmly towards achievement ebbed and he was compelled, by increments, to accept a life dictated instead by his limitations.

The accident had taken away so much; things that couldn't be retrieved; pieces of himself that he hadn't even realised existed until they were gone.

Most of all he missed that grandiose, cocky version of himself, striding boldly into the future. The truth was, he had liked himself for a while, and enjoyed his effect upon life. Now he preferred not to think of himself at all.

He and this old house had something in common: both were frozen in a time they thought would last forever; clinging to the memory of a past that was already faded, already gone.

Turning out the hall light, he climbed the stairs, groping through the darkness to his room.

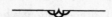

The Bristol Hotel
Paris

12 August 1926

My dear Irene,
I am sorry, my darling, to have given you such a fright.
You must believe me when I say I didn't mean to cause
so much trouble. Anne and I simply wanted a little
holiday and to meet with Pinky for a day or two and
Madame Galliot took it all the wrong way, as usual.
Of course there is no way she would've allowed us to go
had she'd known, so we simply HAD to come up with
a lie – only a little one. We told her we were visiting
relatives of Anne's for the weekend and then, really
quite cleverly, composed the nicest little note in shaky
old-lady handwriting asking for us to come which Pinky
had posted from Monte Carlo the week before. It could
only have been Eleanor who told her it wasn't true.
And then of course it all went horribly wrong. I am
sorry, as I understand now that the papers picked it
up – 'Peers' Daughters Go Missing in Monte Carlo'.
And before we knew it there was a full-scale search on!
All the while we were completely oblivious, wandering
around Villefranche with Pinky, eating ice cream.

*What devastates is the thought that I've caused you harm, my love. Muv has already written a very stern letter, saying my actions have compromised your engagement prospects – can that really be true? Please know that I am silly, and stupid and selfish, but that I would never willingly hurt you – not for all the money in the world! I am too, too crushed! And now Madame Galliot refuses to have either Anne or me and Muv has drafted the Consort's son, Nick Warburton, to bring me home like some defective goods. So now I'm waiting in the Bristol Hotel for him to arrive, under the beady eye of the concierge. I don't even know what he looks like so shan't recognise him and have cried so much my face is swollen and none of the waiters will serve me.*

*Please forgive me, darling! Please send me one small line to say you are still my sister and are still speaking to me! Surely your lovely Honourable will not abandon you just because you have an idiot in the family.*

*Oh dear. Some dreadful fat man has just walked in looking cross. That's probably him. I think I shall cry again.*

*Yours, in floods,*
*The Prodigal D*

Mrs Williams was not the gentle, grey-haired local woman Cate imagined. Coming downstairs in the morning to put the coffee on, she encountered a buxom bleach-blonde in her sixties, wearing jeans and a form-fitting pink T-shirt with the slogan 'Big Spender' spelled out in rhinestones. The radio was on, Madonna pounded out her latest dance tune. She was chatting, laughing away on her mobile while simultaneously chopping up vegetables.

Spotting Cate, she waved. 'Oh, sorry! Gotta go. Call you later, OK?'

Whoever it was took no notice, rambling on without a break. Mrs Williams rolled her eyes and Cate smiled sympathetically. She gestured to Cate, pointing to the coffee-maker on the counter where a fresh pot had just brewed.

'Look, Mum, I gotta go!'

Cate took a mug down from a shelf and poured a cup.

'I'm going to speak to you later, OK? And never mind what he says. You just wait for me before you even think about the guttering, do you understand?' She finally managed to hang up. 'Sorry about that! My mother,' she explained, wiping her hands on a tea towel. 'I'm Jo, by the way.'

'Cate.'

Jo pumped Cate's hand with a firm handshake.

'The woman's in her eighties,' she continued, scraping the chopped vegetables into a saucepan, 'and she still thinks she can go cleaning her own gutters! Insane! I'm telling you, she gets up before I do, goes to bed later than

I do and gets out more than I do. What am I doing wrong? Are you a vegetarian?'

'No,' Cate laughed, leaning against the kitchen worktop.

'Thank Christ for that! There would've been bugger all to eat last night if you had been.' Jo opened the fridge and took out a chicken wrapped in foil. 'Thought I'd do you cold roast chicken for lunch and a chicken hotpot for dinner. I know, chicken, chicken, chicken! A bit dull but I'm trying to clean out the freezer and everything. When you lot pack up that's the end of it. End of an era.'

Cate watched as she drizzled some oil into the saucepan and popped it on top of the Aga.

'How long have you been working here?' she asked.

'I grew up on the estate. My mother was the house-keeper all her life. To be honest, I was dying to get away from here when I was younger. Used to run a bed and breakfast with my second husband over on Majorca. Crazy, really. Just swapped one beach for another. But when that marriage split up, I came back to keep an eye on Mum. And I just fell into looking after Irene as well. She was a good woman. But she used to be very funny about having new people in the house. She paid me twice the going rate just so as not to have to break a new person in. "Let's keep it in the family, shall we?" That's what she used to say.'

'It's a wonderful house.'

'Hmm.' She gave the saucepan a shake. The kitchen filled with the savoury smell of browning onion. 'It has its charms. And what about you? Are you from London?'

'Yes. Well,' Cate shifted, 'yes and no . . . I've been living in New York.'

Jo's face lit up. 'Oh, I love the States! The people are so friendly! If I had the chance I'd move there and never look back.'

'It has its charms,' Cate agreed.

'It's more than that.' Cate watched as she unwrapped a fresh loaf of bread from a shopping basket on the table. 'Have a slice of toast,' she commanded, taking down a breadboard and a knife. 'I mean, they haven't got all this class malarkey going on. No one's listening to the sound of your voice, trying to figure out which drawer they should shove you into.'

Cate took a sip of coffee. 'Hmm.'

Mrs Williams had undoubtedly been seduced by the things all English tourists were enchanted by on their two-week holidays in Florida – the ruthless chirpiness of the American service industry; bright helpful hotel staff, smiling waiters who beg you to 'Have a nice day' while pouring you a second cup of coffee.

'In New York, class matters a great deal. It's just what defines it that's different.'

'Really? I went to Disney World two years ago and everyone was just wonderful. I loved it!'

'It's a great country,' Cate agreed, slicing a piece of bread. It was fresh and soft. She tore a bit off and popped it in her mouth.

'Don't you want that toasted?' Jo moved the vegetables off the heat.

Cate shook her head. 'It's delicious the way it is.'

'My mum makes it. Puts me to shame as a cook. She came to the house as a lady's maid when she was fifteen but when the war started they had to let everyone go. So she taught herself to cook. She has some hysterical stories. Like the time she decided to warm the silver serving dishes in the oven to keep the food hot and when she opened the door, nothing but a bunch of silver balls rolled out! Can you imagine? She only melted some of the best family silver! Bless! Of course she was only a kid at the time.'

'And you grew up here?'

'Yes.'

'It must've been magical.'

Jo leaned back against the worktop. 'It's a wonderful old house. Though we grew up on the estate, not actually in Endsleigh. You're in Irene's room, aren't you? It has a lovely view, don't you think? Of course, you must see houses like this one all the time.'

'Well, not exactly.'

'The library is special. And plenty of people have commented on that dome. Palladian. A very early Robert Adam. Of course it was never properly finished; the restoration work was interrupted during the war.'

'Really? I like the gold room.'

'Gold room?'

'Yes. The way the sunlight dances off the gilding is magical.'

'Gilding?' Jo snorted. 'There's no gilding in this house!'

'Sorry, I mean the one in the far wing, overlooking the rose garden.'

'The far wing?' Jo's expression hardened. 'That room is locked. It's always been locked.'

A flush of colour rose in Cate's cheeks. 'Mr Syms gave us some keys . . . they open . . .' She stopped, mid-lie. Suddenly she felt about five years old.

Jo folded the tea towel and put it down. 'Show me. Let's see what you're talking about.'

Cate marched reluctantly behind Jo out of the kitchen and up the main staircase. At the top of the landing, Jack came out of his room, dressed for the day ahead. Cate was conscious of still being in her dressing gown.

'Hey!' He looked from one to the other. 'What's going on? I'm Jack, by the way,' he introduced himself, offering his hand.

'Jo Williams,' she said, shaking it. 'Your friend here says she's found something – a room.'

He looked across at Cate. 'Really?'

'While you were resting yesterday . . . I had a look around,' she explained, half-heartedly.

'Well, let's see it.' He tried to sound light, but she caught a twinge of irritation in his voice.

She began to feel irritated too. It wasn't her fault the damn thing existed! Heading down the long hallway, she stopped in front of the last door and swung it wide. 'Here it is.'

The morning sun was softer; it was a west-facing room and although there wasn't the same blinding light as the previous afternoon, it was still stunning.

Eyes widening, Jo walked slowly into the centre. 'I'll be damned!'

All traces of defensiveness disappeared. 'Look!' Cate opened the French windows leading on to the terrace. 'Isn't it charming? Have you really never been here? Didn't you ever wonder about it?'

Jo shook her head. 'During the war, most of the house was shut up. They lived in just a couple of rooms, which were blacked out, to conserve energy. And afterwards, there was only the two of them – Irene and the Colonel. They never really opened the house up again properly. When you work for someone, you learn not to look too hard or question too much. Everyone has their little ways, after all.'

'It's beautiful,' Jack agreed. 'Really extraordinary.'

'I know!' Cate was excited. 'But doesn't it strike you as odd that this, this hidden, locked room, is the most lovely room in the house?'

He looked across at her. Standing in her silk dressing gown, face free of make-up, she looked fresh, younger than her years; full of unguarded enthusiasm. Was this the same woman who was so darkly knowing last night? There seemed to be two of her, or rather, at least two.

'I don't know,' he said quietly, turning away. 'Perhaps a touch of our famous English eccentricity.'

'Look at these books. They've never been read. Here.' She pulled one out and handed it to Jack. 'Every single one of them is new.'

He leafed through it.

'Why would anyone lock it up?' Jo wondered.

The question hung in the warm morning air.

'Perhaps the heating didn't work or the roof leaked.' Jack handed the book back to Cate. 'It's not uncommon for old houses to have whole wings sealed off.'

'It's a mystery,' Cate insisted.

He shook his head, laughing. 'A locked door is hardly a mystery!'

It was on the tip of her tongue to tell him about the shoebox. She even went so far as to open her mouth. But then she shut it again, quickly. It was private. Her secret discovery.

'Perhaps you're right,' she agreed, letting it go. 'Perhaps it all comes down to a leak in the roof.'

Cate headed back to her room, adrenalin pumping. The room had been locked for over a generation – not even Jo knew about it.

Something happened; something she felt certain was connected to the box.

Why else would it be locked? she thought, turning on the taps in her bath and putting in the plug. Maybe Irene planned to have a family to fill this old house but her husband was called to the war. Afterwards, when he returned, who knows? Perhaps he was injured or couldn't bear to be touched.

Or maybe she'd fallen in love with someone else.

It was a riddle; a puzzle to be solved.

She opened the bathroom window, looking out across the expanse of green meadow and the limitless view beyond.

What life had Irene dreamed of for herself as a young woman? Here, overlooking the sea, she must've felt that nothing could fail, that she had everything she'd ever imagined. A beautiful house, a titled husband . . . Now there was only an old house with a locked room, books that were never read and a shoebox, filled with strange tokens and memories – like a message in a bottle.

She trailed her fingers in the warm bathwater.

Did she have an affair? Who was the handsome sailor in the photograph? Did he give her the bracelet?

Slipping out of her dressing gown and nightie, she stood in front of the steamy bathroom mirror, pinning her hair up.

It was a mystery, no matter what Jack thought. He was too sure of himself for his own good, that was his problem. Self-satisfied and superior and, yes, prudish. So what if he was dismissive of her? She was the one who had the upper hand now and he didn't even know it.

It gave her a thrill to have a secret in play.

It didn't matter what he thought of her. In another day, they'd be back in London and she wouldn't even have to speak to him again.

God, even at this early hour it was so hot!

She pushed the window wider, stretching her arms high.

Jack was standing on the lawn with a mug of coffee. How did she get into that room? He had the keys. There was no way she could've picked the lock. She didn't look like she'd know how.

He paced back and forth in frustration. She wouldn't conform to anything he wanted her to do or be. In his head he'd composed whole conversations; pleasant little scenes in which he took the lead, showing her what to do and how to do it. But instead she constantly slipped away from him. Despite her golden appearance, she was fast, dark and mutable; like mercury. He couldn't get a grip on her at all.

And he had the unsettling feeling that she was indulging him; that she found him vaguely ridiculous. He was conscious of being constrained by professional proto-col and social niceties while she, in contrast, found her way into locked rooms, landed unfamiliar jobs, slipped into strangely undefined relationships.

There was a noise.

He looked up.

Caught in a ray of light reflected from the window-pane, Cate was standing by the window, naked.

Unguarded and unaware, she stretched her arms above her head, arching her back. Her skin was creamy, her hair white in the sun.

He knew he should look away.

She turned. Her breasts were small, with surprisingly large nipples. They were the same colour as her lips, swollen and pink.

Then she disappeared again, like a fleeting apparition. She hadn't seen him.

Her body was different to what he'd imagined; the vague, classical ideal of beauty he'd assigned her without even knowing it. Her nipples, swollen and erect from the heat, were instantly erotic. His chaste, romantic vision was corrupted by pornographic longings – licking, sucking . . .

Turning his back on the house, he forced himself across the lawn where the road joined a field filled with sheep. It was picturesque; the sky a faultless duck-egg blue above a silver strip of sea.

She'd done it again – knocked him sideways as completely as if she'd kicked his chair out from under him. He was left reeling, grappling with desires that had long been dormant. And he resented it. As much as he loathed the numb monotony of his existence since his wife's death, he hated the effect she had on him; it was narcotic, addictive. She left him longing for more of what he couldn't have in the first place. For a moment he considered the possibility that she knew he was standing there; that she'd deliberately paraded herself in front of him.

Of course that was stupid.

Still, images piled up on themselves.

Stare at the sheep, dammit!

This is a job, he reminded himself, draining his coffee. Tomorrow it ended and then they would go back to London. Most likely she'd end up heading back to New York, to that rich lover of hers.

The memory of her, naked and unaware, flashed up again. He pushed it firmly out of his mind.

He couldn't even trust her.

This girl had no place in his life.

*5 St James's Square*
*London*

*12 September 1926*

*My darling, dearest Wren,*
*I am so, so grateful for your wonderful news and most*
*of all that you have forgiven me! I couldn't have lived*
*knowing I'd caused you pain and now to hear that you*
*are engaged is too, too thrilling! A sapphire ring*
*surrounded by diamonds! I cannot wait to see it!*
*And Muv must be so relieved. But my, you are a dark*
*horse! What became of your shy Honourable? Were you*
*using him as a screen to hide another love? You really*
*have managed the whole thing in record time. Did he go*
*down on one knee? Did he kiss you? I imagine the*
*dampness is less distracting if you are kissing a man you*
*love. How many times? Are you in love with him? You*
*must tell me how Scotland is and his family; if they are*
*terribly grand and if Muv is doing or saying anything*
*ridiculous. (Details, please.) I hope they have given you*
*a decent bedroom and that his mother is kind to you.*

*I'm so sorry to have missed you, but not the Holy.*
*It's bad enough having to be back in St James's Square*
*with the Consort on my own. All he does is stomp*

around glowering at me and lecturing from a book called The Great Threat, which claims the lower classes are poised to take over civilisation and thus end it through a combination of rapid interbreeding and sheer bad manners. It was probably a mistake to tell him I thought civilisation was overrated anyway, as the poor dear seems to take these things very seriously. (There's a single vein on his forehead that throbs violently when he's experiencing an emotion. It turned positively purple.) He called me 'a Bad Seed' and left for his club, taking his precious book with him and muttering furiously. I imagine supper will be unbearable.

Oh my darling! I have a shameful confession . . . Do you recall that Muv employed the Consort's son Nick to bring me home from Paris? Well, he did. And he is neither fat nor old nor anything like the Consort at all. In fact, he's surprisingly handsome and charming – so much so that when he approached me in the lobby of the Bristol Hotel, it didn't occur to me it could be him. He has dark hair, the most elegant features and eyes that seem to be smiling even when his mouth is very serious. I was of course blubbering away like an idiot without a handkerchief. And suddenly I heard someone laughing, and when I looked up there was this man who for all the world looked like Ivor Novello, standing there, shaking his head. 'It's not as bad as all that, is it?' Then he passed me his pocket hanky and sat down. 'Really! You'd think someone had died!'

'You don't understand!' I sobbed, trying to work out who he was, but glad for the hanky all the same. 'I've made the most terrible, terrible mistake!' (And then I blew my nose as delicately as I could, which WAS challenging.)

'Only one?'

'Yes, but a Big One!' I insisted.

And then, my love, he did the most marvellous thing. He called the waiter over and ordered the most expensive bottle of champagne! I could hardly believe it, but the French must do it all the time, because the waiter just smiled and brought it to us straight away. Then he proposed a toast.

'To getting it wrong!'

Well, I've never really had champagne before. I took the tiniest sip and he laughed and said, 'Now, drink up, Baby! It's good for you. Besides, this is a celebration.'

'Of what?'

'It's not every day a person is introduced to their feet of clay.'

And he looked at me with those smiling eyes of his and I had another sip and suddenly the sun started to shine and my nose stopped running and going home to London didn't seem like the most hideous disaster that had ever befallen a human being. And when it was time to go, I felt quite woozy and had trouble walking and he let me lean against his arm. Oh, the smell of him! Too moreish – like freshly cut lemons and warm summer rain. *And on the boat and the train he was so kind and clever and funny. He never once chided or lectured . . . And although he calls me 'Baby' (which I pretend to be vexed about but secretly adore), he is the only person who treats me like a grown-up woman.*

*He's gone back to the Continent now. Apparently he and the Consort can hardly bear to speak to one another, which shows you what good taste he has.*

*Oh Irene! I know he's our stepbrother and old enough to be my father but I can't stop thinking of him. Do you think I'm very depraved? Please don't tell ANYONE! Why has he never married? Do you know?*

*Yours, always,*
*Baby*

That day they worked through the house room by room at an exhausting pace. Jack clearly wanted to finish as quickly as possible; his manner turned brisk, almost curt. Every time Cate asked a question or made a comment, he frowned. The more she tried to soften the atmosphere between them, the worse it got, until finally she gave up. It was clear he couldn't wait to be rid of her.

When they took a break, Cate excused herself and went for a walk into the sheltered Italian rose garden instead of going into the kitchen for lunch. It was still and peaceful; a haven where the minutes felt suspended in amber light. After being indoors for so long the air smelled fresh, of wind and sea, the sun caressing like a warm hand across her shoulders. White roses, plush and fragrant, danced in the breeze, their perfume thick and luxuriant.

Cate wandered over to the sundial, tracing her fingers along the edge. '*The dawning of morn, the daylight's sinking, The night's long hours still find me thinking, Of thee, thee, only thee.*' How romantic and sad.

Sitting on one of the stone benches, she took a deep breath. Despite the lovely surroundings, loneliness pressed like a solid weight against her chest, an unwanted, uninvited companion. It frightened her that she'd managed to alienate Jack; frightened her to be alone, far away from everything she'd grown used to, with a man who clearly found her irritating and inadequate.

She wanted to go home.

But what did the word mean now?

She was brought up in a two-bedroom flat in Highgate with her mother, but that was gone. There was a draughty studio, filled with canvases, above a dry-cleaner's in New York's Alphabet City. That wasn't a home. It wasn't even a refuge.

Home was something else. It was a sense of herself; a mixture of serenity and hope for who she might become. Cate stared at the great Georgian exterior of Endsleigh. Perhaps that's why people clung to land, to houses – so that they could enjoy a feeling of permanence and solidity. Yet even Endsleigh, with all its English-heritage glamour, harboured secrets and unresolved questions, cracks through which the true identities of its occupants slipped into elusive darkness.

It reminded her of a piece she'd made at art school; an enormous foldout drawing of a doll's house in pencil and ink, over six feet tall. At first glance it appeared to be a very traditional, beautiful Victorian structure that, with closer observation, was just slightly wrong. A world that seemed picturesque and charming but was plagued by staircases that led nowhere, rooms with boarded-up windows, doors with no doorknobs. Post piled in a heap, unanswered, blocking the front door; tea things that were never cleared, rotting on china dishes; a hole in the carpet from a stray cigarette; fish floating dead to the surface of the fishbowl – all presided over by stiff, exquisitely dressed dolls, staring blankly into space, passively waiting for someone to determine their next move. Now she had the eerie feeling of living in an equally unyielding world – only not of her own construction.

That piece had won her an award that year. But it all seemed to belong to another lifetime. How long had it been since she'd produced anything original? Could she even do it any more? Or had her imagination completely atrophied? And yet it came about almost by accident, her new career. There was no long discussion; no real debate or even a period in which she'd gone away to think about it. Like so many of the defining moments of her life, it was little more than a wavering; a yielding to what seemed easiest in that moment.

'He's been in the business a long time and is highly respected,' Paul had told her, scribbling Derek Constantine's address on the back of an envelope for her. 'At least he can introduce you to people. You never know.'

She'd rung him as soon as she'd got off the plane. Still jet-lagged, she'd stumbled along the Upper East Side clutching the envelope in one hand and her portfolio in the other, eager to be on time and make a good impression.

Derek's shop was tiny but, like everything about his aesthetic sense, fastidiously and ruthlessly defined. She'd never seen anything quite like it, even in London. It had a lush decadence about it. Here it was permanently evening, forever bathed in dim lighting that mimicked candlelight, softening edges, smoothing out flaws. The walls were lined with black silk taffeta; the air was scented with cedar candles imported from Paris; the bare wooden floorboards were polished till they shone. He had only a few pieces, but they were exquisite, once-in-a-lifetime acquisitions. He made his reputation on being able to provide antiquities of singular quality and rarity. A lone ebony Empire chair was displayed in the window, lit by a rose spot from above. Passers-by stopped in their tracks, arrested by the beauty and symmetry of it; the shocking good taste of displaying it on its own. Derek had an eye for Empire pieces. With their over-the-top opulence and narcissistically soothing classical proportions, they best seemed to fit the personality of his particular clientele.

His *pièce de résistance* was a large, round eighteenth-century convex mirror. Its elaborate gilt frame was fashioned with intricate golden sparrows and twining ivy leaves, shining luminously against the shimmering inky wall. Derek said that there wasn't a week when someone didn't make an offer on it, but he would never sell. He'd dragged it with him all the way from London and practically had to prise it from another dealer, who'd badly miscalculated its value. And it made a statement.

It couldn't have been ten minutes into their first meeting when he suggested it to her.

'Can you fake?'

'I'm sorry?'

'Can you fake, darling? Let me see your portfolio.'

She showed it to him.

Frowning, he leafed through. 'I've got clients who would pay handsomely for some original art. Of a more traditional vein.'

'That's not my forte. But I've got some ideas about a large abstract series based on a modern-day version of *The Three Graces* . . .'

The expression on his face stopped her mid-flow. 'Do you want to rent a broom cupboard in a flat-share in Brooklyn for the rest of your life?'

'Alphabet City.'

'Whatever.'

'No, not at all. But I thought that if I could just get a body of new work together . . .'

Again, he shook his head. 'To start with you get a name, a client base. As a first-class reproduction painter. Then, very gradually, you begin to paint your own subject matter. See, you'll be coming from a much stronger place. And I, my dear, am happy to help you. I know plenty of people who can't even hang their collections because the insurance is so expensive. And some who are too ashamed to admit that they've already sold their most precious pieces. Children's educations have to be paid for in cold hard cash, after all.' He smiled at her. 'Let me help you. Let me guide you.'

'I'm . . . I'm just not sure . . .'

'Would you rather make money painting or waitressing?'

'Painting. Of course.'

He looked at her. 'Well, you wouldn't know it by the

way you're going on. Do you know how many art students flood into New York every year, each of them thinking that they can take this city by storm? It's not as easy as it looks. You need an in. You need help. You need' – he smiled slowly, leaning back in his chair – 'me.'

'I am grateful, Derek.'

'Ava Rottling has just bought the most amazing penthouse overlooking the park. And guess what? She wants a fantastic *trompe l'oeil* in the entrance hall. Of course she doesn't know that yet. But she will, when I'm done talking to her.'

'A *trompe l'oeil*?'

'Yes. Plenty of fat pink cherubs bouncing around on fluffy white clouds. And a nubile Venus eyeing a sleeping Mars, preferably in a state of undress.'

The horror in her voice was unmistakable. 'You mean Romantic?'

'Yes, Romantic. And expensive, my child. Very expensive.'

'I don't know . . .'

His eyes narrowed. 'You don't have to do it if you don't want to. But I could easily tell her that I know just the right artist, a specialist from London, who'll be able to do the work. In fact, there's only one person I would trust with such an important commission. Ava does a great deal of entertaining. Your work would be seen by everyone.'

Fat cherubs. Fluffy clouds. Great, she thought. Everyone would see my derivative Venus; my copy of crap classical bullshit.

'Pretty soon you could charge what you like. But of course if the subject matter is beneath you . . .' he stared at her, unblinking, 'I believe they're hiring at the Chicago Rib Shack.'

'I've never painted a *trompe l'oeil*,' she pointed out.

He reached for the phone. 'How hard can it be? Foreshorten, foreshorten, foreshorten! She's blind as a bat anyway. I'll put in a meeting for tomorrow afternoon.' He started to dial.

She'd thought he might let her work in his shop – not redesign her career.

'Remember,' he continued, 'you're just off the plane. Your portfolio hasn't arrived yet. You're doing this as a favour to me, understand? And whatever you do, tell her that you absolutely don't have time in your schedule. I want you to turn it down flat. Politely, charmingly, but firmly. Allow me to negotiate the whole thing. Rich people are like babies, they only want things they can't have.'

She sighed.

At least she would be painting. And being paid. Perhaps Derek was right. Maybe she didn't have anything new to say artistically. Certainly around him she felt uncouth and adolescent. She'd felt talented in London. Here she felt pedestrian; banal.

Perhaps it was best if she did what he suggested.

Now she had that feeling again, of standing once more at a hidden turning point in her life.

Only what were the choices? Why were they so difficult to see?

There was the crunch of footsteps in gravel. She looked up. Jack was standing on the path, hand across his eyes, wincing in the bright sunlight.

'Don't you want anything to eat?'

'No thanks.' She shook her head. 'Not right now.'

'OK.' He jammed his hands into his pockets. 'I was just . . . you know, checking.'

'Thanks.'

He stood awkwardly for a minute, tracing an uneven circle in the stones with the toe of his shoe. 'You'll never guess what it was.'

'What?'

'Lunch.'

'Oh.' She smiled. 'Chicken.'

He seemed genuinely impressed. 'How did you know that?'

She leaned back on her palms. 'My psychic powers are world-famous, Mr Coates.'

'Really?' He took a step forward. 'Tell me then, Ms Albion, what am I thinking now?'

The garden was sheltered, private. Even the wind came gently there, broken by the high walls.

She tilted her head to one side. 'I wouldn't want to intrude upon your private thoughts.'

'We Olympian slabs of marble have nothing to hide.'

'Certain?'

'Positive.' He crossed his arms across his chest. 'Do your worst.'

'All right.' She stood, turning round to face him, full on. 'Prepare to be amazed.'

A cloud passed in front of the sun, and the sky dimmed, like a hand held in front of a lamp.

At first they were guarded, then smiling, self-conscious; on the verge of laughter. But the longer Cate looked at Jack, the more his features relaxed. She'd never looked at anyone so openly or for so long outside of an art studio. There she'd been hidden behind her easel; a voyeur without danger of detection. But she soon forgot herself, concentrating instead on the dark fringe of his lashes, the gentle creases round his eyes, the black arch of his brow – gradually his expression unfolded, opening, revealing.

And while she stared at him, he stared at her. At the pale green centre of her eyes, flecked with gold; at her fierce concentration. She had the bald, unblinking eye of an artist, a capacity to observe dispassionately, through the layers of colour and form to the substance, the feeling underneath. And he felt himself unravelling, unable to protect himself against the boldness of her attention.

Jack's eyes deepened. Beyond the intelligence and sureness Cate caught a glimpse of something else, a sadness, fiercely defended. And then, slowly, behind even that, a thin shard of fear. Cold and precise, it sliced across the navy core of his iris like a splinter of broken glass.

She recognized it. It too pierced the fragile surface of her consciousness. She felt the same sharp metallic taste fill her mouth as it seeped through, bleeding into her. Suddenly she was aware of the enormous effort involved in avoiding it, hiding it; how vulnerable this moment made them. And, instinctively, she reached forward, placing her hand lightly on his chest, over his heart, as if to protect it.

Confused by her sudden tenderness, he stiffened slightly. 'Is this part of your method?'

'I'm sorry,' she blinked, and began to step back. But he pressed his own hand on top of hers. She felt his heartbeat quicken under her touch.

The fear in his eyes had gone. It had sharpened into something rawer; more visceral and determined. 'Have I convinced you?'

'Of what?' Her own pulse began to beat in tandem with his. 'That you're not made of marble?'

'Precisely.'

'It seems you're flesh and blood after all.'

He released her hand.

It wavered in the air between them a moment, before dropping to her side.

'And yet you haven't answered my question.'

'I'm sorry?'

'What am I thinking?'

She looked again into his face.

The cloud moved on. Once again the sun shone brightly.

Only she knew the fear existed. And she realised that perhaps he'd shown her something even he was unaware of.

'I don't know,' she murmured, turning away. She felt in danger of something she couldn't name or explain. A painful softening; a treacherous, deceptive longing. 'It seems my powers have failed me today.'

'Well, that's a shame.' He shrugged, kicking a bit of gravel across the path. The expression on her face was unreadable; did she find him foolish? 'After all, I was prepared to be amazed.'

He sounded disappointed.

'Who knows?' she said, glancing back. 'These things are famously fickle. Perhaps another day, Mr Coates, I will know exactly what you're thinking.'

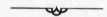

5 St James's Square
London

24 October 1926

Darling,

Thank you so much for your letter – quite the nicest
one I've had in ages. I am so sorry I gave you cause for
concern. I am just a little low as of late and you know
that I am prone to these black spells. Also I'm missing
you terribly. I don't think, darling, that I had quite
realised that you were going to be married and leaving
me so soon. Has he really found a house already?

Perhaps you're right about Switzerland. They
understand these things so much better than we do –
have all sorts of cures and regimes. But I don't want
to go to a clinic. I'm afraid once they get me in, I won't
be allowed to leave. I know I frighten you and that you
want me to be well for the wedding. The truth is, I
frighten myself. I don't know what brings on these
spells. Everything is so different, Irene. Do you really
never miss Ireland, or Fa, or our funny little house?

Father Ryan came round the other day. The Holy
made him. We spent a long time alone with me
gushing and sobbing and him nodding, trying to appear

sympathetic but not wanting to get too close or too wet. In the end he told me to believe. 'Believe in what?' I cried. 'Well, in God's will.' 'How am I meant to know what that is?' He just sat there, all swollen and pink, opening and closing his mouth like a giant fish. In the end all he could come up with was, 'Do as Mother instructs and attend church more often.' Can you imagine God making His will known through Muv? Afterwards, she insisted I have my hair done, since it hasn't been touched in weeks. They put on a rinse which makes it quite golden in colour. She, at least, was pleased. So, apparently, God must be too.

In truth, I'm better than I was. The doctor advocates long walks to lift the mood so the Consort, bless him, has bought me a spaniel pup to keep me company. I call him Nico, which is my little joke. He is the handsomest thing in Green Park. I have been on the lookout for some small token of the Real Nick but there is nothing in the whole of St James's Square. It's quite remarkable how the Consort has removed him from his life.

I so despise this bleak, cold rain we are having! Forgive me if I only write a short note. Some days are such an effort. But I will not fail you on your wedding day, I promise – nothing but smiles and joy and now a blonde head to match!

Diana

When Cate headed into the kitchen, there was a plate of leftover roast chicken and salad waiting for her. Taking a bite, she heard someone in the far pantry. She walked through to find Jo defrosting one of the refrigerators, washing the wire racks in the large sink. To her surprise, she was crying.

'Jo?'

Jo looked up, smiling sadly. 'I can't believe it's come to this,' she said. 'All these years, all this time. It's over. Done.' She rinsed the soapsuds off and stacked the rack on the draining board.

'I'm sorry,' Cate murmured, unable to think of anything else to say.

'And that room. It's strange, don't you think?'

Cate was quiet; she felt somehow responsible.

'All those books. When we were young, my brother and I, we had nothing. Really. We would've killed for books like that. You see, that's not like Irene. She was a generous person. Good. Maybe she forgot they were there.' She wiped her hands on her apron. 'Didn't you want any lunch?'

'No. I just sat in the rose garden for a while. It's really quite beautiful.'

'Yes, it is lovely. Irene used to say that the beauty of nature was proof of God's forgiveness.'

'Why? What did she have to be forgiven for?'

Jo shrugged. 'I don't think it had to do with anything in particular. Maybe she meant original sin, or something along those lines. Catholics are like that, aren't they? Always finding sins where other people only see human nature.'

'I like the sundial. Do you know what the quote is from?'

'No,' Jo admitted. 'That garden was built after the war. The Colonel was very particular about the whole thing. The roses are all the same colour, they've never changed. Always white. Apparently flowers have special meaning.'

'Like what?'

'I don't know . . . Let me see . . .' She sighed, trying to remember, 'White ones are something like purity and innocence, which makes sense. But also something else, something like secrets, or maybe it's silence.'

'Jo, tell me about the people who lived here. I'm curious.'

'Sir Malcolm and Lady Avondale? I think he bought it when they were married as a wedding gift for her. Simple as that really. But war broke out, he joined up and life got in the way. Of course when they first moved in, things were different. My mother came to work for her when she was a bride. A famous debutante, she was. They had house parties, loads of people coming down from London. My mother used to tell me about them – aristocrats, politicians and artists – glamorous, sophisticated young people with the world at their feet. And of course her sister, Baby.'

'Baby?'

'Yes. Well, her real name was Diana but everyone called her Baby. There were only a couple of years between them but Irene always looked after Baby. She was wild, always getting into scrapes. She was part of a set that did silly things like treasure hunts and party games and pretending to be burglars and breaking into each other's houses. Stupid really. That was before she disappeared of course.'

'What do you think happened to her?'

Jo shrugged. 'No one really knows. Over the years there's been lots of speculation. We've had journalists wandering around the place from time to time, looking for clues. What happened to Baby Blythe? When Irene was alive, she never spoke about it. Thing was, Baby was trouble. That's what my mother says. I mean, she was beautiful and popular, but in the wrong way, if you get my meaning. Too many lovers and too many bad habits. Most people think she must've been killed.'

'Killed?'

'Murdered. Or an accident. Though they never found a body.' Jo wiped down the worktop. 'Who knows? She could have died during the Blitz for all we know or fallen off a cliff. Like I said, Irene never spoke of it. There are no pictures of her in the house anywhere. During the war Irene became quite religious. And when he came back, they lived very quietly.'

'I hate to think of it going on the market.'

'It's already been sold. That man Syms came round with the developers a couple weeks ago. As soon as everything is auctioned, they take over. They're going to knock down the old cottage. Begin again. In two years' time, you'll have to have a reservation to see this place at all. God!' She shook her head. 'I've spent more hours here than I have in my own home! It takes over your life, looking after people.'

'And what are you going to do now?' Cate asked softly.

'I don't know. I've always wanted to travel but Mum's so old now. I honestly don't know.' She dabbed her eyes with the corner of the dishcloth. 'I can't believe, after all those years, it's done.'

That evening Cate and Jack had their supper in the kitchen.

Jack stabbed at his chicken hotpot, while Cate, distracted, pushed her vegetables round the periphery of her plate.

'What do you know about Diana Blythe?' she asked at last.

He shrugged his shoulders. 'What everyone knows. She went missing. She was famous for being famous; pretty, reckless. One of the bright young things.'

'You mean like in *Vile Bodies*? Evelyn Waugh?'

He nodded.

Cate pushed the sliced potatoes to one side. 'Don't you think it's strange there are no pictures of her? I mean, they were sisters. But there's nothing.'

'A lot of people don't have photos of family. For some it's just private. Also, perhaps Irene found it painful to be reminded of her, since she was gone.'

'What do you think happened to her?'

'I don't know. Never really thought about it.' He took a gulp of wine. 'Maybe she ran away. Those kinds of people were always legging it at the first sign of real life.'

'And what kind of people would that be?'

'You know, spoilt, beautiful young women with nothing to do.'

It came out sharper than he'd intended. He looked up. She stared back. 'I see.'

They ate in silence; a band of tension stretched between them.

'Have I upset you, Jack?'

'No, I'm just tired.'

'You seem upset.'

His mind turned. 'How did you get into that room?' he asked suddenly.

'I picked the lock.'

He blinked at her. 'Oh.'

Suddenly she was laughing.

He laughed too.

'Yes. I can pick a lock, Jack. I can also hot-wire a car if necessary.'

'And where did you learn how to do that?'

'From my father. Professional piss artist.'

'You're not what you appear to be.'

'Which is?'

'The phrase "butter wouldn't melt in your mouth" springs to mind.'

'Appearances can be deceiving.'

'I should've remembered that's your stock-in-trade.'

He didn't know why he said it. For a moment things had been easier between them. So why did he have to toss out some sideways comment? It was as if he couldn't help himself.

'Not exactly,' she said finally, folding her napkin, getting up. 'It's been a long day.'

'Look, I'm sorry.' He tried to stand too but knocked into the table, spilling the wine across his plate. 'Dammit!' It dripped onto his trousers. He grabbed his napkin and began mopping it up.

'Here.' She passed him a dishcloth and continued stacking the plates in the sink.

Her calmness was more irritating than his clumsiness. He tossed the napkin down, ignoring the spill.

'Cate . . .' He took her hand.

She looked up, alarmed. For a moment, he'd unmasked her.

He reached for her other hand.

'I know you don't like me.' Her voice cracked like a whip, warning him off.

'That's not true.' He tightened his grip.

'But we might at least be civil.' There was something unfinished, almost pleading in her tone.

'It's not true,' he said again, quietly, leaning in. The faint scent of her light citron-based perfume blended with the darker warmth of her hair and skin. Her body yielded ever so slightly against his. 'It's not true.'

Deep in the house, a phone rang – shrill and insistent.

He relaxed his fingers and she backed away, head bowed, disappearing down the dark passageway.

There was an extension on the drawing-room table. She picked it up.

'Hello? Hello?' The line was crackly, muffled.

'Yes, Hello?' Cate answered. 'Rachel? Is that you?'

'Katie! Thank God! I've been leaving messages for you. Isn't there any reception down there?'

She shifted, thinking of Jack's fingers on her skin, the look in his eyes. 'Ah, yes . . . well, sometimes,' she lied, trying to concentrate. 'Why? Is everything all right?'

'Yes . . . well . . .' She hesitated. 'Sort of.'

A knot tightened in Cate's stomach. 'What do you mean, sort of?'

There was a silence.

'I've had a visitor,' Rachel said at last. 'A man, wanting to see you. Someone from New York.'

Driving back to London, they were courteous, formal. Overly polite.

The inventory of Endsleigh was finished now. All that

remained was for the catalogue to be drawn up and the
auction to take place.

Jack switched on the radio. The delicious tension he'd
experienced on the way down, the hope, was dulled by
frustration and disappointment.

Cate sat next to him, stomach tight, mind racing. A
visitor from New York. A man. He had stopped in the
office, made enquiries; left an envelope.

'What did he look like?' she had asked.

'Well . . .' Again Rachel had paused. 'Not exactly good-
looking but well dressed. Tall. With glasses.'

'Glasses?'

'Yes.'

'Oh. I see.'

He'd sent a messenger.

'Do you want me to open it?' Rachel had suggested last
night. 'I have it right here.'

'No.' Her answer was sharp, terrified.

'Do you want me to throw it away?'

Silence.

'Katie? Shall I throw it away?'

'I don't know.'

Cate sighed, twisting round in her seat. She was gone –
starting again in another country. So why was Rachel's
question so baffling?

Jack looked across at her.

He'd blown it. The only thing he couldn't work out was
if he'd blown it because he hadn't kissed her or because he

almost had. Whatever the answer, she was gone now, far away in the concerns of her own life.

So they drove home, through the rolling hills, the picturesque seaside villages and national landmarks of this green and pleasant land. They drove without speaking, the radio losing and gaining reception, each occupied with their own thoughts.

Halfway home, the sky darkened. Jack pulled over and cranked the top up. Almost immediately thick drops fell, lightning seared across the sky. Their progress was slow, windscreen wipers squeaking furiously across the window, sheets of grey rain obscuring the view.

Cate closed her eyes. Her life seemed as torrential and unfathomable as the storm rumbling around them, slipping through her fingers like water. Automatically, she thought of the shoebox, hidden inside her overnight bag. It drew her, pulling her away from her tangled thoughts; filling the void of her loneliness. She was a thief, stealing fragments of the past from the old house; peering into the private life of a dead woman. More than that, it was dangerous; illegal. She'd taken a Tiffany bracelet; personal belongings from a client of Rachel's. Part of her dreaded what would happen if anyone found out. And yet to put it back had been unthinkable.

Was it her imagination, or was the connection she felt to the house, to the mysterious sisters, real?

The wheels hummed beneath her. In another hour they would be back in London.

Cate wondered what Irene looked like when she was younger. What perfume she wore; what her favourite song was.

They crept forward, lorries whizzing by them, buffeted by the wind.

Suddenly she could see her, sitting next to her new husband as he pulled up the long arched drive of Endsleigh for the first time. It was an early-autumn afternoon; bright and clear. He brought the Daimler to a stop, turned off the engine. Overwhelmed with excitement, Irene climbed out of the car, eyes wide, laughing in amazement.

She turned to face him, the sea breeze tossing her dark curls around her lovely face. 'Is it really ours?'

'Yes,' he nodded, smiling. 'It's really ours.'

He took a set of keys from his coat pocket. And, wrapping his arm around Irene's shoulder, he led her to the front door. 'We're going to be happy here,' he promised, pressing his lips to her forehead.

'Yes. I know we will.' Her eyes were gleaming.

Her husband turned the key in the lock. 'Welcome to Endsleigh.'

# Part Two

Part Two

5 St James's Square
London

13 July, 1932

My dearest Wren,
Oh how I miss you! Though I must say last weekend at
Endsleigh was nothing short of divine. You are the most
accomplished hostess – I don't know how you managed
to get Lord Rothermere to sing 'Mademoiselle from
Armentières' without his teeth but it was too killing!
It's impossible to imagine him advising the PM after
one has seen his gums. And Jock Witney, who shall
be hereafter known as the Rover, cheated miserably
during the midnight egg-and-spoon race. He tripped
me mercilessly and those roving hands of his are most
tiresome. I'll bet he's every bit as foul in business as he
is on the field. Of course your cook is so good, which
makes all the difference. Such a quantity of fresh
oysters – the sheer extravagance! But I do wonder
about your lady's maid. I know she's local and very
young but there seems something amiss with her; as if
she's watching all the time. Do keep an eye on your
jewellery.

    And the most wonderful thing is you look so well,
darling. Healthy and relaxed and – dare I say it? –

rounded! They say the third time is the luckiest and I feel certain this will be true for you. I know the whole thing has been torture and you've been so endlessly brave about your disappointments. Not the least because Muv will go on and on about feeding the blood and making a sticking place for it. She is so ceaselessly foul about blood. I can't wait until we can go properly shopping for furniture and new curtains – I shall be the most spoiling aunt ever!

Now, what news of London? Well, Pinky has taken to going round with Gloria Manning, who has hair like a poodle and the eyes of a frog. I cut him dead at Grosvenor House on Saturday, but really, there are only so many times a man should be allowed to propose – every time Pinky has a glass of champagne he goes down on one knee. It's just tiresome. Harpers Bazaar have printed pictures of me dancing at Four Hundred, looking just this side of hysterical, which I cannot decide is good or not. And Cecil wants me to pose for him again – Venus. I can't tell you how bored I am already by it. But he's hounding me; says it will be novel and daring. I'm tired of people taking my photograph. I feel like a national monument. It is incredibly overrated to be a 'beauty'. Especially as people feel as if they have the right to stare at you openly and say anything they like to your face. I was outside Wilton's the other day when two fat American women walked right up to me, gave me the once-over and then declared loudly in those foghorn voices of theirs, 'Well, I don't see what all the fuss is about!' I felt I should die from mortification and rage. If Anne hadn't been there, I'm certain I would've run after them.

Anne is so lovely. And I admire her taking her own flat. She works in a bookshop just off Piccadilly doing accounts and posting out orders, which sounds too dull but she says is blissful. I fear she's becoming a communist – she's in a fever over the Spanish and their new Republic. Keeps calling it the dawn of a new age, though to be honest, it feels very much like the same old age to me. Her fiancé Paul is some sort of big cheese in the movement – that is if communists are allowed to be big cheeses. He wears nothing but black and brown, with a little red kerchief around his neck, which I suppose he needs when he's out tilling the soil and must wipe the sweat from his noble brow. And he never speaks to me directly, but only refers to me in the third person as the 'decadent bourgeoisie', which is not as endearing as it sounds. Anne spends all her time apologising to me for him, and to him for me. I wouldn't mind so much only I know he went to Eton and his father is a peer.

As for me, I wander lonely as a cloud! Mrs Digby Smith is having a masquerade ball for Esme's twenty-first

tonight and I'm going as Cleopatra. Donald Hargreves
is going as my asp. Donny's a terrible lush but a terrific
dancer. And then on to the Kit-Cat Club, I suppose.
Don't allow the Holy to force-feed you like
a goose, darling.

 Masses of love from your own,
 D xxx

Cate walked up the steps of 1a Upper Wimpole Street, to the first floor, where Rachel's flat was situated above a dentist's office. It was a sprawling collection of rooms, spread over two floors, every surface crowded with books, paintings, objects gleaned from various commissions. Last decorated in 1984, it was frozen in an age that had been the highlight of hers and Paul's marriage. Bright red walls adorned the dining room, sunshine yellow in the kitchen. A mossy-green carpet buckled, faded and shapeless, throughout. Once they had entertained frequently, generously – open-house luncheons and parties that went on into the early hours of the morning. The dining table seated twelve with ease and there were extra chairs everywhere, lining the walls of the living room, tucked into corners, ready to accommodate the overflow. Nothing had been altered since Paul's death. But it had been a long time since anyone had crashed in the upstairs guest rooms or sat down to enjoy one of Rachel's famous roast beef suppers.

Cate put her bag down in the hallway.

It was waiting for her in the centre of the dining-room table; the thick white envelope. Rachel came out of the kitchen, wiping her hands on her apron. She was making chicken soup in celebration of Cate's return; the air was filled with the savoury aroma of fresh stock. 'Hello!' she smiled, giving Cate a hug. 'How was it? I hope Jack wasn't too difficult.'

'No. He was fine.'

'Good.'

Cate looked past her, into the dining room.

Rachel turned, following her eyeline. 'Oh . . . yes,' she said significantly.

Cate walked over and picked it up.

Her name was written across the front, 'Cate Albion'. But it was not in his handwriting. She was surprised by how both relieved and disappointed she felt – how much she'd longed to see something of him and yet dreaded it at the same time.

Rachel sat down. 'Do you want to tell me who it's from?'

Cate shook her head.

'Do you want me to sit with you while you read it?'

'No.'

'You know you don't have to open it.'

Cate said nothing.

Frowning, Rachel ran her hand over the tablecloth in front of her, smoothing out the wrinkles. She was unused to playing the maternal role and was unsure how to proceed. 'I only want to help you, darling.'

'Yes. Yes, I know.'

'But you're still not going to tell me anything,' she deduced.

'Not yet. That is –' Cate looked at her, her eyes anxious – 'if you don't mind.'

Sighing, Rachel got up. 'Fine. So, do you want rice in your soup or noodles?'

'Noodles, please.'

'OK.' Resigned, she headed back to the kitchen, closing the dining-room door behind her.

Cate sank into a chair, turning the envelope over and over. If she opened it, she couldn't quite be sure of what would happen next. It had happened before; she'd watched her good intentions and firm resolves melt away with a few simple words. And yet there was an excitement – a tangible energy. He wanted her. Why else would he contact her at all? Her ego swelled, inflating like an empty balloon. She was desirable, alluring and, as long as the envelope remained unopened, in complete control.

The fire alarm blared. Rachel rushed into the dining room. 'What's going on?'

'Sorry!' Cate was wildly fanning the air around an old marble ashtray, the envelope crumpling and curling, consumed by flames. 'Sorry! So sorry! I was just . . . you know . . . getting rid of this.'

Rachel flung open the windows and began flapping her apron. 'You know, you could just throw it away.'

'Yes, but . . . but I don't trust myself!'

Rachel grabbed a plant mister from the mantelpiece, spraying until the flame fizzled out. 'Well –' she surveyed the remains – 'you won't be reading it now.'

They both stared at the sodden, charred mess.

'No.' And for the first time that day, Cate found herself laughing. 'I'm sorry, darling. I'm all on edge. I don't want you to worry. There's nothing to worry about. I promise.'

Rachel wrapped her arm around Cate's shoulder and gave her a squeeze. 'Except perhaps the house burning down!'

'Ah! Yes. There is that.'

Rachel took the ashtray, emptying it into the kitchen bin and wiping it clean.

Cate followed her into the kitchen. 'Tell me, if you had some old piece of clothing and you wanted to know more about it, like, for example, a handbag or a pair of shoes or something, where would you go to find out more?'

'Clothing?' Rachel gave the soup a stir. 'What clothing?'

'Just something I found at one of the local antique shops in Devon.'

'Well, I suppose you could take it over to Alfies Antiques Market. Or go to the library in the Victoria and Albert Museum. They have the largest resources about fashion history.'

Cate leaned against the worktop. 'That's a good idea.'

'Actually, I've got a contact there, in the fashion department. Occasionally they bid for pieces that go up for auction. It's been a while but I could put you in touch with him.' She concentrated, her brow wrinkling. 'Theodore. That's it. He might be able to help you. Are you becoming a collector too?'

Cate shrugged. 'I'm just curious. That's all.'

'I'm surprised you didn't find anything in Endsleigh. You know it was owned by one of the Blythe sisters?'

'Yes, I think Jack mentioned it at one point,' she admitted lightly.

'Now there were two sisters who were chalk and cheese!'

'Really?' She picked at a sliver of raw carrot, left on the cutting board, sweet and crunchy.

'The older one, Irene, was devoted to charity work, especially around refugee children during the war. But Diana was the exact opposite – wild, promiscuous, Trouble with a capital T.'

'What do you think happened to her?'

'Personally, I think she ran away.'

'Why?'

Rachel rolled her eyes. 'Why does anyone run away? I like to think of her as a wizened old woman living quietly in a trailer park somewhere in Arizona.'

'Slightly far-fetched.'

'Far-fetched is what life usually serves up, my dear.'

Cate smiled. But inwardly she knew all too well why people ran away. It was difficult, almost impossible to change who you were. Could anyone really be faulted for settling for a change in landscape instead?

Perhaps Rachel was right; somewhere out there, in some unassuming corner of the world, Diana Blythe had managed the impossible – she'd managed to elude herself once and for all.

'Do you want me to give Theodore a ring in the morning?'

'Sure, that would be great.'

'What is it, anyway?'

'Nothing much. Just bits and bobs. Listen, I'm sorry again about the fire alarm.' She landed a kiss on Rachel's cheek. 'I'd better unpack.'

As she headed upstairs with her bag, there was a tangible sense of relief. It was over. The letter was destroyed. But why would he send a third party all this way to deliver it? Why not simply post it?

She stopped, gripped the banister hard.

Unless, of course, he was in London now.

There would be no need to post it if he were here. And he would never come to the house himself. It wasn't in his nature to take a risk; to do anything of which he wasn't already assured of the result.

He was content to bide his time.

After all, this wasn't a question of love.

It was a matter of ownership.

Rachel emptied the remains of a box of egg noodles into the simmering soup. Popping open the lid on the bin to throw the empty container away, something caught her eye. It was shiny and black, curling and twisting like a misshapen claw, reaching out of a sheaf of seared, soggy writing paper, among the damp ashes. Gingerly, she picked it out, her curiosity getting the better of her.

'Good God!'

It was the remains of a black American Express card;

the kind that had no credit limit. The kind that was only offered to clients who were privately referred; whose bank balances were in the millions rather than the thousands. She had come across only a couple of them in her business, used to purchase items no ordinary card would cover. 'Ms C. Albion' it read in gold letters across the bottom. She turned it over. Just visible on the back was Katie's faded signature.

Quickly, Rachel unfolded the sodden paper that had been wrapped around it.

It wasn't the love letter she was expecting. In fact, only three words were typed across the centre.

'Paid in Full.' A. Monroe.

5 St James's Square
London

14 July 1932

Oh my darling!!

I write to you in the early hours of the morning, with a shaking hand – Eleanor Ogilvy-Smith has lunged at me at Esme's fancy dress party! She cornered me in the cloakroom and for a moment I thought she'd just lost her balance but then I realised her mouth was about to collide with mine and that she was trying to kiss me! Oh, the horror of it! And when I told her I couldn't possibly she began to cry and begged me not to tell her mother. I swear she was half-cut but she clung onto my hand (she has a grip like a sailor) and said she's been in love with me for years. It was all extremely shocking. It wouldn't have surprised me a bit from Brenda or Liz, but Eleanor? I suppose the Romeo costume she was wearing ought to have given it away. She's really quite large and rather alarming. Oh, what shall I do? I so preferred it when she despised me.

Advice please at your earliest convenience!

Mortified and Terrified to Leave the House Lest I Am Pounced Upon,

D xxx

The vast lobby of the Victoria and Albert Museum was a mixture of classical marble architecture and sleek modern interiors; a winding, undulating Chihuly chandelier hung over the information desk; azure and emerald glass twisting in long serpent tentacles like an aquatic, faceless Medusa.

Cate's heels echoed as she walked in, stopping to open her bag for the security guard to check inside.

He took out the old shoebox and, eyeing her suspiciously, opened it.

'I have an appointment in the fashion department,' she explained, slipping the lid back on.

He directed her to the front desk. There she was asked to wait, while they rang through to Theodore's assistant. Walking slowly around the periphery of the enormous hall, she watched the groups of people passing in and out, feeling her nerves tense. There was nothing to be afraid of. And yet she was aware of a growing possessiveness around the shoes, the objects, the entire discovery. She wanted to know all the answers but didn't really want to share the secret. What if this man, this Theodore, took the shoes away from her? What if she was found out as a thief?

Strolling slowly, she concentrated on the inlaid marble pattern on the floor, hugging her bag to her chest. She would ask a few questions and leave. That was all.

'Ms Albion?'

She looked up.

An attractive, dark-haired girl stood in front of her, wearing a pair of thick black tights, flat ballet shoes and a dress that appeared to be fashioned entirely from brown wrapping paper and packing tape. The word 'DRESS' was written on the front of it in red ink.

She smiled. 'I'm Sam, Mr Whyte's assistant. His office is downstairs. Would you like to follow me?'

Cate blinked. 'Yes. Of course.'

Sam turned and Cate followed her through the maze of galleries and into the fashion section of the museum. There was a reverent hush in the dimly lit rooms where mannequins were posed in long glass display cases, modelling exquisite examples of couture through the ages. Sam's incredible outfit made a crisp, rustling noise. People turned and stared as they passed, but Sam seemed unperturbed. Eventually they arrived at a thick mahogany door with a security lock on it. Sam swiped her pass key through and they descended into the bowels of the building, along a winding warren of workrooms and offices in the basement of the museum.

Fluorescent lights blinked and buzzed above them and there was the smell of various dyes and adhesives, mixed with the comforting aroma of strong Italian coffee brewing. A radio played in the tapestry repair shop; there was the sound of raucous laughter as they passed the hats and accessories room; some sort of heated discussion was taking place in small leathers on the merits of glue versus rivets. The further back they went, the quieter it became.

They passed vaults and vaults of hanging garments, smashed together in automated rails that hung in rows up to the ceiling. There were piles of boxes, and corridors crammed with posters and old brochures, hanging rails laden with Victorian greatcoats, Mary Quant minidresses and Armani evening gowns. Mannequin parts were everywhere; arms poking out of black bin liners, heads balanced on filing cabinets. It was bursting with treasures, rare fragments of past lives salvaged, researched and restored with a loving, dedicated eye.

They rounded a corner to a small office tucked away from the main jostle of the department. There, sitting at a long desk piled high with fabric swatches, piles of papers, magazines, reference books, old coffee cups and a state-of-the-art G3 Mac computer, sat a slight, older man in his sixties with a shock of bright pink hair. He was wearing a pair of original Vivienne Westwood red tartan bondage trousers and a shirt with the sleeves rolled up. Thick black glasses framed his bright blue eyes. On the wall behind him was an extensive collection of Virgin Mary memorabilia.

He stood up. 'I'm Theo,' he introduced himself. 'Please, have a seat. Would you like something to drink? Coffee? Water?'

'No, thank you. I'm fine.' Cate balanced on the edge of her chair.

He laughed. 'Don't be nervous! We're preparing for a new show exploring Dada and punk. "The Radical Voice in Fashion". Sam and I occasionally get a bit carried away, don't we?' He gave Sam a wink.

'Actually, I like the dress,' Cate assured them.

Sam's face lit up. 'It's taken from an original 1960s Pierre Cardin pattern I found on the Web. I'm interested in disposable clothes for a disposable society. And recyclable. Disposable and recyclable,' she corrected herself. 'I'm working on a Burberry-style mac made entirely from black bin liners at the moment.'

'How's that going?' Theo asked.

'I have to admit, it's not draping very well.'

'You need industrial-strength bin liners. The kind builders use.'

'Hmm.' She nodded. 'I think you're right.'

He turned to Cate. 'We like to live our research around here. Last year was "The Fashionable Farewell: The Tradition of Mourning through the Ages". Everyone without exception wore head-to-toe black all year. But enough. Did you say you wanted coffee?'

'No. No thank you.'

He gave Sam a nod.

'Excuse me,' she said, taking her leave.

He settled back behind the desk, cocking his head to one side. 'You don't remember me, do you?'

'I'm sorry . . .' Cate stumbled, desperately trying to place him, 'I can't quite recall . . .'

'It doesn't matter. It was years ago. Your end-of-term show. Your aunt introduced us.'

'Oh. I apologise. I have the most shocking memory.'

'Well –' he looked at her through the thick glasses – 'you seemed a bit the worse for wear that night.'

Cate felt her cheeks reddening. 'I hope I wasn't rude.'

'Not at all. You were just . . . well, celebrating. It was an extraordinary show. I'll never forget the piece with the babies and the bed sheet.'

'*Medea.*'

'Yes! That's it! Very dramatic stuff.'

Cate had forgotten that painting, deliberately. The blood-soaked bed sheet, the limp child. That was the year her father died. She'd struggled with her work; struggled with herself.

She stared at the floor. 'It didn't sell.'

Theo laced his fingers together, pressing them to his lips thoughtfully. 'It was very powerful.'

'It was ugly.'

'But art isn't just about beauty. It's about truth. And I for one don't believe the two are always related.'

She focused on the madonnas behind him, the bright, garish colours of their robes; the gentle inclination of their long-suffering heads.

'What are you doing now?' he asked, leaning forward. 'I hope you'll be exhibiting again soon.'

'I'm doing some . . . some more traditional pieces. Reproductions.'

'Really?' He sounded surprised.

'Commissions.'

'Oh. Yes, well . . .' he conceded. 'What I loved about your work was the sheer scale and audacity of it. Like a modern-day female Caravaggio. So –' he settled back – 'what can I help you with?'

Opening her bag, she took out the shoebox and pushed it across to him. 'I wonder if you could tell me anything about these?'

He opened the box and examined the shoes. 'Yes, Pinet of Bond Street, I'd say from about 1929–33. A very expensive shoe shop, even in those days.' He turned them over. 'Hardly been worn. Evening wear, obviously. But the evening must've been cut short. And they're broken.'

'Really?' Cate leaned forward.

'Just here.' Theodore showed her where one of the straps was severed. 'They wouldn't have stayed on for long. Where did you find them?'

'I was in Devon recently. They come from an old house. Actually . . .' she hesitated, 'I think they belonged to Irene Avondale.'

He sat up, eyes gleaming. 'You mean Irene Blythe? As in the Blythe sisters?'

'Yes.'

'Ah! I have a special fondness for the Beautiful Blythe Sisters! Who doesn't? But sadly the answer is no,' he said firmly, putting the lid back on.

'What do you mean, no?'

'No, they couldn't have possibly belonged to her.'

'But how can you be so sure?'

'I like to collect things.' He gestured to the wall behind him. 'You may be admiring my collection of tacky madonnas right now. Or not. Be that as it may, one of my earliest passions was collecting shoe lasts.'

'Pardon me?'

'Lasts. They are the exact moulds of feet, carved out of wood that are kept at bespoke shoemakers. A customer has them made once and then they're stored until that person dies. Each pair of shoes is custom-made to fit their feet exactly. As a result of my own personal passion, we launched a show about five or six years ago called "If the Shoes Fits" on the history of bespoke shoemaking. And as chance would have it, several lasts belonging to Irene Blythe were purchased by the museum at great expense. One set from Foster & Son in Jermyn Street and another from Ferragamo himself. Lady Avondale was afflicted with that crippling condition that made her right at home in the upper classes – long, very narrow feet and fallen arches. She would never have purchased a pair of ready-made shoes, no matter how expensive. She wouldn't have lasted two seconds in them. Besides –' he pushed the box back to her – 'they're the wrong size. Long narrow boats, that's what her feet were like. Really most extraordinary.'

'Oh.'

'What you have there, my dear, is a lovely pair of vintage shoes possibly worth fifty pounds in today's market. Oh, and quite a nice box.'

'I see.'

'Would you like to see the lasts?' he asked eagerly. 'They're stored just a few rooms down. The craftsman-ship is incredible!'

'Ah, no. That's not necessary.' She put the box back into her bag.

'You seem disappointed.'

'I . . . I just thought . . .' She stopped herself. 'It doesn't really matter.'

He leaned back, folding his hands in front of him. 'Certain people are enigmas. They have a glamour that captures the imagination. The Blythe sisters are like that. They were the living embodiment of the spirit of a romantic, highly charged time between the wars. You're not the first person to have fallen under their spell.'

'No,' she sighed, 'I suppose not.'

He stood up. The interview was over.

'I'm sorry I can't be more helpful. But listen, do drop me a line if you are exhibiting again in London. And if you want to see anything, any of the shows, let me know and I'll be happy to arrange some tickets for you.'

'Thank you. That's so kind.'

He opened the door.

Cate had a thought. 'What about her sister?'

'Baby?'

'Yes. Could the shoes have belonged to her?'

He frowned, wrinkling his nose. 'Baby Blythe went missing in . . . I can't recall . . . it was shortly after the war began.' He shrugged. 'I mean, I can't say for certain. After all, no one knows what became of her. Anything's possible and yet it's unlikely.'

Sam was hovering again, waiting to guide her back through to the main gallery.

'It's addictive, isn't it?' he laughed, patting her on the shoulder.

'What do you mean?'

'Once you've caught the collecting bug, it's a hard habit to shake – isn't that right, Sam?'

Sam nodded. 'Every piece tells a story.'

'Unfortunately,' he added, 'only once in a blue moon do we discover what the real story is.'

'Yes, yes, I guess you're right,' Cate said.

Trailing after Sam through the corridors her heart sank. Once again the larger, unsolvable problems of her own life loomed like dark shadows on the periphery of her consciousness, bringing with them a familiar feeling of dread.

Before she realised it, they were back in the main fashion gallery; long rows of dimly lit display cases arcing round. Suddenly Sam stopped.

Cate looked up.

They were standing in front of a simple bias-cut halter-neck evening gown of smooth, pale pink satin. It was form-fitting, sensuous, almost flesh-coloured. Its owner must've been slight; the waist was diminutive and yet the bust generously cut.

Cate turned to Sam. Her eyes were sparkling.

'This is an original Vionnet,' Sam whispered. 'From Paris.'

'Yes . . . ?'

'It belonged to Baby Blythe!'

Cate looked at it again. The proportions were stunning; at once tiny and voluptuous.

'The thing is,' Sam continued, 'it's never been officially confirmed. There's a scandal around that dress. It came to us from a very unexpected source.' She took Cate's arm, pulling her closer. 'Rumour has it we received a bequest from the Rothermere estate. Lord Rothermere was most famously one of Chamberlain's chief advisers during the lead-up to the Second World War. But he was also an avid hunter; used to fox-hunt with the Prince of Wales and owned an entire estate in Melton Mowbray for that purpose alone. The bequest was meant to be riding habits and military uniforms. Fancied himself as quite the Dapper Dan. But hidden in one of the trunks, tucked into a silk pillowcase, was this dress! Diana's name was embroidered inside. Apparently it still smelled of perfume – Worth, Je Reviens. And' – she leaned in – 'it was torn – in the back!'

'Really?'

'There was a note with it. "Paid in full." Signed, "B". Lord Rothermere was married and very moral and uptight. And believe me, no oil painting. God only knows how it got ripped. The repair department had a devil of a time fixing it; that's why it's positioned that way.' She pointed to the angle at which the dress was displayed. 'I'm sure if the family knew it was in that old trunk, we would've never received it in a thousand years. But I suspect he kept it hidden, some little trophy from his past. Of course, no one can prove a thing. And the note got filed away somewhere, lost in a sea of bureaucracy. But it's a beautiful example of Madame Vionnet's tailoring. It must've cost a fortune at the time.'

Cate stared at it. 'She was really very tiny, wasn't she?'

Sam nodded.

'How big do you think her feet were?'

'Oh, I don't know . . . small . . . Maybe four, four and a half?'

Cate smiled to herself. There was a slim chance still.

'When I heard you mention her I thought you might be interested,' Sam said.

'Yes, I'm interested in anything to do with the Blythe sisters. Thank you for showing it to me.'

'My pleasure. Have you tried looking in the National Portrait Gallery? You never know. They have the most amazing collection of famous faces in there. We use their archive all the time.'

'That's a good idea.' Cate made a mental note.

Sam sighed, turning back to the mannequin. 'But why? That's the thing that gets me.' She shook her head in disbelief. 'Why would anyone that beautiful, that sought-after, end up shagging some bald old man? I just don't get it.'

Cate's eyes were trained on the perfect satin folds of the exquisite dress.

'Not everything we do makes sense,' she said at last.

Cate walked out into the close, hot air, on to the crowded pavement of Exhibition Road and headed towards the bus stop. If the shoes belonged to Baby Blythe, then everything, all the other objects were likely to be hers as well. The key, the bracelet, the photograph . . . could these be missing clues to the mystery of her disappearance? Perhaps she was the only person alive able to piece the puzzle together. And she thought again of the dress, the note; the tear which could never completely be repaired. Her mind buzzed with questions and possibilities. Who gave her the bracelet? Why was it hidden? Was the sailor a lover?

A bus pulled over. She climbed up to the top deck, taking a seat next to the window.

Looking out across the neat little garden square opposite, she admired the creamy Georgian terraced houses and the Brompton Oratory. At once imperious and lopsided, its walls were pitted and scarred from bombs during the Second World War. It was amazing how much the war still influenced London, its very fabric still marked, the wounds as fresh as if they'd happened last night. And she wondered if Baby Blythe had ever walked these streets –

perhaps visiting someone in the square or attending a wedding at the church. Cate felt an eerie sense of their lives intertwining, overlapping one another across the decades.

Someone was staring up at her from the pavement. A man; tall, thin, with glasses, frowning intently at her.

A man . . . with glasses . . . like the one who delivered the envelope.

Turning away, she shielded her face with her hand, her mind racing.

Had he been following her? Was it just a coincidence or had he been sent, hired to report on her whereabouts? He was still staring, she was sure of it.

The bus pulled away from the stop, lurching into traffic. Automatically she turned and looked back. A fresh swarm of foreign students crowded around the bus stop. She couldn't see him. Maybe she was being ridiculous; the product of an overstimulated imagination. And yet she couldn't be sure.

Her heart thumped. Suddenly London was no longer the safe haven she had imagined; at each turning, on every street corner, a sinister stranger might appear.

5 St James's Square
London

30th July 1932

My darling Wren,
You will never guess who I ran into, quite literally,
at the Black and White Ball – Nick Warburton –
looking every bit as handsome as I remembered him –
beautifully dressed and with those same smiley eyes. I
was flinging myself quite wildly around on the dance
floor, wearing the most divine silver gown and shoes
(after all, silver is black and white mixed together and
one doesn't want to simply fade into the crowd), when
suddenly I heard a familiar voice say, 'Those feet of clay
don't seem to weigh you down at all.'

I turned and there he was, sipping champagne and
smiling at me. 'Here.' He put his glass down and took
my hand. 'Let me show you how the grown-ups do it.'

Oh, what heaven!

We danced. Of course, Pinky behaved very badly
about it all, lurking around the edge of the dance floor
and STARING. I just ignored him in the end. And
Nick howled when I told him about life in St James's
Square with the Holy and his father. I told him all

*about how she wants to have me thrown in a convent to
save my wicked soul while he wants me married to one
of the chinless set – anything with a title. He says
I want spanking. I told him he was welcome to try.
And things did go quiet – only deliciously so.*

*Then I told him I had quite a full dance card
and couldn't be detained any more by men without
prospects or decided intentions. To which he laughed
and told me he had very decided intentions, then took
the liberty of pulling the strap off my right shoe! 'Now,
Baby, you'll twist your ankle dancing in that. Time to
come with me and sit down, like a good girl. You know
how fond I am of those feet of yours.' And we spent
the rest of the night sitting in lounge chairs outside,
overlooking the park, eating strawberries and talking.
He put my foot up on a little cushion and every time
someone came to get me, we'd point to it and make
noises about its fragile condition. But, my love, I
could've spent all night there with him. Have you ever
found someone who perfectly understood every little
thought in your head, every twist and turn, every
sentiment, so that half of what you wanted to say is
said by them before you can even voice it? And there
is an ease about him that's so attractive; a firmness of
character that young men don't have.*

*He didn't take me home. But this morning a
bouquet of long white calla lilies arrived with a card
that said, 'With Deepest Sympathy For Your Shoe.'*

*And of course it was addressed to 'Baby Blythe', which drove Muv mad. 'I will not have you wandering around town with some ridiculous nickname!'*

*And then the Old Guard started as well, 'What if the papers should get hold of it? Who is this man? Who are his family?' (Too funny!)*

*I simply waltzed away on a cloud.*

*Oh, my angel! Is this what love feels like? Like having no stomach and no desire to sleep and a constant buzzing in your head? I only want the conversation to continue and never end.*

*Sending you every inch of love,*

*Baby xxx*

Rachel had found the piece of paper with her sister's number on it. It had been in front of her the entire time, dangling on a Post-it from the computer monitor. She held it, turning it over in her fingers thoughtfully.

It was early; she was alone in the office. She liked travelling in to Holborn before the morning rush, especially in the summer months. These were hours, precious and golden, which would disappear come autumn. But they were gifts now. As she got older, she learned to appreciate and use them. In a little while the area would be swarming with people, but right now it was quiet; the day unfolding.

She took another sip of her coffee. The room was filled with pieces, trophies from the jobs she and Paul had done and their adventures together. The ebony pug dog from the Queen Anne house in Cheshire. The oak reading table from the old public library in Aylesbury. The fake Canaletto from Bath. This business had been their lives. Today, especially, it seemed impossible, as it always did, that these things should remain but that he was gone. He was more real than any of it and yet here she was, staring at paintings and planters; empty chairs.

She forced herself round, picked up the phone and began to dial.

Then she stopped, putting it down.

What would she say? That Katie was in trouble? That she was worried about her? Or just that she was visiting?

Perhaps if she left a message, Anna would ring back and speak to Katie herself.

She sighed, running her fingers through her hair.

Why was it so complicated – the basic facts slipping through her fingers like water?

This is what happened around Katie; what used to happen around her father too. The simplest things became elusive, complex. Two minutes in their company and you didn't know where you were or what you were doing.

Feeling around in her handbag, she searched for her cigarettes but the pack she found was empty. Scrunching it up into a ball, she aimed for the bin but missed. It landed on top of a box of old catalogues she'd intended to file months ago.

She missed Paul. It was an aching emptiness across her chest; physical and real, as if her heart were straining, like a dumb animal, reaching out for a touch that it couldn't understand was no longer there. Despite the years they'd had together, the good years, it hadn't been enough.

And now, she realised with a stab of irritation, she missed her sister Anna too. But this was different. It wasn't a comfortable sentimental longing, but rather an older feeling; childish and petulant; a feeling she should've out grown long ago. She was jealous, as simple as that. She envied her sister her new life. And suddenly the objects around her ceased to feel like precious mementoes but instead like burdens; weights binding her to a past she couldn't escape.

Why was it that she always wanted what Anna had?

She should be happy for her. She owed her that.

And without wishing to, she thought of Ryan, Katie's father.

Getting up, she opened the door, clearing her lungs and her mind with fresh air.

But once summoned, the memory lingered, haunting her still.

That awful, disgusting summer. The house they'd rented by the shore.

Her thoughts were interrupted by a car horn, tooting. Across the street she saw Jack pulling up in that funny little Triumph of his, which so belonged to another age. It wasn't like him to come in so often or so early. She waved back at him.

'Want a coffee?' he called, climbing out.

She shook her head and he walked off towards the cafe.

Rachel closed the door, went back to her desk.

She would make the call later. When she was alone. There was work to do. And today was the day she would sort things out, get things done.

Cate was sitting at one of the computers in the cool marble interior of the Marylebone Library. She'd been there most of the morning. The librarian had helped her locate several glossy picture books about the Blythe sisters, which she'd skimmed through eagerly. It seemed Baby in particular had inspired a great many people with her starlet looks and mysterious disappearance. But there was very little evidence about what actually became of her – only romantic speculation. Now searches under 'Baby Blythe' or 'Diana Blythe' yielded plenty of the same photographs but no significant new material.

She was stuck.

'Irene Avondale' she typed in.

The screen flashed to life, bringing up a page of fresh links, most of them obituaries from her recent death. She clicked on one.

'Irene, Lady Avondale was born on 13 September in 1907, married Colonel Sir Malcolm Avondale, Bt, in 1927, died in Devon, England, 19 March 1999.

Irene and her sister Diana (1910–?) were born to an Irish writer and historian, Benedict Blythe, and his young wife, Gwenevere, in Dublin. Their circumstances were extremely modest; however, that changed dramatically following their father's death in 1918 when their mother married Lord Warburton, the wealthy heir to the Warburton fortune, in 1921. Both sisters were launched into society and were widely regarded as the two most beautiful debutantes of their years. They were extremely popular, devising elaborate party games and masquerades to amuse their friends. One was the famous St Valentine's Day treasure hunt when the girls persuaded

Lord Beaverbrook of the *Evening Standard* to publish a series of clues in the paper, leading to secret locations all over London. The winner was guaranteed a kiss from his favourite sister, though the proceedings were declared to be rigged when the lucky winner was revealed to be one of their own close set, claiming his prize as a kiss from both.

Irene, the more conservative and quieter of the two, went on to marry Colonel Sir Malcolm Avondale, Bt, in 1927, a popular member of the Conservative Party who rose to prominence as an effective public speaker in opposition to Chamberlain's appeasement policies and an early supporter of Churchill. He later distinguished himself serving in Burma with the Army, gaining the rank of colonel. Irene also worked during the war as a nurse at the Devonport Naval Base in Plymouth. After her sister's mysterious disappearance in 1941, she retreated from social life, finding solace in the Catholic Church and her faith. She and her husband had no children, although she worked extensively in later life with UNICEF and was awarded an OBE for her services in this field in 1976. After her husband's death in 1985, she lived almost exclusively at their Devon home, Endsleigh, until her death in March earlier this year.

Cate leaned back in her chair, considering.

She hadn't realised the Blythe sisters' background was quite so modest. What a shock, as young girls, to come into so much wealth and position – to be transported from the outskirts of Dublin into the very centre of glamorous London society between the wars. They must've been extraordinary personalities to rise to the top of that set so quickly, distinguishing themselves among a class of people punch-drunk from endless rounds of parties, balls and events.

And they were outsiders. She'd always known that and yet somehow it hadn't sunk in. They weren't born into this class yet they managed to conquer it. Had they referred to their upbringing; made jokes about it? Or had they simply sidestepped it, as she'd done hers, allowing it to be recreated in the fertile imaginations of others, fed by rumour and deliberate, subtle misinformation?

She thought about how Derek had introduced her in New York, at gallery openings, restaurants and gala events. Her name became shortened to Cate and her personal history suddenly became vague and amorphous, gaining a great deal by omission. He'd send her to the bar for drinks and then he'd lean in, his voice dropping seductively. 'She's a Londoner, of course. But now her mother spends most of her time on the Continent. Her training is extensive – from all the best schools. Her father is sadly deceased but he had a home in Mayfair; part of the music industry. I'm trying to convince her to stay in New York but it's difficult because she's had so many other offers.'

The first time she heard him do it, she hadn't realised who he was talking about. When she finally made the connection, she took him aside. 'My mother vaccations in Malaga and my father never owned anything. He lived in a Peabody flat behind Bond Street Station.'

'Spain is the Continent, my dear. And anything behind Oxford Street and before St James's Park is Mayfair, regardless if it's a penthouse or a park bench.'

His sureness disarmed her. She stared back at him, unable to combat his logic. Had she really had such a glamorous upbringing and just not noticed it?

'It's called reframing,' he explained. 'If you emphasise the negative that's what you'll get back. You're in America now. They like success; positively adore social climbers. In fact, they celebrate it. None of this misplaced English modesty. Believe me, it won't get you anywhere. Fast.'

She hadn't realised it then, but a crack had formed under her feet. Initially it felt thrilling, full of hope and possibility. For the first time in her life her history didn't dominate her experience of herself. But unchecked, it widened into an abyss; a gaping hole between who she really was and who she pretended to be. She no longer knew what was real any more and found she couldn't trust her own perception.

Now it occurred to her that there was nothing particularly negative about her background at all, certainly nothing worth hiding. It was just sad. And perhaps most damning of all, common. It was of the one-size-fits-all variety of dysfunctional family drama that's so frequent as to make the 'normal' families the rarity.

Had the Blythe sisters been 'reframed' too? Had they struggled with the tensions of what and who they imagined they should be?

Rubbing her eyes, Cate looked up at the massive clock above the reception desk.

Time for a coffee.

And taking a stack of books with her, she headed out into the bright sunlight, in search of a cafe on the Marylebone Road.

Rachel was sitting on a bench in Gray's Inn Gardens with her tuna sandwich. One of the largest public squares in London, it was neat and symmetrically composed, gravel pathways cutting across manicured lawns, bordered by imposing red-brick law chambers. Already it was filling with office workers, making the most of the unprecedented good weather, lounging in the cool shade of the plane trees with their lunch.

She took a sip of cold Diet Coke. How would Anna bear the high temperatures of Spain? Automatically her fingers reached for the Post-it with Anna's number on it, which she'd shoved into the pocket of her dress before leaving. Of course, it was different, wasn't it? England wasn't made for intense weather conditions. Everything was easier on the Continent.

She unwrapped her sandwich but it sat untouched on

her lap. Instead she watched as a young couple holding hands searched eagerly for a private spot. Eventually they settled for a sloping enclave of grass behind a high wall of hydrangea bushes. Soon they were wrapped in each other's embrace, any thought of food quickly forgotten.

Suddenly Rachel felt old, invisible and alone.

The memories she'd tried to sidestep this morning were back. Only now there was nothing to distract her.

Was it his fault? Or hers?

Part of her was desperate to assign blame. Yet the bulk of her resentment fell on Anna, which was insane. Of course she knew why.

Katie. She was only small then. A toddler.

Perfect. Unmarked.

Again, the shame pressed in.

It was during a time when Ryan, Katie's father, was working as a roadie for the Stones. She couldn't remember how he'd got the job but for that brief period of time he might as well have been one of them for the way he acted. He had all the arrogance, all the glamour of a rock star. And for once in his life he had money too. He talked about how he was going into the recording industry. How Mick could see he had a lot of talent and wanted to help him. He called him Mick, like they spoke all the time, hung out. Apparently there were invitations to spend the weekend at Jagger's country house that never quite materialised.

Rachel had felt middle-aged and stuffy by comparison. She and Paul were valuing and emptying old houses. They seemed like just one step up from junk men. No one lived in Marylebone in those days, it was a wasteland. Hip and Happening London was in Chelsea, the King's Road, Hampstead . . . anywhere but where they were.

And there was no child. It had become an obsession for Rachel. Everywhere she went she saw them; pregnant women, round and soft, children, babies, families. Her lack was like a vacuum, sucking all the joy of life into a single, concentrated, black hole. But no matter what they did, she couldn't conceive. They'd stopped trying; it became too tense an exercise. That's what sex became for them; a futile exercise, a job they failed at each month.

So they decided to take their minds off it; have a holiday instead. Relax by the beach.

Anna and her family had come down to join them for a long weekend. And she was so lovely and glowing, really properly happy. Laughing, wearing miniskirts that showed off her long legs and so proud of Ryan, who was confident, masculine; darkly sexy. They were going places, succeeding at life. And there was Katie. The first child of many.

Rachel had hated Paul then. He seemed so staid, so prissy and inadequate. They'd been married six years. This was not the life she'd planned or signed up for. He'd married her under false pretences.

Her bitterness was poison, seductive and silent, so much a part of herself she couldn't separate from it, see clearly. And it seeped out, spreading to include Anna.

Rachel looked again at the young couple, tucked into the shadows, oblivious now to anyone around them. Was it an office romance? Or something clandestine; hidden?

She'd bought a new dress. From Zandra Rhodes. She knew when she bought it, a week before they came down, that something was wrong. She didn't buy the dress for her, or for her husband. It was low-cut, flowing. It was a dress that grabbed attention and kept it, that made her feel sexy and alive – like a real woman.

There'd been too much red wine that weekend, too much marijuana.

And she'd moved just that bit slower, more sensuously. Spent the weekend catching Ryan's eye. Laughing at his jokes. Leaning in closer when he spoke, giving him her undivided attention, allowing her hand to rest on his shoulder just that bit too long. And he'd lapped it up, felt it was his due. It was only right that he should finally get the recognition he deserved. And she'd watched Paul, watching her . . . his face strained, eyes furious. She'd done it right in front of him; punishing him.

Anna had been busy with Katie, chasing her as she veered from one disaster to another. And Rachel had let her.

She wasn't used to having a child in the house. She didn't realise how things had to be cleared away. Put back.

How intent they were on touching everything.

Rachel looked up at the sky, cottony wisps of cloud sailing slowly across an expanse of blue. The years hadn't made it easier to remember.

Her body had still been taut, magnificent. Anna had had a baby. She was softer, rounded; she had worn an all-in-one bathing costume, with a pointy built-in bra. Rachel had shown off her figure, wearing a purple crocheted bikini. Oiling her limbs with baby oil. Thick, square, Jackie O sunglasses.

She'd sent Paul to the shop for food.

They'd headed down to the beach. Katie spent too much time running straight at the water and eating sand. Soon she was tired, overheated and badly in need of a nap. Anna took her back to the cottage, lugging her up the steep pathway. She was tense, irritable.

Rachel had slipped her bikini top off, lain flat on her stomach. Ryan had passed her a joint. She'd reached for it without bothering hide her breasts, lazily turning over, sucking hard on the joint. Playing the sophisticate. He'd ignored them, ignored her. Closed his eyes, rolled over.

But she had known.

Later on, early evening, freshly showered and per-fumed . . . 'I've left my glasses down on the beach. I'm just going to get them.'

'I'll go,' Paul had volunteered.

She'd turned on him. 'You don't even know where they are,' she'd snapped.

He had given her a look. A look she'd never forget.

Then he'd got up, taken the car keys. 'I'm going for a drive,' was all he'd said before he'd left.

And she had let him. It had been a turning point. They'd both known it. And yet, it was as if she was being driven by something larger; a compulsion she couldn't control.

Ryan had been outside, sitting on the steps, having a smoke.

Rachel had walked past him. 'I left my glasses.'

That was all she'd said. All she'd had to say.

He'd got up.

She'd walked on, a little ahead.

He'd strolled slowly, lazily after.

It was dusk; the beach was all but abandoned, some man walking his dog.

There was an alcove, a high, narrow wall of rocks. By the time she'd reached it, he'd been right behind her, moving quickly, urgently. There had been none of the delicious, dangerous tension of that afternoon on the beach. As soon as she'd turned round, he'd been upon her, grabbing at her. She'd banged her head on the side of the cliff; her hair caught in the rough surface. And then he was inside her, tearing at the sheer fabric of her blouse, fingers digging into her thighs. He was bigger than Paul; it hurt. She'd tried to pull away but he'd held fast, pumping harder. And suddenly, with dreadful clarity she'd come to, into the shocking, incestuous, reality of what was happening, what she was doing.

They'd heard Anna calling. Her voice was strained, like she was crying. She was looking for her husband . . . for her sister.

Rachel had struggled but he'd clapped his hand over her mouth, carried on.

And then he'd come; it had seemed to go on for ages, to be running down the inside of her leg.

Rachel winced again, the memory burning with shame and self-loathing, as fresh thirty years later as if it had happened yesterday.

Katie had been left alone in the house. When they'd found her, she was bleeding, crying. She'd banged her head on something. Thank God she had been all right. Thank God nothing more dreadful had happened to her.

Rachel hadn't got pregnant.

She'd got herpes instead. A disease she'd had to explain to Paul, with everything that meant. A disease she'd had for life. Paul had left for a few weeks; there was talk of divorce. But even when he came back, every time they made love after that, it was tainted.

After a while, people stopped asking when they were going to start a family. After a while, they stopped asking why too.

Standing up, Rachel threw the uneaten sandwich into the bin.

Anna never knew.

Or did she?

Rachel could never be sure what Ryan might say when he was drunk; what bitter and cruel truths may have been levelled at her. It was a wound that never healed; her secret, the weight of which was unbearable at times.

That summer, that particular obsession, had cost her her identity. After it had passed, she could never look at the world in the same superior way; could never hold her sister in contempt; could never win an argument with Paul. She'd fallen, like some biblical figure, from grace and she'd lived in a permanent purgatory ever since. Now she deferred not so much to others as to the knowledge of her inadequacy to negotiate with any dignity or character the loss of her dream.

As she left the park, she scanned the faces of the people she passed. Had any of them, relaxing on the grass on this beautiful summer's day, ever betrayed the people they loved most? Or betrayed themselves?

Walking back to the office, her heels clicked along the pavement.

Rachel was, in fact, not fond of red shoes. But in wearing them, she acknowledged what no one else knew or could know; it was an outward sign of an inward failing.

When she got back to Jockey's Fields, the office was locked. Jack was on his break. Turning the key in the door, she made her way straight to the desk and took out the number. She dialled, breathing a sigh of relief when she got through to the answering machine. 'Hello, this is Anna. Please leave a message and I'll call you back.'

It beeped.

'It's Rachel. Darling, Katie's here. She's come back. Something to do with her boyfriend though I can't get a straight answer. I . . . I thought you should know.'

She put the phone down. Pulling her chair out, she sank into it, staring at the pile of paperwork.

There were all the things she didn't say, like, 'Katie's in trouble. I'm frightened for her. And I don't know what to do.'

But then her relationship with Anna had always been defined by the unsaid.

5 St James's Square
London

8 August 1933

My darling Bird,
How brave you are to tear round the countryside
giving speeches and electioneering for Malcolm in
that rackety old car of his! I'm certain you are his
greatest asset, but are you sure it's a good idea for
someone in your condition? No doubt I'll feel differently
when you invite me to join you for tea at Number 10 in
a few years' time but until then I remain concerned.
I had secretly hoped that you might be the one person
in the world who hadn't gone mad and that Endsleigh
might be a haven from the blight of radical political
thinkers that have descended upon us poor philistines.
But now I see I alone shall have to fly the flag of
decent conversation at your table. I cannot bear to go
down to Nancy's this weekend for that same reason,
except that Nick is going and London is so hot and
sticky at this time of year and I am aching for a swim
in their lovely pool.

Lord R has come back from Paris and today his
office sent over the loveliest gown. I hardly knew what

to say! I telephoned to say it must be a mistake but he came on and assured me that his wife wanted me to have it and that they should love to see me wear it at Wooton next weekend. The frightening thing is it fits like a dream. I simply cannot make him out.

Nick is leaving for Portofino soon and I am doing my very best not to throw myself in front of a train. I wonder how fast it has to be going to really be effective? Do you think it's possible to expire from sheer physical longing? Of course, Muv won't set foot out of England for at least another nine months so it's up to me to try and wheedle an invitation from someone. Oh! And Pinky has proposed to Gloria Manning and, poor dear, she's said yes! He looks utterly terrified, like a man permanently on his way to the dentist.

I wonder if she knows how wet his kisses are?

Plotting and Pining,

B xxx

Sitting in an Italian cafe, drinking strong cappuccino, Cate leafed through a book of Beaton photographs the librarian had recommended – page after page of high-society life between the wars. It was an undeniably golden era. They gazed back at her, these darlings of another age, with the confidence of youth and the steely arrogance of privilege. Protected by their wealth and beauty, they seemed untouchable; far removed from anything too real or too unpleasant.

Then she stopped.

Here was a photograph of several young men in bathing trunks, laughing beside a swimming pool on a bright summer's day.

And one very familiar face.

She searched through the captions. *'David Astor, Nicholas Warburton and Bill Farthing sunbathing, 1931.'*

It was the young man – the sailor from the photograph in the shoebox. He was taller than the others; trim and well muscled, with the same lively black eyes. There was something charismatic about him; not only was he incredibly good-looking but he appeared to have a natural ease and athleticism.

Cate stared at the photo a long time. Nicholas Warburton. He was her missing sailor, she was sure of it. And she recognised the name. Could the sailor in the picture be related to the Blythe sisters' stepfather? Turning to the index, she searched for any more photographs. Unfortunately, there was only one.

Leaving her coffee half finished, she quickly paid her bill and headed back to the library, ducking and weaving through the lunchtime crowds.

Once there, she entered the name 'Nicholas Warburton' into the computer system and eagerly pressed return.

Up came a dental surgeon in Harley Street, a professor in Canada, a website for a hotel in Mayfair and a link to the Warburton Baked Goods site, extolling the virtues of Warburton's Wholegrain.

She tried again. But again, nothing.

It didn't make sense.

She typed in 'HMS *Vivid*', the name that had been stitched into his naval uniform.

Pages of Plymouth Naval History came up. 'The Royal Navy Barracks at Keyham were first known as HMS *Vivid* but 1934 it was renamed HMS *Drake*.'

So Nicholas Warburton had been a naval officer some-time before 1934. Could he have served in the Great War? That would mean that he was considerably older than Diana.

She went back to the pages of Plymouth Naval History and made a note of a few names and the address of the naval base. Perhaps if she wrote to someone in the archives department, they might have some more information.

Sighing in frustration, she entered instead 'Lord Warburton'.

Up came links to Warburton's Wholegrain again, a

large National Trust estate in Hampshire, and some of the related links to Baby Blythe she'd already explored. She clicked onto the National Trust site.

Hargraves House is an extensive private estate and one of the pioneers of the organic farming movement in England. The land and late-Gothic-revival Victorian house were bequeathed to the nation by Lord Warburton upon the death of his wife, Lady Warburton, in 1972. Hargraves House was purchased as a retreat for Lady Warburton from the turmoil of London life between the wars and also played a pivotal role in her considerable charity work, providing accommodation for Catholic refugees from all over Europe. It was, in fact, her interest in nutrition and in particular her experience providing homes for evacuee children from the East End of London during the Second World War, many of whom were suffering from rickets and malnutrition, which, in her later years, inspired Lady Warburton to begin experimenting with the sustainability of natural farming techniques. Lord Warburton preferred to remain in London and spent his final years living an independent life centred around politics. His Mayfair mansion at 5 St James's Square, is now the London headquarters of right-wing Conservative special-interest group, the Wednesday Club, and open to public viewing by appointment only. Today Hargraves House produces a wide range of organic products and houses a cafe, shop and is a much sought-after place for agricultural work experience in addition to playing host to regional agricultural events.

Cate paged through the many images of green, abundant fields and well-tended gardens, followed by interiors of the dark, mahogany-laden house and bright, contemporary cafe transformed from one of the barns.

Frowning, she worked her way back through the various screens she'd brought up.

Here was something odd.

She clicked on the link to the hotel in Mayfair.

It took her to a page devoted to the history of a small, privately owned boutique hotel in Hill Street.

Opened in 1923, the Belmont was originally built as a series of small but luxurious bachelor apartments with a restaurant and concierge service on the ground floor. It functioned like a private gentlemen's club and members had to be referred. Ladies were strictly forbidden on the premises except in the basement bar, which became popular as an exclusive after-hours club and casino, where one founding member, the baked-goods heir, the Honourable Nicholas Warburton, famously lost £20,000 on a bet on what colour tie Edward VIII would wear to his abdication. 'Whatever colour it is,' he remarked, 'you can be sure he won't have chosen it himself.' Today, although the Belmont has become a leading luxury hotel in London's exclusive Mayfair, the club, known simply as

'106', remains a private members' casino and cigar room, which all guests are automatically invited to join upon registration.

Cate reread the passage again. So Nicholas Warburton was Lord Warburton's son and heir – and Baby Blythe's stepbrother by marriage!

When she'd found the box, she felt sure it was filled with the mementoes of a love affair. Had she got it wrong? Or had Baby Blythe and Nicholas Warburton crossed a very delicate social boundary? Perhaps that was why the box was hidden. Maybe the entire relationship had been a secret.

But if that were true, why was it hidden at Endsleigh?

She cradled her hand in her chin, concentrating.

Lord Warburton had a son. And yet he left both his vast properties to the nation.

Why? Had Nicholas died in the war?

It was almost as if someone had wanted to erase all trace of him entirely; to pretend he'd never existed.

5 St James's Square
London

14 September 1934

My darling,
So lovely to hear from you. I'm sorry if I gave you
offence by dancing in the fountain at Piccadilly Circus
but the truth is I can't remember any of it. If it weren't
for all the photographs in the papers I should've sworn
I was tucked up in bed. But I do recall it was a hot
night and there was absolutely no place to go after the
Café de Paris closed. I suppose now that you are a
rising MP's wife such behaviour reflects badly but
perhaps you can console yourself that the more
outrageous I am, the more respectable you seem by
comparison. So I'm really doing you the most enormous
favour. We are all off to Goodwood this weekend and
then to Nice after so you can relax for a few weeks at
least and read The Times in peace.

I know you're only trying to be sensible when you
suggest that I should consider the amorous advances of
Geoffrey Tynedale and it's true that he is good fun and
very well off. He's also as ugly as two toads. And you'd
be mistaken if you thought that I didn't have to listen

*to advice like that from Muv every second of the day.
Some day soon I will marry but right now life is too gay
and exciting to be spent wandering down aisles
wrapped in tulle. And I think we both know who
I have in mind for the job when I do accept!*

*Please let's do be friends, darling. You really will
laugh when I tell you that I saw Eleanor in Purdy's
last week ordering safari clothes and stacks of new
guns; she's agreed to marry some decrepit old coffee
plantation owner in deepest, darkest Kenya – some
friend of her father's she last met when she was six.
I've really never seen her so animated, though she'll
look like a giant tent kitted out in so much khaki.
I shouldn't think she'll need a gun – any lion would
be terrified to go anywhere near her. And Anne has
renounced communism entirely after she came back
to the flat early one afternoon to hide a new hat and
caught Paul in flagrante with some impossibly hairy
lady writer from The Week. Apparently they were
lowing like cows and didn't hear her come in. Poor
darling. She is devastated but at the same time one
could tell she was longing to eat caviar and read Vogue
again and take off those dreadful sensible shoes and go
out dancing. I took her immediately to Scott's for a
truly decadent bourgeoisie lunch and then we tottered
over to Simpson's in a champagne haze and bought her
the most killing new coat in peacock blue. Her father's
already contacted the lawyers even though Paul's*

*written four times to ask her to come back. But she says she'll have nightmares till the end of her days, remembering that moment when she was standing in the doorway, trying to work out what it was he was doing to that small dark man with the moustache and the flabby chest.*

*I'm thinking of you all the time – opening fetes, giving speeches and cutting ribbons at local libraries. How good you are! I've only seen Malcolm in London very briefly as he dashes from one room to the next, a kind of pinstriped blur. As you can imagine, we travel in very different sets. I'm sure he disapproves of me, despite what you say. And he will keep going on about the 'ruling classes'. No wonder the Consort turns pink with delight every time he sees him. (Quite seriously, he does blush! I think he may have the tiniest crush which is perhaps understandable given that he's married to Muv.) We were meant to have supper one night at the Dorchester months ago and I'm sure I was in for a stern moral lecture but there was a vote at Parliament and he was called away at the last minute. I know he's dear to you but I can't say I was disappointed.*

*But my angel, if I can't tell you the secrets of my soul . . . who can I tell? You who know me best of anyone.*

*All my dearest love,*

*B xxxx*

The National Portrait Gallery was not as daunting as its neighbour, the National Gallery. It was smaller, narrow; less all-encompassing. Room after room of famous faces wound upwards in a meandering sprawl, in every conceivable style, from Tudor portraits to modern paintings, photographs and sketches. All tastes were catered for – royalty, celebrities, statesmen, women and men of the arts and sciences, politicians, film stars. They gazed out, some confident, others defiant or self-deprecating, still others oblivious and unaware. It was a complex record of centuries of shifting social standards and fashions; of accomplishments, controversy, self-promotion, heroism, humility; unfolding in an ever-expanding Vanity Fair.

It always struck Cate as a distinctly English institution designed for a people who found looking at one another or, worse still, being seen, anathema. Here, one could finally stare openly, and recognize, in a thousand different faces, something of the fine human thread which made up the ever-changing national character.

Knots of tourists clogged the central wooden staircase as Cate made her way up. She paused, feeling suddenly tired and strangely light-headed. Too little sleep and not enough food. The rarity of an English heatwave, and the nation's stubborn refusal to invest in any air conditioning, had kept her awake. Also she'd had doubts about burning the letter. Perhaps she should've read it. After all, what did she have here, in London? Round and round her thoughts ran, little knives stabbing at her confidence.

As she reached the top of the landing, she sat down on a bench. If only she could stop thinking; simply switch her head off. After a while, one of the security guards came over, a spotty young man in a uniform.

'Are you OK?'

'Yes,' she nodded. 'Just thinking.'

'If you need something . . . I mean if you don't feel well, I can call someone.'

She stood up. 'I'm fine.'

'Are you sure?'

'Yes. Thank you.'

Walking on, she plucked a gallery guide from the nearby information booth and headed into the next room, moving out of visual range of the security guard. It was the main contemporary gallery with high vaulted ceilings, bright skylights and clean white walls. It reminded her of New York; positive, bold and absolute.

She took a seat on one of the benches in the centre and opened the guide, looking for what she had come to see, room 32, the work of Cecil Beaton. Digging around in her handbag, she unearthed an old packet of mints. Sucking hard, its sugary sharpness cleared her head.

She had so many memories of the free public galleries in London. The Wallace Collection, the Tate, the National Gallery . . . How many Sundays did she spend as a little girl walking through them, holding tight to her mother's hand, killing time? Waiting for her father to wake up from where he'd passed out on the living-room sofa and go out again to the pub. Waiting for it to be safe to go home. So they trailed around galleries and museums, anything free; her mother trying to be light and cheerful, as if it were just a wonderful educational adventure that she'd planned all along for their Sunday afternoon. But despite the circumstances, something penetrated. Within the walls of these glorious institutions, Cate was transported. She came to view art, and painting in particular, as something sacred; a refuge against the unpredictability and chaos of life.

She used to visit the galleries alone in New York. Her favourite was the Guggenheim. She'd sit in front of the massive Pollock paintings for hours. She loved how angry Pollock was; how unrestrained. Here was a religion she could believe in – one that gave voice to all that was unknowable, irresolvable and truly holy. She dreamed of one day sitting in front of one of her own paintings, hanging on the wall opposite; of finding her place among what she believed in most.

But then she met Derek Constantine and he redirected her vision. 'That Pollock is flaking. Its value diminishes every day. Besides, he died a drunk.'

His words sliced through her. He died a drunk. Even the painting was dying, peeling slowly away. The nobleness of art, its smooth promise of marble-like immortality, was as transient as everything else she held dear. It too was vulnerable to the caprices of time.

She couldn't look at it now without thinking that something was missing, that it was cracking and fading away before her very eyes.

'We can do better than that,' he promised.

London was a city of pasts, histories, shadows and sneering social subtleties. New York was going to be the blank canvas on which she'd create a new life; a new persona. He'd show her the way; guide her through the pitfalls.

But she'd tripped and fallen anyway.

Getting up again, Cate searched through the winding rooms, heading deeper into smaller, more intimate annexes. The paintings gave way to black-and-white photographs, mounted against dark walls. At last, she found it. Room 32. The work of Cecil Beaton. Society portraits and film stars, dating from the early 1920s through to the 1970s, lined the walls. Edith Sitwell gazed imperiously, Wallis Simpson conquered, and her husband the Duke of Windsor looked wistfully into the distance as if the camera were a subject too lowly to be acknowledged. There was Winston Churchill winning the war, Marlon Brando sulking, Salvador Dali clowning about . . . Douglas Fairbanks Jr smouldering and the twin sisters, Viscountess Furness and Mrs Reginald Vanderbilt, two bodies with the same striking face, mirroring each other with eerie symmetry.

Cate stopped. *Four Debutantes.*

There she was. Diana Blythe. She must've been all of seventeen, a child. By far the most striking of the four girls, she was dressed in the traditional long white gown of the coming-out ball. She had a young, hopeful, impossibly beautiful face.

A debutante. It was another world, full of beautiful society princesses in floaty pristine gowns.

A little further on there was another portrait, this time of Irene and Diana lying head to head on a lawn, sunbathing. Diana's blonde hair contrasted with Irene's dark curls. They were laughing, eyes closed.

There was also a portrait of Irene, alone, stiff and formal, when she was newly married. She was wearing a dark serge suit, a pillbox hat and a fox fur. She could only be in her early twenties but already she was sophisticated and serious; an up-and-coming pillar of society.

And then there was another. Diana 'Baby' Blythe, dressed as Venus – a rather staid, arty shot. Swathed in layers of sheer fabric, the curves of her figure showing provocatively through, only just hidden by careful lighting. Gone was the girlish naivety of the earlier photos. She had the direct, unnerving sexual energy of a Hollywood starlet and the unearthly, sculptural beauty of a goddess. The caption underneath explained: 'This portrait was considered far too daring and explicit to be displayed when it was first taken and remained in the gallery's archives for almost sixty years. It is one of the few nude portraits to be taken by Beaton. Diana "Baby" Blythe was a famous society beauty whose high spirits and unorthodox ways gained her quite a reputation before her mysterious disappearance in 1941.'

High spirits and unorthodox ways. Here she was all but naked. The boldness of her stare was overwhelmingly erotic. And yet there was something self-conscious about the whole exercise. Perhaps it was that the rather staged conceit of Venus was unworthy of her naturalness and warmth.

Later, in the shop, Cate purchased some postcards of the Blythe girls, slipping them into her bag. It was nearing five.

Heading out, she crossed the street to St Martin's Lane, lined with famous theatres – the London Coliseum, the Duke of York's, the Albery. So little had changed about them since the time the Blythe girls sat, enjoying musicals and comedy reviews in their crowded, smoke-filled auditoriums. She wandered down Cecil Court, a narrow passageway between St Martin's Lane and Charing Cross Road, lined with specialist second-hand bookshops. Rare first editions were displayed in the windows and outside bins were piled with prints and books, inviting passers-by to browse.

One stall had floral and fauna prints, another fashion plates, a third old political cartoons. There was something irresistible and comforting about the nostalgia of the past. Cate stopped, leafing through the various wares.

Browsing among the political section, she pulled out one of the framed cartoons. It was from 1936. It portrayed a handsome gentleman in black tie with a glamorous young woman in evening dress. They were entering a theatre and saluting another equally fashionable couple at the bar, while a portly, elderly couple looked on in confusion. 'It's all the rage!' the wife explained to her husband. The caption below read: 'Dress Circle Fascists.'

Fascists?

Cate took the cartoon into the shop. A chime on the door rang as she entered. It was a narrow, dark establishment lined with floor-to-ceiling bookcases; its shelves sagging with dusty volumes. Boxes and prints were stacked high on every available space, while at a desk in the back an elderly gentleman was reading the *Independent*, drinking a steaming mug of tea.

He looked up. 'May I help you?'

Cate handed him the cartoon. 'I wondered if you could tell me anything about this. I don't understand it. What's it about?'

He peered through his glasses, examining it closely. 'Yes, well, it appears to be a joke about a certain class of political thinker in the early 1930s. As for the couple, I'm fairly sure they're meant to be socialite Anne Cartwright and the right-wing conservative MP James Dunning. He was very outspoken in the years before the war. And she had all sorts of dubious political leanings, veering from communism to fascism. He was interned for a while when war broke out.'

'Interned? Why?'

'For being pro-German. Unfortunately, it was very fashionable to have fascist leanings during those times – from Mosley to the Mitfords to the Cliveden Set.'

'The Cliveden Set? I've never heard of it.'

'The Cliveden Set was a name made up by the communist newspaper *The Week*. They were supposed to be, though no one's really quite sure, a sort of 1930s right-wing think tank. All upper class, all friends of Nancy Astor,

Viscountess Astor to you and me. They used to meet at her home, Cliveden. It's a famous hotel now. You may remember it from the Profumo affair. Between the wars they were incredibly influential in both politics and public opinion. Apparently they were in favour of the appeasement of Hitler and maintaining friendly relations with Nazi Germany at all costs. The group included Geoffrey Dawson, the editor of *The Times*, Phillip Kerr, Edward Rothermere –'

'Rothermere? As in Lord Rothermere?'

'Yes, that's the one. He eventually became the American Ambassador. At least for a while.'

'And these people were fascists?'

'Well,' he sighed, 'no one really knows any of it for sure. It was a complex time. Made more complicated by the involvement of an entire set of hedonistic young people whose experience and idealism were naive to say the least. But the press loved them. So people like Anne Cartwright with her pick-of-the-week politics were prone to a great deal of publicity, both good and bad.'

Cate looked at the cartoon again – at the wide-eyed young woman in the evening gown.

'What happened to her?'

He shrugged his shoulders. 'The war came. The party ended.'

'Your history's very impressive,' she admired.

'Well, this is my specialist subject. And otherwise,' he grinned, 'if you don't know the story it's impossible to get the joke. And I like a good joke.' He handed it back to her.

'So –' he cocked his head to one side – 'would you like a bag for that?'

Cate smiled. 'That depends.' She took out her purse. 'How much?'

'Five pounds.'

He put it into a brown paper envelope and she slipped it under her arm.

'Thank you. And thanks for the history lesson!'

'What are old men for?' And he gave her a wink.

She walked back out on to Cecil Court.

Here was a dark seam to Baby Blythe's world that she hadn't even realised existed. Under the parties and glamour, a powerful current of political extremism tugged like an irresistible undertow. Had she fallen prey to such fashionable ideas?

Weaving her way down towards the Strand, Cate negotiated the crowds around St Martin-in-the-Fields, and headed towards Holborn.

She was missing something, she was sure of it. Something obvious yet important; right in front of her eyes.

If only she could go back to Endsleigh, just once more, she might see it more clearly. Especially to that extraordinary gilded room. Had it been her imagination or did it have an eerie calmness, a sense of expectation about it? As if it were holding its breath.

As if it were waiting for someone.

Rachel had gone home early, complaining of a headache and Jack was alone in the office. He checked the notes again from Endsleigh. Cate's handwriting, careful and neat in the earlier pages, had deteriorated. He frowned, trying to decipher the description and match it with the best photograph for the catalogue. He'd been working diligently all day. His shoulders ached from hunching over the computer. Normally he would do most of it at home, delivering the finished product on a disk by courier.

He didn't usually spend this much time working in the office. He knew it. Rachel knew it. But neither of them commented on it. She didn't even bother to tease him, which was telling. They both understood what he was doing – throwing himself in the way of Fate; upping his chances of seeing Cate again. But it hadn't worked. She hadn't been in all week. And instead of enjoying the solitude of his own routine, he spent his days waiting; poised for the moment when the door opened and she walked in.

And then what would he do? What would he say when he finally saw her? He was resolved in some vague way to be nicer to her. But there was no plan.

He took off his glasses, rubbed his eyes and concentrated again on the notes in front of him.

'Regency commode, mahogany with white marble top, turned supports . . . stripped bare . . .'

Stripped bare?

What was that about?

He looked at the corresponding photographs. Here it was – a perfectly ordinary piece. He was certain he hadn't said anything about it being stripped bare. Above it, in the photo, hung a mirror. Just visible in its reflection was the curve of her shoulder, a bit of blonde hair.

Pushing his chair back from the desk in frustration, he stood up and, opening the back door, stepped out into the small courtyard between the buildings, stretching his cramping legs. He would finish this today, even if he had to work late into the night. Then he would go home and stop mooning about like a fool.

Cate pushed open the office door. 'Hello? Rachel?'

The office was empty, the back door open. Where was she?

'Rachel?'

A soft breeze rustled the papers on the desk and the computer was still on.

She couldn't be far.

Sinking into one of the leather club chairs, Cate pressed her eyes closed. She was so tired. She relaxed back into the cool leather, wrapping round her like an embrace. She needed to rest. Just for a minute. Just until Rachel returned.

When Jack came back in, she was asleep, head lolled to one side, hands folded on top of her chest, making small sighing noises.

'Cate?'

He said her name quietly, too quietly. The truth was he didn't want to wake her.

'Cate,' he said again, half-heartedly. She looked as if someone had pulled the plug, switched her off.

Jack stood back, hands in pockets. He had wanted her to come. Now she was here. Was that the way the universe worked?

If only.

He rubbed his eyes. He should get back to work. Or wake her up and take her home. That was the logical thing to do.

Instead he sat down in the chair opposite.

Was there anything more vulnerable than sleep?

There was a time when he was first married that he used to watch his wife sleeping. He used to wake up in the middle of the night and marvel at the beauty of her face; her long dark hair spilling out across the pillow, her mouth, pursed into a delicate pout, and hands pressed like a child's against her chest.

Then, gradually, as the years passed, he forgot to watch her sleep. Often she would go to bed before him. 'I'm shattered,' she'd say, with that tone in her voice that was at once warning and blaming. 'So don't try to touch me,' was the unspoken ending to that sentence.

He learned to let her go without resistance; spent time on the computer or watching TV. It was easier than taking offence. When he came in, she was already asleep, with her back turned towards him, claiming her side of the bed. All the vulnerability and openness had vanished.

Cate shifted, nestling deeper into the old chair.

What was this? He sat forward. A small faint scar, white, like the ghost of a crescent, near her right temple.

After a while, Jack made himself a cup of tea, turned on the desk lamp. It cast a soft circle of light in the darkening room. Cate slept so deeply that she hardly stirred.

Time passed, thirty minutes, an hour. The light drained from the sky. The area changed after hours. No longer bustling with droves of upmarket office workers, it took on a desolate, lonely quality. The council estates and pubs came to life; noisy customers spilling out into the high street. But Jockey's Fields was deserted, Dickensian in the eerie glow of its old gas street lamps.

Jack put his teacup down on the floor next to him and settled back.

She was here. He had wanted her to come and she was here.

Cate flicked her eyes open and sat up, blinking. 'What are you doing here? Are you OK?'

'Yes,' he laughed, 'I'm OK. But you fell asleep.'

'God, how embarrassing! Did I drool?'

'Apart from the snoring you were fine.'

Yawning, she sank back into the chair again. 'I'm in complete denial about any snoring. Though occasionally I do sigh rather loudly through my nose.'

'That'll be snoring.'

'No, that's breathing – with emphasis.'

'Or snoring.'

She smiled at him, her features soft, bathed in the warm glow of the single lamp. 'You aren't very romantic, Mr Coates.'

'Since when is lying romantic?'

'It's the very foundation of romance.'

He leaned his chin on his palm. 'Is that what you want?'

'More than anything. I'm longing to be lied to.'

'You're a cynic.'

'That's what happens to romantics gone bad. We never fully recover.'

'So, educate me. What is it that romantics want? Besides lies of course.'

'I suppose,' she sighed, stretching lazily, 'underneath it all, we want to believe in some sort of beautiful rightness to the world, a grand, heroic, emotional symmetry to love.'

'And snoring doesn't fit into this vision.'

'No, not at all.'

'Which is a shame. Because I found your emphatic breathing rather charming.'

'Did you?'

'Well,' he considered, 'I always knew where you were in the room.'

'See! That is not romantic!'

He shrugged his shoulders. 'But it's true. Have you no appetite for reality?'

'None. Reality is too loud and noisy!

He smiled. 'Like a brass band?'

'Exactly. What time is it, anyway?'

'After nine.'

'Really? Where's Rachel?'

'She left hours ago. I don't think she knew you were coming.'

'Well, *I* didn't know I was coming, so I guess it serves me right.'

'I'll drive you home,' he offered, standing. There was a crick in his neck. He gave it a rub.

'Are you sure you don't mind?'

'No, no of course not.' He gathered his papers together, saving his work and turning off the computer. 'What have you been up to all day?' He tried to sound nonchalant.

'Nothing much.'

'Shopping?'

'Actually, I went to the National Portrait Gallery. I was doing some research.'

'Research? On what?'

'The Blythe sisters. There are some really wonderful photographs there.'

'Are you planning something – a painting?'

'No I'm just curious, especially after seeing Endsleigh. Don't you find them fascinating?'

He shook his head. 'No. Not really.'

'But they had such style, such beauty.'

'Maybe, but they didn't do anything. Being beautiful is in itself not an occupation.'

'Stop trying to be reasonable. It's really very tedious. Besides, I wouldn't expect you to understand. It's a girl thing.'

'Thank God.'

She wandered over to the window. 'I'm famished.'

He stacked his papers into his briefcase, closed and bolted the back door. 'Yes? Well, we could always stop on the way home. I haven't eaten either.'

'OK.'

'Great.' His mind raced. Where to go? Not too fancy, not too cheap . . .

'Jack?'

Picking up his briefcase, he turned off the desk lamp. The darkness was thick around them. 'Yeah?'

Cate was standing in the pale blue halo of light from a street lamp outside, looking out of the window. 'Why didn't you just wake me up?'

'I didn't want to.'

She turned to look at him. 'Why not?'

He considered his reply. Because I'm obsessed with you? Because I wanted to stare at you for as long as I could without interruption?

'You seemed tired,' he said at last.

He opened the door. They stepped out into the street and Jack locked it behind them.

He held his arm out and she took it.

She looked up at him. 'I have a craving for ice cream.'

Was it his imagination, or was she leaning towards him?

'What about real food?'

'And what exactly do you mean by real food?'

They rounded the corner. His car was parked across the street.

'You know, meat, potatoes, veg. Real food,' he insisted.

'If you want real food, we'll have real food too.'

He unlocked the door, holding it open for her. But she stopped before climbing in, her eyes fixing on his. 'That was kind of you – to let me sleep. Thank you.'

'My pleasure. Any time you feel the least bit drowsy, you know where to find me.'

'Yes.' She smiled again, tilting her head. 'Yes, I do.'

They drove into Primrose Hill, to a little Greek restaurant. They were seated outside, side by side at a square wooden table facing the street. Cate ordered rice and chicken and Jack the lamb and roast potatoes.

'How do you know about this place?' she asked, picking at an olive.

'I used to drive by and see people having dinner here on the pavement in the summer. The place was always crowded. I figured it must be good.'

'But you've never been here before?'

'No.'

She seemed to relax a little into her chair.

'Why? Did you think this was an old haunt?'

She looked out at the gentle curving crescent of Regent's Park Road. 'Every place in London seems to be an old haunt.'

'I've never been here before,' he assured her, taking a bit of warm bread and dipping it in olive oil. 'This is uncharted territory.'

'Good.'

Her possessiveness pleased him; she wanted somewhere exclusive to them.

'So,' he smiled, 'you were talking in your sleep.'

'No! Really?'

'Well, not talking so much as murmuring.'

'I had a dream.'

'What was it?'

She blushed. 'I'm not telling you!'

'Go on! How bad can it be?'

'Pretty bad!'

'Well –' he rubbed his hands together – 'now I have to hear it!'

'Oh . . . all right.' She smiled shyly. 'I was walking with someone . . . a man, across an open space, like a common or a park or something, and . . .' she was surprised by how difficult it was to say, 'and he was holding my hand.'

He waited for her to continue.

'Is that it?'

'Yes, well, it was one of those dreams where when I woke up, the feeling lingered on; that kind of lovely warm feeling of being close to someone.' She stopped, suddenly self-conscious. 'It was . . . nice.'

'Nice?'

'Yeah, nice.'

'I was hoping for something more than nice.'

'Like what?'

'Oh, I don't know . . . perhaps something involving a circus pony, a pair of nubile twins and a large tub of whipping cream.'

'You're exposing yourself, Mr Coates.'

'Now that's just wishful thinking, Ms Albion.'

'Besides –' she rolled her eyes – 'whipping cream is so passé.'

'I'm an old-fashioned guy.'

'Yes. Quite the conservative.'

They sat a while.

'Of course,' Jack admitted, 'it has been a long time since I held anyone's hand.'

'And this is surprising?'

Whistling a snatch of Mozart, he stretched his arms out, fingers brushing lightly against hers.

'Oh no!' she warned. 'Don't even think about it, buster!'

'Buster? Wow. You really know how to hurt a guy.'

'And that's the last time I confide in you, pal!'

'Pal! Stop. I can't take any more.' He grabbed her hand, plopped it on the table.

'What are you doing?'

'I'm going to hold your hand,' he announced. 'Stop pulling it away.'

'Stop taking the piss!' she squirmed.

'I'm not! I'm offering you a moment of . . . of . . . Jesus! Would you sit still?'

'You're taking the piss!'

'I am, in all seriousness, Cate, desirous of holding your hand.'

'Katie.'

'Pardon?'

'My real name is Katie.'

'I suppose I should be relieved it's not Frank. Is there anything else you want to tell me?'

'Not at this time.'

'Now, down to business.' He turned his palm over.

'Stop it!' she laughed, giving him a swat.

'Why not?' he asked, offering his hand in earnest. 'After all, it doesn't mean anything, does it?'

She didn't answer. Instead she let him lace his warm fingers through her cool ones, pressing them close.

'See, that's not so bad, Katie.'

'It's dreadful.'

Still, they sat looking out at the street for some time; letting go only on the arrival of their supper.

Afterwards they walked over to Marine Ices where he bought her a pistachio ice cream and a chocolate for himself. They strolled, in the warm night air, along Primrose Hill, sitting on a bench at the top, overlooking London.

'It's late.'

'Yes.'

'Shall we go?'

'If you like.'

They didn't move.

After a while, Cate pointed to the dim shadow in the far distance. 'What do you think that is?'

'Some structure of great architectural and cultural importance.'

'Hmm.'

He indicated a guidepost a few feet away from them. 'We can look on the map over there.'

'Yes . . .'

They sat, gazing up at the few stars that blinked in the filmy night sky.

'You have a scar on your forehead.'

'Yeah. I don't remember getting it. I fell or something when I was a baby.'

A gust of wind tossed the branches of the trees. London glimmered in the distance, like a faraway fairground, all the attractions, music and noise packed up, put away for the night.

'Do you miss New York?'

She turned. 'Why?'

'I don't know. There's no need to be cagey – it's a harmless question.'

'I'm not cagey.'

He smirked.

'Stop smirking.'

'Fine, smirk-free, do you miss New York?'

'Sometimes.'

He stretched his long legs out in front of him. 'And what about, you know, your . . . relationship?'

'Why? Why do you want to know?'

He shrugged his shoulders. 'Oh, I don't know.' 'I'm conducting a survey or maybe I work for MI5 or perhaps I'm just asking a normal question. You decide.'

She sighed heavily.

'Is it that bad?'

'The thing was . . .' She stopped, folding her arms tightly across her chest.

'What?'

'It wasn't straightforward.'

'Few things are nowadays.'

She looked across at him. 'I was a mistress.'

She'd never said it out loud before. It sounded overblown; distinctly eighteenth century.

He laughed. 'Pardon?'

She said it clearer this time. 'A mistress.'

He stopped laughing. His eyes changed, the warmth retreating.

'You don't approve,' she deduced, looking down at the space between her feet. 'That's all right. Neither do I.'

'So why did you do it then?' He tried to keep his tone neutral, but the very fact that he was asking sounded judgemental, like a schoolteacher.

She looked up, suddenly small, out of her depth. 'I don't know.'

He felt unreal, slightly numb. 'Do you love him?'

'I'm sorry?' She blinked back at him, unseeing.

'Let's leave it.'

She was afraid to talk about it. She was afraid not to talk about it. And now she'd gone too far.

'It's not love.'

'What is it then?'

'Some sort of soul sickness.'

Her answer unnerved him. This was not the history he had in mind for her; not the romantic, seductive end to the evening he had been looking forward to. He felt cheated. Instead he sat, staring out across Primrose Hill, blind to the view, unable to summon the necessary social dexterity to say anything mitigating, yet unwilling to leave the subject alone.

'Is he rich?' It was a sordid question; instantly he regretted it.

'Richer than some.'

'A client?'

She stared at him, hard. His questions were intrusive, yet compulsive.

'We don't have to talk about it,' he relented.

'No, you're right: we don't need to discuss it. I'm sorry.'

'I didn't mean it that way . . .'

'Of course not.' She stood up. 'Look, I can make my own way home.'

'Don't be ridiculous.' He got up too.

'I'd rather go on my own.'

'Katie . . .'

The look she shot him was fierce.

Shoving his hands into his pockets, he gave up trying to talk to her, staring into the darkness instead.

'We're headed in different directions.' She picked up her bag, flung it over her shoulder. 'Besides, it's late. Far too late now.'

He stepped back, let her go.

And as she passed in front of him, he bowed his head slightly; a strange, formal gesture from another age; an acknowledgement, perhaps, however awkward, of the privileged, if unwelcome, nature of her confidence.

If Cate registered it, she gave no sign; walking on, back straight, chin held high, into the night.

5 St James's Square
London

12th August, 1935

My dearest,
I am so sorry.

So sorry, my love, for your loss. I long to comfort you
but don't know how. Perhaps if it had lived it would've
been ill. The truth is, I don't understand God at all.
Perhaps Anne is right and He doesn't exist. Still yet
another part of me screams, have faith, believe. But I
don't know what in and I don't know why. And yet,
against all reason, I do believe. We must. You are only
young. Please don't give up hope.

I am on my way.
Yours always,
Dxxxx

In the dream she wasn't running. She should've been, but she wasn't. She could feel the danger, a swell of sickening adrenalin in her stomach. Around her the air changed, cooling, quickening.

She looked around. The landscape was shadowy; she'd arrived here all of a sudden, like coming to from a powerful narcotic. What was this place? A house? Was that the sound of the sea? On the floor a doll, naked, hair matted, limbs twisted, stared up at her, its blue eyes unseeing. She bent but couldn't reach it. How did it get so damaged?

Somewhere, at the end of the corridor, the thing approached.

She wanted to move but her legs didn't work. She tried to scream – her throat tearing at notes that couldn't be heard.

It was coming, black, slippery, shifting. Nearer, nearer . . . limping, panting, running at speed across the bare wooden floor.

Cate woke covered in cold sweat, heart racing and disorientated. The room was pitch black and close. Where was she? What country?

Getting up, she felt in the dark for the light switch, then stumbled to the bathroom, sitting on Rachel's avocado-green toilet, staring at the balding patches between the bath tiles.

What made her tell him? Did she imagine he would understand? Or that he might console her, smoothing over her self-contempt?

Now he knew her true character. And he was repulsed.

Standing up, she splashed her face with water.

Why shouldn't he be?

Her reflection blinked back at her, pale, swollen.

Wasn't that the way she felt about herself?

She went back to her room and turned on the bedside lamp. Propping the pillow behind her, she lay back, closed her eyes.

Her mind turned again to the restaurant, holding his hand. She'd never held a man's hand before. Or rather, she'd never *just* held a man's hand. There was no context for the experience in her history; she didn't understand what it meant or didn't mean. All she knew was it felt unusual. Comforting; tender; frightening.

Reaching into her handbag she took out and lit a cigarette.

She wanted to hide now. How was she ever going to be able to look him in the eye again? At the same time, she wanted to be back at that table, with his fingers firmly wrapped around hers.

She got up, opened the window wider. It was a still, airless night.

He probably still loved his wife. It was clear that he'd been devoted to her. She was most likely a wonderful woman. Beautiful, accomplished, kind. The sort of girl you would scour London for in search of the perfect mirror.

Her head ached.

She took another drag. There was no way she was going to be able to sleep now.

The book of Beaton photographs she'd taken out of the library was on her bedside table. Reaching across, she opened it, leafing slowly through the pages; sedating herself with image after glossy image.

Katie. He'd called her Katie. She'd liked the way it sounded.

She continued to turn the pages.

Here were the now familiar photos she'd seen at the National Portrait Gallery. And one new one of Baby Blythe, taken on a lawn: a close-up of her lying flat, golden curls spread out in a halo around her head. A little spaniel was curled possessively into the crook of her arm, a shimmering diamond-studded collar round its neck. Diana was laughing; it was a portrait of unrestrained joy, rare among Beaton's work for its spontaneous, unstudied nature. 'Diana "Baby" Blythe and her dog, 1931.'

Searching for something to flick her ash into, she found an old glass. The embers fizzed as they hit the dregs of water at the bottom.

Then something caught her eye.

*'Lord and Lady Rothermere at Wooton Lodge, Leicestershire, 1931.'*

She sat forward.

Stiff and formal, the powerful figure of Lord Rothermere stared out; an intense, formidable gaze. Next to him sat a gaunt, dark-haired woman in her mid-forties;

a woman of undistinguished features and vaguely maternal bearing, her mouth drawn into a tense little smile. She gave the impression of someone who was horrified by the prospect of being photographed; who would've sprinted away given half the chance but who'd been caught off guard. They were sitting at a tea table set up on a lawn at the back of a strange Gothic house. Her face was partially hidden under the shadow of a large sun hat; his hands were folded stiffly in his lap. Cate was struck by his huge, overbearing physicality and how old he seemed. Suddenly she shared Sam's amazement that he'd ever touched Baby Blythe. There was something incomprehensible, revolting even, about the pairing.

Behind the Rothermeres, a wide terrace led to French windows opening into the dark, shadowy recesses of the house beyond. There was a curious black blur near one of the doors; flashes of light reflecting off the windowpanes.

Cate leaned in, squinting to see better. Then she remembered a pair of Rachel's reading glasses sitting on the side of the bathroom sink.

Padding along the hallway, she got them and returned, pushing the magnifying frames back on her nose.

Her eyes adjusted. The blur solidified.

It was the running figure of a small dog.

A jewelled collar glinting around its neck.

5 St James's Square
London

2 April 1936

My darling,

Yes, I saw Malcolm for lunch. And just as I predicted
it was a chastising monologue of epic proportions – he
didn't draw breath from soup till Sauternes. In the end
I gave up trying to get a word in edgeways and amused
myself instead by thinking of various ways I could kill
him using only the objects found on the table. Once
you get past the obvious ones – knifing someone,
forking them to death, hanging them by noose fashioned
from the tablecloth – things get considerably more
challenging. I'm particularly proud of asphyxiation
through excessive amounts of mint jelly, dowsing them
in brandy then setting them on fire, and the forceful
ramming of a napkin down the throat. (I spent a long
time imagining that one.) Of course all the methods
rely on your victim being either very drunk or really
tremendously obliging. I failed to come up with
anything viable involving a spoon.

Why do you do it to me, my darling? I cannot
understand what you hope to gain by throwing us

together all the time! He hates me and thinks I'm
a fool. No amount of time spent picking at lobster
thermidor at the Dorchester will make the slightest bit
of difference. Now you, on the other hand, I'd be only
too happy to meet for lunch — at any time or any place!

Please, please don't make me dine with your
husband again. I may not have come up with anything
wicked to do with a spoon yet but it's only a matter
of time . . .

Yours,

Baby xxx

Jack sat on his roof terrace, drinking red wine. The heat, like a giant sweaty palm, wrapped around him. He pushed his hair off his face.

A mistress. Was that the same as a lover?

A mistress was colder, more calculated. It usually involved finance. And, more importantly, betrayal.

A sick feeling flooded him, followed quickly by frustration.

She was right, he didn't approve of her.

But neither could he prevent himself from thinking about her. His psyche, his whole body was already in play, inclining towards her, in conflict with his better judgement. His reason was useless; no match for the reality of her, no matter how contradictory.

Forcing down another swallow, he filled up his glass again.

He couldn't sleep; didn't even try.

This time of year was difficult anyway. It was the build-up. And the heat didn't help. It reminded him of those first awful weeks . . . just after the accident.

He remembered all too well walking through the days after his wife's death, numb, devastated. Now the feeling was back; the same terrifying loss of control.

He shifted, as if changing his position would ease the internal discomfort. It didn't.

It was the stupid things that had overwhelmed him, then, grinding his whole being to a halt, like what kind of flower arrangements there should be at the service, the wording of the obituary, the endless sympathy cards. What to do with all her clothes and personal belongings.

He took another sip.

Her personal belongings.

For a while he'd lived with them. He couldn't grasp that she wouldn't need them. There was a lingering feeling that she'd be upset if she came back and he'd thrown them away. So he did nothing for over a year. It was all he could do to get up, get dressed, go to work.

Paul was alive then. Paul, who'd hired him, mentored him; given him a safe place to fall apart. After the accident, he'd let Jack come in even when there wasn't much to do, just to sit in the office, be among people. He'd made mistakes, stupid, careless blunders; things anyone else would've been fired for. Instead, Paul had quietly got on with it, correcting the errors without even bothering to point them out, letting him fuck up. But then Paul was like that. He just got on with stuff in a non-dramatic way. He didn't press Jack either; didn't fuss over him or worry. Sometimes he'd take him out for a pint at lunchtime; let him ramble on about anything he wanted to. He remembered talking to Paul about the clothes. It had seemed a terrible dilemma at the time. Paul had offered no advice. He just listened, nodding every once in a while, looking interested. Jack must've banged on about it for months. But Paul always gave the matter his undivided attention; always acted like it was the first time Jack had ever mentioned it. It was only later, maybe a year and half later, that

Jack realised he'd been mad. Insane from grief. At the time, he'd thought he was pulling off a fairly credible imitation of a man going through a difficult time. In fact, it had been merely his own amazement at being able to do anything at all that substantiated the illusion of normalcy. But the truth was, he'd been demented and quite obviously so; only one step up from the person talking to themselves in the street, punctuating their monologue with the occasional rant at passers-by or pigeons. He too had felt the pull of the abyss and teetered, for a very long while, on its edge.

Or had he fallen?

He considered, drinking. The wine was warm, bitter.

Was he still there, scaling his way slowly, painfully up the edges even now?

In the end it was Suzanne who had taken care of the clothes. Suzanne had been the sister of the man in the other car. There'd been a joint memorial service, in which she'd played a very active role. She liked to organise; events, careers, lives. Tall, blonde, horsy, with a good education and bad teeth, Suzanne had relished being really rather amazing under the circumstances. She ran a recruitment consultancy. She was bright, efficient, eager to please. And after the memorial service was over, she'd turned her attention to Jack.

She'd set up a kind of informal support group for the friends and relatives affected by the accident, and under this guise, sent Jack a great many emails keeping him updated about how everyone was doing, organising various get-togethers. Jack didn't want to make casual conversation or to be supported by other grieving, shell-shocked people. He wanted to be left alone, wandering around London with a gaping hole where his heart and memory should be, and to be mad, in the great English tradition of madness, talking around the edges of his loss with eloquent stoicism rather than striding boldly into the centre of it with a bright searchlight and a lot of American therapy-speak.

But Suzanne hadn't let him off the hook that easily. And he didn't always have sufficient inner resources to resist. She'd rung, always on the pretence of making sure he was all right, asking if there was anything she could do, and once, just once, he'd made the mistake of hesitating. 'Well, I'm not really sure what to do about her clothes . . .'

There'd been a sharp intake of breath. 'You still have her clothes?' She made it sound as if he'd been cross-dressing; fondling them of an evening.

'Well, yes . . .'

'Right. That's it. I'm coming over tomorrow and we'll clean out the cupboards.'

'No, I'm sure that's not –'

'No, Jack, I insist. Someone needs to get it sorted. This situation can't continue.' Again, she made it sound as if he hadn't emptied the rubbish in a year; that there was some-thing morally unhygienic about his behaviour.

She'd found her way in. And Jack felt the horror of her being on his private territory with her tall, blonde loudness; her flowery perfume; her terrifying self-possession. She assaulted all his senses; the ones that had been dimmed, requiring soft noises, dull light; slow, predictable movements.

In the end, she'd been rather useful. She brought her own bin bags and sent him out for a walk. When he got back, she'd done it, even moving his belongings into the empty spaces of the wardrobe so that it didn't look so bleak or bare. They loaded them into the back of her Ford Fiesta.

'Shall we have a quick drink?' she suggested.

He paused. She'd come all this way, done something incredibly intimate . . . something he couldn't seem to manage on his own. He owed her.

They'd gone to a local pub, sat in a corner. It was late afternoon. They'd drunk warm whisky and she'd done all the talking, pulling her jumper off to reveal a low-buttoned oxford shirt over surprisingly large, rather distracting breasts. She'd told him about her business, chatted easily about the troubles with staff, holiday plans, family dilemmas; leaning in, making lots of eye contact; laughing just that bit too readily when he'd made any sort of comment, no matter how banal. And to his shame he'd responded; had felt the physical ache of attraction come clumsily, blindly to life beneath the leaden surface of his grief.

They had stayed too long. He hadn't offered to buy her dinner; hadn't even pretended to be amusing or charming.

Walking back to her car, he'd made a fumbling sort of lunge at her, which was immediately reciprocated. She'd bent forward, guiding his mouth to hers, orchestrating the contact that, in his state of drunkenness, was bound to be hit-and-miss. They'd stumbled back into the flat, him groping at her; unfamiliar with her body, her shape and smell. Once or twice there had been head-on collisions. She seemed to go right when he was heading left; up when he went down. It had been a tangled, desperate business, over before it had barely begun, without any pleasure or even relief.

To her credit, she'd left fairly quickly afterwards, gathering up her things, moving away as if on cue. But later it had struck him as pathetic how quiet she'd been; how little she'd felt she could intrude upon his patience or time.

There'd been a few occasions after that, simply because he'd felt so awkward about the whole thing. He'd had a desperate desire to mask his aversion to her by sleeping with her; a strategy that was demoralising for both of them.

It was she who had ended it, two months later.

She'd driven off, slightly huffy despite her sympathetic, understanding speech about how she hoped he looked after himself; she needed someone more emotionally available.

That's how Jack got more closet space. And another black period he hadn't reckoned on. Just when he'd thought he was out of it, back it spiralled, in and around itself, sucking him into the vortex.

It wasn't the loss of his wife so much as the loss of everything around her – a basic belief that life was good and some form of justice would eventually prevail.

Now he sat on the roof terrace of his flat in Canonbury, thinking about another woman – a girl with small, cool hands and a tiny white scar on her forehead. A girl he couldn't make out; didn't trust. And yet the memory of her touch, her stillness, lingered.

It had taken so long to come this far. How could he risk losing himself again? He was teetering, in danger of falling into another void of feeling.

A smart man would stop while he could. A clever person would learn from past mistakes.

He took another drink.

Was he smart?

After Suzanne had thrown Julia's clothes away, Jack had emptied the flat of the details of their life together. He hadn't done it in the same way, with the same brisk purposefulness or resolve. But he'd done it. Bit by bit. First he took the photos, stacked them in a box that sat in the front-hall cupboard. And then he began to replace the pictures that she'd bought, with pieces he found from either work or the antique shops around Islington. Gradually he made it his practice that any time he happened across something in a drawer, something that reminded him of her or that she'd owned, he took it out, either throwing it away or putting it into the box in the hallway cupboard. Over time the objects went from being quite obvious, like her passport or a small porcelain figurine, to much more subtle things like a book of matches from a favourite restaurant or a kitchen knife that she'd brought with her when they first moved in together.

All these things went, until finally he was satisfied that he could move around his flat in any room and not come into contact with anything that had belonged or, indeed, been specific to her.

In this way, he exorcised his home, his surroundings, from the traces of her.

For as he recovered from the dark, dragging days, Jack began to see what had been there all along. It rose like a sudden sprawling landscape from a veil of blinding mist, spread out before him all at once and in unmistakable detail.

Everything about their former life had been a lie.

5, St James's Square
London

23 May 1936

Darling Bird,
Tell me plain – what is it that men want from us? I
cannot make it out. One minute they're so attentive you
imagine they'd die if you moved even two paces to the
left. Thirty seconds later they're off without so much as
a goodbye. I seem always to have too much of the men
I don't want and not enough of the one I do! Am quite
morbid today. Feel a great big wave of Black building
and the only way out of it is to dance harder. Or
perhaps to stop dancing all together . . .

Say something kind to me, my love. Even if you have
to lie. And do tell me another story about that funny
little maid of yours! Did she really darn the leg of your
knickers together? Do you think perhaps she works
for Muv?

If you wanted to come to London, I would be your
constant, devoted companion. Please don't leave me
alone with all these plotting politicos! The city is simply
crawling with ambassadors and foreign royals with the
most impossible names and even more impossible

*manners, lounging around in damp basements drinking too much and fondling each other. Am certain they're all spies. Lord R spends all his time trying to make me dance with them in the hopes that they'll be indiscreet. Of course they are indiscreet, but hardly in the way he means. Now, Mr Paul Robeson – there's a man I'd really like to dance with! Can you imagine what the Old Guard would say to that!*

*Oh, I do hope I've made you blush!*

*Sending piles of chaste, Rome-approved kisses,*

*B xxxxxx*

The woman turned it over in her fingers, frowning. 'I've never seen anything like it,' she admitted, handing it back to Cate. 'It's not really my area of expertise. It looks like an old Girl Guide badge or something like that. Why don't you ask Laurence at stall twenty-eight? I have a feeling it's something to do with the war. That's his particular passion.'

Cate slipped the little badge back into her jeans pocket. 'Where is stall twenty-eight?'

'Through the passage on your left and right to the end,' the woman directed her. 'Laurence Friedman.'

'Thank you.'

Cate walked through the passageway of Alfies Antiques, through the close, crowded stalls, filled with furniture, clothing, some bursting with fine antiques, some cluttered with kitsch memorabilia. All tastes were catered for here at Alfies. Spanning over four floors, it was one of Europe's largest antique markets and a great treasure trove where the past came to life in the wonderful collections of passionate enthusiasts.

Right at the back, Cate spotted stall twenty-eight. It was a jewellery concession – watches, diamonds, brooches, pearls; all of them pre-1950 and a few even from the Regency period. A bearded man in his fifties sat reading a copy of the *Sun* newspaper. He looked up, folding the paper away, as she approached.

'Hello,' Cate smiled, 'are you Laurence?'

'Absolutely.' He stood up. 'What can I do for you?'

'I wondered if you could help me.'

'I'll try.'

'I've got something that I can't place.' She took the badge out and put it on the glass counter between them. 'I was told you might be able to help.'

He picked it up. It was battered, a dark racing green. In the centre there was a golden candle with the letters SSG. Around the edge it read: '*The Prize is a Fair One and the Hope Great.*'

He looked up at her, frowning. 'Where did you get this?'

'I found it. What is it?'

'Well, I've never actually seen one before,' he said slowly, 'but I believe it's a badge for the Society of St George.' He turned it over. 'Hold on a minute . . . what's this?' Taking out a jeweller's glass, he examined the back carefully. 'It's got an inscription. God, it's small!' He squinted. '"God said let there be light and there was you."' He looked up. 'Very odd.'

'I hadn't noticed that before. What's the Society of St George? I've never heard of it.'

'No,' he said, 'you wouldn't. In fact, I thought it was probably just a legend. That is, until now. Apparently it was a dilettante organisation formed between the wars. The goal was a purer, more culturally superior Britain. Thus the St George imagery. Britain ruled by the British, for the British. That sort of thing. It didn't last long. Quite a popular concept at the time, unfortunately. Especially among the upper classes.' He turned it over again. 'This is a real find. They were meant to be more influential than even the Cliveden set. And very exclusive. An underground, secret movement.'

'Are you sure?'

How did that fit in with the laughing socialite, posing as Venus or clutching a pedigree dog with a diamond-studded collar? It didn't make sense.

'Well, like I said, I've never actually seen one before. But I've read about it. There was a newspaper called *The Week* which was dedicated to flushing these private political organisations out. Exposing them. The only shame was that, because it had communist leanings, it wasn't taken seriously enough by the Establishment. It's always the same: the few rule the many. All behind the scenes too. I'll give you fifty quid for it.'

'I wasn't intending to sell.'

'You won't find a fairer price.'

'No, I don't expect I will. Have you ever heard of Nicholas Warburton?'

'Who?'

'Nothing. Never mind. You've been really helpful.'

He shook his head. 'Let me know if you change your mind. I could probably go as high as seventy-five.'

She held out her hand.

Reluctantly he handed it back. 'Here's my card. Just in case.'

'Thanks.'

'Promise you won't go anywhere else, OK?'

She put it in her pocket. 'OK, sure,' she promised. 'And thank you again.'

Wandering back down the passage, she turned the badge over, running her fingers over its worn enamel surface. Why would anyone even make a badge for a supposedly secret organisation? Surely the point would be not to advertise. The whole thing felt wrong.

She slipped it back into her handbag and checked her mobile phone.

Nothing.

No messages, no texts.

She pressed the power button, just to make sure it was working. It was.

Not even a missed call.

Heading out of the dim, dusty half-light of Alfies into the hard, bright glare of the afternoon sun, she was aware of feeling weightless, like a bit of flotsam, cut off, drifting aimlessly downstream.

Had he really stopped trying to contact her?

She should be relieved. It's what she wanted, after all. Wasn't it?

Stopping at the corner of Church Street and Lisson Grove, she wavered.

She was unsure of which way to go, what to do next. London felt alien, overwhelming; stifling. She went and sat in the shelter of a nearby bus stop, grateful for the shade. And taking out her diary again, she paged through, looking at her notes from the library.

But as she flicked through the months, her eye was caught by certain, memorable dates, starred or circled with red pen. And she was transported to private booths in restaurants, out-of-the-way hotel rooms, secret trysts that had shaped her days, then weeks. Unconsciously she ran the tips of her fingers along the smooth strand of pearls around her neck.

Why had she worn them today? Out of habit? For luck? Or perhaps to remind herself that, once, someone had loved her?

It had been snowing when he had given those to her; presented in a dark blue leather box, the pearls luminous against the folds of the black satin, like the great feathery flakes that filled the night sky outside.

'Think of me,' he had said, placing them around her neck, fitting together the gold clasp as he kissed the top of her spine, the soft curve behind her ear, and then, very slowly, moving down to kiss the rest of her . . .

And here she was, thinking of him, in the heat of summer, so many thousands of miles away.

He wasn't handsome. He was striking. Tall, black hair, blacker eyes. But there was a flash of fierceness, a moody darkness. His features were out of balance; they didn't have the evenness for handsomeness. Yet when he smiled, his face came alive, the room shone. He had charisma, power.

And of course, the first time she saw him, he was wearing black tie. Men look different in a tux. In a ballroom. And women feel different in a gown.

She'd gone with Derek. Derek spent a lot of time socialising at parties and grand events. He had business to do, clients to line up. He liked to be seen. And it mattered enormously to him who he was seen with. In all the time she knew him, he never once attempted to touch her. She was fairly sure she was what was known as a beard; more of an expensive accessory than an actual companion. Besides, she had no money or connections. Had she been wealthy, he might have found it in himself to do almost anything. He was unknowable like that. His true self was so subverted that she was never entirely sure of anything, even the most basic truths about his character.

But that night had been a big one; an exclusive charity ball. He'd asked her months ago but she'd been so busy she'd nearly forgotten. In the end, he'd sent her to an upmarket hair salon and manicurist, even selecting her dress himself. It was emerald-green silk, Calvin Klein; the most striking dress she'd ever seen let alone worn. It was simple, sophisticated, draping luxuriously over her torso. It was strange how he'd known her dress size so accurately; known what would suit her to such an alarming degree. And she'd imagined, for a few minutes, that perhaps his interest in her did go deeper. Even more disarming was the fact that she didn't know exactly how she felt about that. Yet it gave the evening a certain sexual tension, and driving in the car on the way over, she'd been careful to say as little as possible, to feel her way gently into this strange new chapter between them.

When they'd arrived it had taken a minute for her to realise what was wrong; that everyone else was dressed in black and white and it wasn't a mere coincidence but the dress code. 'I'm the only one out of place!' she'd hissed at him, blushing and bowing her head to avoid the surprised looks of the other guests. 'It looks as if I've done it on purpose!'

'An honest mistake.' He'd smiled slyly. 'But my darling, it's a ballroom crowded with faces, and only yours stands out. Now, that's got to be a good thing.'

And he'd been right. Not all the glances were disapproving; many were admiring.

'Stand straight, pull your shoulders back. And put that accent on with a trowel, will you? I've got work to do, which means you do too.'

And so she had. Whatever illusions she'd had in the car evaporated. Laughing, she breezily explained how she hadn't known it was a black-and-white ball, how she felt an absolute fool and people warmed to her, assured her she looked stunning. And before she knew it, she was dancing, commanding unprecedented attention. Mostly with the older husbands of the women who were Derek's clients, women who wanted to whisper about each other into his attentive ear, while someone removed their husbands from the table, distracted them on the dance floor.

Alone with them, Constantine would tease and flatter, joke and cajole, mentioning ever so casually about a piece he was expecting from France that month, one that was incredibly rare and that he really had promised to someone else, but, since they were such good friends, he might be able to arrange an exclusive preview . . .

And he had his eye on one client in particular. Hailey Cashelle, patron and organiser of the ball, society belle and the wife of Henry Cashelle, the publishing mogul. She'd recently bought a two-storey penthouse which she was remodelling extensively. With her icy demeanour and statuesque, slender figure, she dominated any room she entered with her commanding arrogance. Her looks were honed to that demanding standard of New York perfection: deep auburn, expensively highlighted hair, wide tawny eyes, and a high forehead. She had ambition – political, social – and a fiercely driven nature, masked by an almost comically clichéd Southern charm. When she turned her smooth smile in your direction, the warmth of her attention was impossible to resist. Her husband, Henry, seemed coarse by comparison. He was a businessman, pure and simple. And they were rarely seen in public together due to his advanced years and overwhelming work schedule. She had instead a series of 'walkers' or 'beaux', as she jokingly referred to them; men who escorted her to various functions, some of them straight, some of them not; some of them lovers, others just very attentive, highly photogenic friends.

Cate was aware of a kind of hush that surrounded her as she made her entrance, well into the evening, quickly followed by a trail of gossipy hysteria. Her gown was fitted to within an inch of her life, a shimmering silver strapless affair. And in her wake another woman followed, less obvious but no less striking for it, with long dark hair, regal bearing and clear grey eyes, wearing a black jersey sheath of impeccable tailoring.

Derek came to get her. 'Time to get to work, angel. I need you to stand over here.' He placed her next to the bar.

It was like awaiting an audience with the Queen. Hailey made her way slowly through the throngs, shaking hands, laughing and blowing kisses. Then she caught sight of Cate, in her green dress. Her eyes narrowed, though her smile remained as wide as ever. Laughing, she walked towards them.

'My, my, my! Well, there's always one every year!' She posed next to her while a flurry of photographers descended upon them, cameras flashing. 'Let me guess, you're an actress. Or a would-be model.'

'N-no, I'm so sorry,' Cate stammered, overwhelmed by the sudden attention, 'you see, I had no idea . . .'

The other woman came up behind Hailey, placed her hand gently on her elbow. Hailey turned. 'What do think, Anne Marie?'

Anne Marie regarded Cate coolly, as if she were nothing more than a chair or any other inanimate object. 'Personally,' she sighed, in a soft French accent, eyes busy scanning the room, 'I thought this year the dress would be red.' She gave Hailey's arm a light squeeze then moved on, already bored by the subject. Soon she was engulfed in a crowd of her own, punctuated by air kisses and little shrieks of delight.

'It's my fault,' Derek intervened, slipping his hand around Hailey's. 'The poor girl's a painter of all things. I've been so busy I forgot to tell her about the dress code. Derek Constantine. I'm a friend of Gloria Rawlands, and Rhona Klein. And of course, I'm longing to make amends.'

Hailey's eyes fixed on his. 'Are you now?'

'I'm mortified,' he assured her.

She considered this a moment, then turned again to Cate. 'A painter?'

'Yes. I really had no idea.'

'You're English.'

'Yes.'

'Well, that might explain something. Usually it's an actress wanting to get in the papers.' She turned back to Derek. 'You're not the dealer who found Gloria that sixteenth-century Spanish table, are you?'

He nodded. 'You have a wonderful memory.'

'I remember that I tried to buy it from her and she wouldn't part with it for love nor money!' Hailey twisted round, scanning the room, her brow wrinkling in irritation. 'I don't know where my date has got to! They'll be wanting a turn on the dance floor in a minute.'

'Shall I see if I can find your husband?'

'My husband!' She gave a trill of a laugh. 'Lord, no! I haven't come this far in life just to dance with my husband! No, I've got some divine young man from the Harvard rowing team at my disposal this evening, only these young peacocks do like to disappear and stand in front of a mirror. Once they're mesmerised it's hard to tear them away!'

Derek flashed a row of unnaturally white teeth. 'Well, I know I'm a poor second, but perhaps you might allow me,' he said, offering his arm.

Cate watched as he escorted her to the centre of the dance floor, slipping his arm about her waist, and the music began to play. He was whispering in her ear and she was laughing, tossing her head back, a ripple of applause making its way round the room. He was in, exactly where he'd planned to be. All it had taken was one gauche English girl and a bright green dress.

A stray photographer snapped Cate's picture again, laughing. 'Nice try, kid!'

Cate felt her cheeks burning. The green dress should've made her feel invincible; instead she was humiliated. Her head was throbbing, as if it were twice its normal size. She escaped to the ladies' room. A uniformed attendant was wiping down the sinks, emptying the change bowl; doing all those strange things attendants do, like filling up basins with water and putting out little towels. And it was overflowing with other guests, gossiping, powdering their noses and checking their make-up. As soon as she walked in, she was aware of the looks and whispers of the other women. Pushing into a cubicle, she locked herself in, slumping on the toilet seat, cradling her head in her hands.

If only she could get out of here; go home. But Derek had spent all this money on her. She felt beholden, trapped.

She left the ladies' room and stopped, unsure of what to do next, dreading going back in.

The ballroom was to the right.

The hotel bar was to the left.

She put a tenner on the bar. 'Jack Daniel's, please.'

Without even bothering to sit, she downed it in one. She needed courage.

She signalled to the barman again. 'Another please.'

'Take it easy,' a voice said.

She looked up. He was older, in his mid-forties, nursing a beer.

'Mind your own business.'

He laughed. 'Quite right. Nice dress, by the way.'

'With all due respect, fuck off.'

He grinned.

There was something about him – the way he looked at her. From the very first moment, she felt as if she were a small glass marble rolling down a hill towards an inevitable conclusion.

She turned back to her drink.

'English, huh?' He tapped the end of a pack of cigarettes. 'It's the way you guys say it that's so charming.'

She tossed the second shot back, put her money on the bar.

'Only, if you're going to drink like that, you really shouldn't drink alone,' he pointed out, offering her a cigarette.

She ignored it. 'The company's better on my own. Besides,' she decided, 'I'm going home.'

'Good idea.' He put two cigarettes into his mouth, lit them both and passed her one.

She leaned against the bar. Already it had hit her; hot, burning the back of throat, easing its way down to her stomach. And already her head was that fraction slower. The pressure valve had been located and any minute now it was about to be released. She felt dangerous, free. 'What if I don't smoke?'

'Then I guess I've made an ass out of myself,' he smiled.

He wasn't even handsome. She remembered thinking that at the time: he's not even good-looking – that is, not in any traditional sense. But he was so sure of himself.

She slid onto one of the bar stools, took the cigarette. 'Aren't you going to buy me a drink?'

He shook his head. 'I figure you've had enough.'

She took a deep drag, exhaling slowly through her nose. 'All this and a mind-reader too.'

'Where's your date?'

'Dancing with someone else. And yours?'

He flicked a bit of ash into an ashtray. 'No doubt doing the same thing.'

'Well, it is a ball.'

'My name's Alex, by the way.'

'Cate.'

'What do you do?'

'I'm an artist.'

'Would I know your work? Are you famous?'

'Oh, sure.' She looked at him sideways. 'Now's the time to invest, before my value hits the roof.'

He laughed. 'Is that so?'

'What about you?' She leaned her chin in her palm. 'Are you famous?'

'Yeah.' He took a drag. 'Rich and famous.'

'So why don't I recognise you?'

He shrugged his shoulders.

'What do you do?'

He looked across at her. 'You really have no idea who I am?'

'Sure. You're the guy who won't buy me a drink.'

He nodded to the barman, who poured out another two shots. Again, Cate tossed it back in one go. 'Thanks.' Then she stubbed her cigarette out, slid off the stool and picked up her evening bag. 'Have a nice night.'

'That's it?' He slipped his cigarettes into his breast pocket, stood up too.

'Yeah, that's it.'

'What's your last name?'

'What do you care?'

'Are you always this rude?'

'Think of it as direct.'

'Do you ever eat?'

'All the time.'

He shoved his hands into his pockets, rocked back on his heels. 'How do you feel about strange men?'

'They're my favourite kind.'

'Is that a fact?'

'Yeah,' she nodded. 'And I like them to stay that way.'

Turning away, she smiled to herself, as she walked out of the bar.

Back in the ballroom, the party was in full swing. The whiskey gave her courage. By now her dress had ceased to be a novelty anyway. Derek was flitting around Hailey Cashelle and her table, refilling her glass, leaning forward to attend to every comment she made and laughing loudly. He had the glow of someone who'd made it. She'd served her purpose. Now was probably a good time for her to make her apologies and leave.

She was heading through the crowds towards him when someone caught her hand. She turned.

He fixed her with those dark eyes. 'May I have this dance?'

'I was just going to –'

He pulled her close. 'Shut up and dance with me.'

He smelled good, his hand caressing her bare back,

swaying to the music. He twirled her round. 'I have a commission for you.'

'You don't even know me or my work!'

'So what?'

'And I don't know you.'

'What do you want to know? My favourite colour is black. I like dogs not cats. If I have a star sign, I don't give a shit about what it is. And I don't believe in luck, I believe in balls.'

'Clearly. Where's your date?' she asked again.

'She's not my date. Don't you want to hear my offer?'

'No.' She pulled away. The other couples turned and swayed on the dance floor, their images reflected in the mirrors that surrounded them.

'I see. Some people are afraid of success. Afraid of really being alive.' He was taunting her now.

'I'm not afraid of anything.' She walked away, made her way out of the crowded ballroom without saying goodbye. She knew if she wanted to escape entirely, all she needed to do was move with slightly more purpose; a little more speed.

But she didn't. She moved languidly, aware that he was bridging the distance between them, that in another moment he would catch up to her.

When he did, he took her arm

'What are you doing?' she laughed, allowing him to ferry her down the hallway. 'I have to go home!'

He was leading her into the foyer, towards the exit. 'Do you?'

She turned to him, leaning too heavily on his arm, pressing her body against his. 'What are you doing?' she asked again, softer this time.

'I'm abducting you.'

'What if I don't like you?'

'What makes you think I'm so fond of you?'

'Do you abduct every woman you meet?'

'No.' His eyes were unblinking. 'Never.'

They were outside now, standing on the pavement. It was dark, the air cool. A doorman stood focusing on the middle distance, ignoring them.

He put his hand in the air and a long black Mercedes pulled up.

She laughed incredulously. 'Don't tell me that's yours!'

'Yeah.'

'So, you're one of those guys who has their own private driver?'

'Yeah, that's me. Own Private Driver Guy.' He swung the door open. 'Get in.'

'Why?'

'So I can escort you home.'

She looked up at him. For a moment, he reminded her of her father, the smell of him, the swagger, the danger and sex that rolled off him in waves, indiscriminate, corrupting. It was disorientating; yet familiar. She felt exhilarated, alive with desire and nerves. 'I don't do that.'

His voice was low but clear. 'Sure you do. But only with me.'

How long had it taken from the time she'd walked into the bar to the time she was lying in the darkness of the back seat, kissing him, fingers lacing through his dark hair?

An hour?

How much longer until the green silk gown was crumpled in a heap on the floor and he was pressing into her, as if he owned her; would always own her?

A bus pulled up to the stop, its doors creaking open.

'You getting on?' called the driver.

He had loved her, hadn't he? In his own way.

'Hey, lady,' he called louder, 'you getting on or what?'

Cate looked up, at the driver's red, sweaty face, at the tired faces of the people behind him, staring at her in irritation.

'In or out? On or off?' he elaborated.

She shook her head and the door slammed shut; the bus pulled away.

Now she was sitting here, with nowhere to go, chasing after ghosts.

It didn't take long to fuck up your life.

———— ❧ ————

*5 St James's Square*
*London*

*3 June 1936*

*My little Bird,*
*Anne and I are to have a flat together! I have finally*
*persuaded She Who Must Be Obeyed that Anne will*
*be the most wonderful stabilising influence and that*
*working alongside her in the bookshop will be excellent*
*for my character. The Old Guard, as you can imagine,*
*is only too happy to be rid of me. So we shall live in the*
*most delightful little hovel on Birdcage Walk, which*
*has glorious views and very little actual floor space. I*
*cannot tell you how excited I am! It's only a few blocks*
*away from the Belmont and within spitting distance of*
*Fortnum's (does one spit and go to Fortnum's?), so we*
*shall never want for either good company or tea and*
*fresh crumpets.*

*Oh! And thank you so much for the badges from the*
*Sunderland School for Girls – they are too, too perfect*
*with their fantastically cryptic slogans! Anne and Nick*
*and I have been wearing them everywhere and now*
*even James is in on the joke . . . It is simply the best*
*tease ever and everyone believes we have suddenly*

become terribly serious and politically minded and all are dying to know what it all means! We have even devised a kind of 'secret' salute which drives the press insane with curiosity. Serves them right – especially that foul little paper The Week. Of course Paul is mortified as Anne has been seen everywhere with James Dunning, that very funny, very rich MP who is simply tossing diamonds at her which she catches eagerly and with both hands. She says she'll marry for money this time, as marrying for love has no earthly use. I think Paul's father has forced him to get a job in banking to pay the alimony. So gone are the days of the little red kerchief and the brown felt hat. Ho-hum.

Long live the decadent bourgeoisie!

BB xxx

Jack hadn't been sure, even as he stood on the train platform, if he would actually go. He had his briefcase with
him, in case he changed his mind and decided to go to the
office instead. But when the train pulled in, he felt himself
get on – travelling in the opposite direction from people
heading into the City.

Part of him knew, that if he didn't do it, he'd regret it.
And yet he'd wrestled with the idea; the complicated
mass of feelings. And mostly the anger. It was monumen-
tal, like the stones that surrounded him now, heavy,
dark marble, in the leafy calm of the Fortune Green
Cemetery.

Here was one that looked like an angel, arms crossed
over its chest holding a single lily, head bent, a filmy veil
across its face. Was that what grief was? A sheer filter
through which the beauty and hope of this world could no
longer be perceived? He passed a cumbersome family
crypt, bolted with black wrought-iron gates. On top there
was a great stone urn, wrapped in winding drapery. This
was the common theme; in death, the living were cut off
from their loved ones by doors that were shut forever, the
great mass of despair covering them like thick folds of
fabric, weighing them down.

He walked up the wide central pathway, stones crunching beneath his summer shoes. The air was clear and the
sunlight glorious. There were a few people walking their
dogs; a pair of white Labradors panted and frolicked off
their leads, playing chase between the headstones, their

exuberance and vitality strangely not at odds with the dark solemnity of the place.

He'd forgotten it was so beautiful. And so quiet.

There was a flower stall by the front entrance of the chapel. He stopped. He hadn't brought anything. He needed to mark the day, but not in any traditional sense. He had a feeling that if he could just see, finally, that it was over, that she was gone, he would be released. And he wanted to be free now. He needed badly to put it behind him.

The word 'forgiveness' came to mind. Inwardly, he balked. His anger had protected him; seen him through the first annihilating year and given him the only energy he'd had to move forward. He was afraid to let it go, for fear of what lay behind it. But now it felt like the encroaching tentacles of tough ivy winding up the boughs of a slender tree, taking over, until the thing it clung to was obliterated from view.

He walked on.

Heading down a sloping side path to the far edge of the cemetery, his heart beat a tattoo, a queasy half-excitement, half-dread running like ice water through his veins. Could he see it? Would he recognise the headstone? He'd selected it with her father. It had been an awkward, excruciating task. Neither of them had been able to look at the other. But Jack would never forget her father's face, frozen in a grim mask of unbearable determination to do the thing he dreaded most, by way of saving his wife the pain.

Then it was in front him.

Or was it?

He frowned, blinked. Then felt the hot flush of rage fill him.

It was the right stone. Only someone had been there before him.

The bouquet of full white roses wasn't from the stall by the chapel. They were expensive, hand-tied, their ivory petals tinted with a subtle, translucent green. And they were scented, their tender perfume rising in the growing heat, filling the air around him. Encased in a small emerald vase, they were the kind of sophisticated arrangement that could only be purchased from a West End florist. And they were flawless, romantic. Not the kind of flowers her parents, Donald and Fay from West Sussex, would ever have bought.

He stared at them, his vision blurring; the words 'Beloved Wife' on the tombstone melting together, separating again when he blinked.

It was meant to be a private moment. A private marriage.

He considered crushing them with his foot; grinding the flowers flat underneath his heel.

Then he spotted the card, dangling from a bit of rough-hewn twine wrapped around the base of the bouquet, fluttering like a butterfly.

He didn't want to look at it.

But he did anyway, stooping down, turning it over.

It was as if a heavy foot had landed a blow to his ribs, driving all the air from his lungs, winding him. The card slipped through his fingers, dancing in the light morning breeze.

As he rose again, he had the bizarre feeling of leaving his body, of his feet being on the soft, grassy earth but his real self flying out, hovering just above. And from this vantage point, he had a clear view of the expression on his own face; the hollow, defeated look in his eyes, the slack jaw; once handsome features suddenly aged by bitterness and confusion.

Turning away, he somehow made his way back along the gravel path that led to the long main road, past the parade of shops and eventually the train station.

But the word on the card stabbed, slipping like a knife underneath the sealed folds of his heart.

'Forever' it said.

12 Bird Cage Walk
London

2 September 1936

My darling,
I so enjoyed our time together – it is wonderful to see
you and far too rare an occurrence nowadays. I shall be
up all night thinking about the thrilling dance scenes
from Swing Time and the way we shrieked and clapped
with delight when Fred Astaire sang 'The Way You
Look Tonight' – I think everyone in the cinema was
laughing at us! It was so like old times, my love. I do
wish you came to London more often!

   I can see that you're very hopeful now that
you've been talking so much with Nancy. She's very
compelling at times and her views are so passionate.
I've often been transfixed by her myself. But I must say
I'm concerned that you are putting too much store in
her ideas. Firstly, you know the Holy will positively
collapse if she gets wind of you and this Christian
Science Movement. She will have the entire Roman
Catholic establishment camped upon your doorstep
in a flash. And secondly, I don't like the fact that it
sounds as if you're blaming yourself for your ill luck.

It can't all be down to your own thinking and praying —
Lord knows, no one prays more than you do or more
earnestly. And you have been a good wife, even
if God hasn't blessed you with children. To my
knowledge, Malcolm has never complained nor has
reason to. (He would have me to contend with if he
did!) I cannot bear it that you think there's something
defective in you, my love. For I'm certain you're just
as God would have you be. I know my opinion matters
very little in these concerns; I'm neither a pillar of
virtue nor faith. But as one who loves you dearly I urge
you to consider Nancy's convictions in a larger light —
as fancies rather than certitudes. She is American,
after all, and so much more susceptible to these trends.

When can I see you again? Perhaps we could go to
the theatre next time? Oh, I do miss you so!

Yours always,

B xxx

As Cate approached la Upper Wimpole Street, she saw Jack's Triumph. And a wave of unexpected adolescent excitement washed over her as she turned the key in the lock. It was the first time she would see him since their night together on Primrose Hill. And yet, despite their difficult conversation, suddenly things seemed more manageable, better. Rachel would cook something, they would eat and relax around the dining-room table . . . She was looking forward to seeing him; and the pleasure of being near him again.

Flinging her bag down in the hallway she walked through to the kitchen. Sure enough, Rachel was standing at the worktop, chopping some vegetables and Jack was standing at the far end of the narrow room, hands in pockets, looking out of the window. They turned as she walked in.

'Hello,' she smiled. 'This is a nice surprise. Are you staying for dinner?' She was aware of sounding slightly forced, like a 1950s hostess in a film.

'I'm trying to convince him. Look.' Rachel nodded to the table. 'He's finished the catalogue proofs in record time!'

Cate picked up the thick sheaf of paper from the table.

'It looks marvellous, doesn't it?' Rachel beamed.

'Yes.' Cate leafed through the pages of photographs; it was odd to see it all laid out so dispassionately. She'd imagined it would take longer. 'Well done.'

'Thank you.' Jack had turned round again, staring out onto the street below. He seemed far away and unapproachable.

She looked to Rachel who gave her a reassuring smile.

'What are you making?' she asked, giving her a hug.

'Risotto. Listen, I'm going to pop out to the shops. I need to get a few things. You two can amuse yourselves, can't you?' She wiped her hands on the front of her apron and then untied it from round her waist, tossing it over the back of a chair. 'There's some wine in the fridge. I'm going to buy some strawberries, cream and meringue, and then I can whip us up a pavlova. I won't be long.'

'No problem.' Cate looked over at Jack.

But his back was still resolutely turned to her.

Rachel took her bag and keys from the hallway and headed off down the stairs. The door closed.

Cate sat down at the kitchen table.

'Are you well?' He spoke without turning round.

Cate picked up the sugar spoon. Began twirling it on one end. 'Fine. And you?'

'Fine.'

'Do you want something to drink?' she asked.

'No, thanks.'

'How long have you been here?'

'Not long.'

She nodded to herself. The spoon fell over onto the wooden table with a clang.

He turned.

'Am I disturbing you?'

'No. I'm sorry. I'm not . . . I'm just tired, that's all. So, how are you?'

'Fine. We already did this bit.'

'Yeah. Well.' He tried to concentrate, then seemed to give up, rubbing his eyes. 'The other night, on the hill, why did you tell me?' he asked suddenly.

'I don't know.' His bluntness felt accusatory. 'I'm sorry.'

'Are you in trouble?'

'Why? Are you offering to rescue me?'

'No, of course not. I just meant, if you need help, I mean, if there's something I could do . . .'

'No. It's all done, anyway.'

'What do you mean?'

'When it began, I didn't know. And when I knew, I mean, when I really knew . . .' She stopped.

'You left,' he concluded.

'Yes.'

'So –' his eyes searched her face – 'it's over now?'

She twirled the spoon around. 'Yes. Yes, I suppose it is.'

'Well, it is, isn't it? You didn't know he was married and when you did, you left. And now it's over, right?'

'You want it all neatly tied up in a box. First this happened and then that –'

'Facts. They're called facts.'

She looked up. 'Is your life a collection of facts, Jack? Bullet points on a timeline of upward achievement?'

He sighed, running his fingers through his hair in frustration. It was all going wrong.

'You want to like me, don't you?' she continued. 'Only it's really proving a challenge.'

'I do like you. That's the problem. I'm sorry if I gave you the impression otherwise.' He picked up the proofs from the table. 'I'm not very good company tonight. I'll see myself out.'

He made his way to the door; she heard it shut behind him.

Suddenly her eyes stung with tears. She wiped them away with her fist, resenting them; resenting him. No matter what she did, he was determined to find fault with her.

A few minutes later, Rachel walked in, putting the groceries down on the table.

'Jack left,' Cate said flatly, helping her to unpack. 'I'm sorry.'

'Yes, I saw him.' Rachel retied her apron round her waist. 'He's going to take some time off, go away for a few weeks.'

'A few weeks?' She felt personally affronted. 'Why?'

Rachel, on the other hand, seemed completely unperturbed. 'He needs some time off. It will do him the world of good.'

'Well, he might have said something sooner, don't you think?' She flopped into one of the old wooden chairs, jabbing her finger into the sugar bowl and sucking the sweet granules off.

Rachel looked across at her. 'Did you have a fight?'

'A fight? Why would we fight?'

'I don't know,' Rachel shrugged, pouring a bit more

chicken stock into the risotto and giving it a stir. 'All the usual reasons, I suppose.'

'And what are they?'

Rachel ignored her question. 'What you have to understand is it's a difficult time of year for him, darling. It's the anniversary of his wife's death – two years ago . . . today.'

'Oh.' Cate blinked, feeling as if someone had just slapped her across the face. 'I had no idea.'

'She was killed in a head-on collision. Both drivers died instantly.'

'How awful!'

'But that wasn't all.' Rachel ran a bunch of flat-leaf parsley under the tap before chopping it roughly and stirring it in. 'He used to confide in Paul quite a bit. Seems the accident happened on a secluded stretch of road, in the early hours of the morning. Her car was headed in the wrong direction. Not away from her sister's, where she'd supposedly spent the night, but towards it.' She paused. 'It took him a while to piece it together. I think the sister covered up for her. Said she'd gone to the shops. But of course the shops out there aren't open 24/7. And her overnight bag was still on the back seat.'

Cate's blood ran cold. 'You mean, she was having an affair?'

Rachel nodded. 'I don't think he wanted to believe it. And the family didn't help; they stuck by the sister's story, even when it became clear that it couldn't possibly be true.'

Cate thought about all Jack's questions; his need to know that she'd ended her affair as soon as she'd known her lover was married. 'Oh God!' She ran her hand wearily across her eyes. 'What an appalling way to find out!'

'It's a difficult thing to get over.' Rachel lifted the heavy iron pan off the heat. 'The police had the sister identify the body before Jack arrived. But even when they gave him her effects afterwards, he said there were things, clothes in her bag he didn't recognise, that he'd never seen before. It was as if it was a bag belonging to a completely different woman.'

'A double life.'

'Yes.' Rachel's face clouded. 'Infidelity is very much a Jekyll and Hyde existence.'

'Did you know her?'

'Of course.'

Cate hesitated, her stomach tightening in a knot. 'What was she like?'

'Smart, very intelligent. She was a researcher for a television company. Quite ambitious.' Rachel wrinkled her nose, remembering. 'I think in many ways she was very demanding. But she had a great deal of personal charm.'

'And –' The words stuck in Cate's throat. She tried to sound light. 'I mean, was she attractive?'

'Oh yes! A very pretty girl. But then, Jack's a good-looking man, don't you think?'

'Yes . . . yes, that's true,' Cate agreed. She hadn't really thought of it before.

'They made a handsome couple.'

'Where's he going to go?'

'Probably back to Devon. Everything has to be checked before the auction. And it will give him some time away from London.'

'It doesn't sound like much of a holiday.'

'I know,' Rachel smiled. 'But Jack's not like that. And in a way, I understand. On the one hand you don't want to be around people, and on the other, you don't really want to be by yourself, doing nothing. It's a time you just have to get through.' Again, her face tensed and Cate thought of Paul – of how much she must still miss him. 'Wash the salad leaves, will you, darling?'

Cate no longer had an appetite but she washed them anyway, turning the bright green leaves of watercress and spinach under the cool water of the tap, shaking them out into the colander.

'What was her name?'

Rachel was busy slicing strawberries. 'Sorry?'

'Jack's wife . . . what was her name?'

'Oh . . . ah, Julia.'

Somehow this cut right through her.

Julia. It was an elegant name, with subtle, musical qualities.

Suddenly she was no longer a distant figure. She was here . . . walking around London, in the room with them now, sitting at the kitchen table, eavesdropping. More importantly, she filled Jack's waking thoughts; haunted his dreams. Julia was real, more real than she'd ever given her credit for. It was Cate who was the ghost, the one with no real substance or purpose in his life.

Moving mechanically, she took a wooden bowl from the shelf and began tearing the leaves.

Julia.

She was a very pretty girl. They made a handsome couple.

She was unfaithful.

No wonder Jack left.

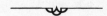

Wren,

It was an accident. You must believe me. I simply forgot how many I'd taken.

You see, things keep me awake at night. Things I wish I could forget about and I cannot sleep, so the doctor gave me some pills.

But then, I don't expect you've ever done anything you regret.

It was an accident. Please don't let her send me away again.

He will never marry me. He never will. And I can't imagine what I've done wrong!

D

Jack stayed at a bed and breakfast in Lyme Regis, driving up to Endsleigh to spend the day working alone. Since his last visit it had grown still more wild and unkempt. Without Jo to clean, polish and air the old house, a filmy grey layer of dust settled upon everything, dulling sounds and giving it a muffled, crypt-like atmosphere. Most importantly, Cate wasn't there. She was so closely linked to his experience of the place that without her it felt bereft of charm or any sensual beauty. The rooms had seemed better proportioned, more pleasingly decorated when she was either in them or about to enter. Now he wandered through them alone, his mind drifting from one memory to another, untethered and unfocused.

After a while, he found an old record player tucked into the corner of the study and a pile of thick vinyl opera recordings. He put them on, loudly and opened the French windows at the side of the house. The majestic tenor voice of Jussi Björling filled the vast, empty rooms, echoing through the main hallway with its marble floor and cavernous ceiling.

And so he worked, making himself endless pots of strong black tea, moving methodically through the rooms, labelling and cross-checking, work which required only the smallest fraction of his real attention. Against the backdrop of grand emotion, *Madama Butterfly*, *Faust*, *Lucia di Lammermoor*, he wrestled with his own feelings, and the ghosts that stubbornly dominated his thoughts – Julia and her lover, who even now, two years later, continued to maintain an intimacy with her that he knew he'd never enjoyed.

It was one thing to lose his wife. It was another thing to realise the love they'd had was meaningless, like a bad cheque.

Like a record with a deep scratch, his mind kept repeating, stuck in the moment when reality came crashing down on him, playing and replaying the phone call, early that sunny Sunday morning; a call he thought must be from Julia but which turned out to be from a Berkshire police officer, saying things that didn't make sense, that couldn't possibly be true. One minute he was comfortably drowsing, enjoying the freedom of having the bed all to himself, listening to the birdsong outside and planning his day off. The next he was sitting up, the birds sounded as if they were screaming rather than singing and he was falling, internally, at a terrifying speed with nothing to grab hold of.

'She's at her sister's,' he kept insisting. 'It can't be her.'

The officer spoke slowly, patiently. 'Her identification says Julia Coates. She has dark brown hair, drives a black Mini Cooper.'

'Yes, but . . .'

'You need to come in, sir.'

'But it can't be her!'

'Sir –' the man paused – 'how can you be sure?'

There it was; how could he be sure? A crack formed, a single hairline fracture across the eggshell surface of his ego. It grew wider, more devastating as the day unfolded, till any sense he had of being able to trust his own senses or interpretation of life disappeared forever.

'Sir?' The officer was waiting. 'Would you like me to contact her sister for you? If you give me her name and number, I'd be willing to speak to her directly. Sir? Are you still there?'

Jack had heard about people whose world had turned upside down in a moment. He'd outwardly sympathised but felt secretly immune, even superior to such twists of fate. He didn't believe in fate, after all. It was all about attitude and effort. He was self-determining.

Only that turned out to be an illusion too. He wasn't self-determining. Or rather, the only thing now that he got to determine were his responses, his attitudes, how he would deal with what life doled out. That wasn't good enough. He wanted more than that.

The Greeks called it hubris. What the fuck did the Greeks know?

More about tragedy than he did, he thought wryly.

Her sister hadn't spoken to him herself. The family that had once welcomed him and been his as well, especially after his father deteriorated, took a step back. And he found he was instantly isolated, separated by their loyalty to Julia. No one ever said anything directly; no acknowledgement was ever made of how she was found. They were grieving the loss of their sister, their child. He was alone in grieving the loss of his marriage as well. The gap widened. An unspoken hostility grew between them, built from the unsaid words; a kind of defensiveness on both sides, which gradually hardened into a wall. Had they believed he had something to do with her infidelity? That he'd driven her to it through some neglect or unfaithfulness of his own? Had she confided in them about her lack of marital satisfaction? And so it spread outwards like a kind of web; extending to embrace her friends – friends he'd thought of as belonging to him too until they struggled to make eye contact with him at the funeral or no longer bothered to ring.

He hadn't been the one who'd cheated. But he was the one who felt punished for the affair.

The one who was left.

'It's time you moved on,' people began to say, as little as six months later. 'You need to let go of that now.'

Yes, he needed to let go of it, accept it, and endure the increasing indifference of those he thought had loved him. He needed to grow up, get on.

Life wasn't fair. Who ever said life was fair? So she cheated. Time to get a girlfriend; buy a house . . . start again.

Yet the wound went too deep. He'd lost what he couldn't afford to lose. Hope. A basic tangible belief in the goodness of people, of love.

Could he have prevented it? Is that what they thought?

The words on the card ran through his mind. *Forever.*

He thought of Cate.

Did forever even exist any more?

And so his thoughts ran, endless, obsessive, battering him through the long, still days, like waves pummelling into the rocks, wearing his spirit down. He made no attempt to stem the tide and gave up trying to shake himself out of it. For too long he'd strained every inch of his being, trying to avoid the overwhelming mass of feelings. He couldn't do it any more. He surrendered. So what if he fell, tumbling into a bottomless abyss? He no longer had the energy to pretend to be normal. And here it didn't matter. He was alone. He could wear the same clothes, forget to shave, eat or not eat as his fancy took him. Here, in this abandoned old house, miles from anywhere, he could be mad and no one would hear if he ran from room to room, screaming.

Endsleigh was as eloquent and grand as his rage and fear; as wild and neglected as his grief.

So instead he listened to Renata Tebaldi singing 'Un bel dí', over and over, drinking cold tea, wandering from one room to another, occasionally doing work, and occasionally lying down in the cool, overgrown grass at the side of the house, dozing in the sunlight, allowing his mind to be stilled briefly by the gentle breezes and birdsong.

On the fifth day he arrived at the house to find a familiar car in the drive.

Rachel was sitting on the front steps, dressed in jeans, a smart white button-down shirt and a pair of flat red ballet pumps, smoking a cigarette.

'It's more beautiful than I imagined,' she said, standing.

'Which,' she added, 'is more than I can say for you! Lost your razor, have you?'

Jack laughed, hopping out of his convertible and shutting the low door. 'What are you doing here? Come to lend me a hand?' Walking over, he wrapped an arm around her shoulders and gave her an affectionate squeeze. It was good to see her; she smelled reassuringly of cigarette smoke and Chanel No. 19. He hadn't realised how lonely he'd been. 'Is Cate with you?'

She shook her head. 'Sorry, darling, just me. And no, I haven't come to help so much as to check on you.' She reached out a hand, running her fingers lightly along his dark unshaven beard, glistening with silver strands. 'It looks as if I'm just in time. You've gone a bit Grizzly Adams, kiddo.'

He nodded. 'Yes.'

Her face softened. 'It's a shit time of year.'

'Yes,' he agreed again.

'I've got a grand idea. Show me the house and then let's bunk off and go and have a slap-up lunch somewhere, on me. What do you say? I'm just guessing but I'll bet you haven't had a proper meal in days. Am I right?'

'How well you know me!' he smiled, and then stopped. His face changed, suddenly serious. 'Paul . . . he died in the summer. It's that time for you too, isn't it?'

She took one last long drag on her cigarette and, tossing it down, ground the end out under her heel. 'Well remembered.'

They stood a moment, looking out over the horizon to the sea beyond. The wind blew but the sky was cloudless, limitless, a scorching sun beat down, like an eye that wouldn't blink or close.

'I cannot bear it,' she said at last, matter-of-factly.

He took her hand.

She looked up at him. The bright armour slipped away; she seemed to age before him, her eyes had a hollow, helplessness he recognised.

Turning the key in the lock, he pushed open the heavy oak door. 'Come inside.'

*12 Birdcage Walk*
*London*

*30 October 1936*

*My darling Wren,*
*This business of living on one's own is a bit more*
*difficult than I imagined. Of course Anne is terribly*
*good at it but I'm hopeless. For example, washing*
*clothes seems to take forever and all I end up with are*
*piles of soggy soaking woollens which of course shrink*
*and then I look like I've pulled a sock over my head*
*instead of a jumper. And the washing-up is even worse.*
*I've already broken two glasses and chipped a teacup*
*that Anne says I must replace or the landlord will*
*become cross. Little balls of dust blow across the living-*
*room floor like tumbleweeds. I practically wept when*
*Mrs Lynd, the charwoman came today. I have rarely*
*been so pleased to see anyone in my life!*

*I'm forever forgetting to buy any food, and when*
*I do, I don't know how to cook it. Scrambled eggs*
*aren't meant to be crunchy, are they? The instant*
*Anne leaves the house, I pounce on whatever she's*
*left behind like a starved animal. (She's taken to*

hiding her bread and honey and now it's a real trick
to find it!)

The job is coming on. I have graduated from
wrapping and posting orders and am now allowed on
the shop floor. The Old Guard came in the other day
to order a book called, Wellington: The Man and the
Myth, which I'm fairly certain he already owns but
which is expensive and so gave me quite a good sale
in front of Mr Thurberton. Then he offered, a bit
reluctantly, to take Anne and me out to lunch. It was
only because we stood in front of him, gazing up like
a pair of puppies and refused to budge. We went to
Lyons, which I don't think he's ever been into in his
life and seemed to confirm his worst fears about the
decay of modern civilisation. Of course Anne and I
were too busy cramming food into our mouths to care,
as we only had a short break, and even pocketed the
bread rolls for supper later. TOG was horrified but
slipped me a five-pound note before we left. He is dear
in his own way.

I haven't seen much of Nick. Some Canadians are
in London, friends of his family, making their rounds.
I got quite upset about it; behaved stupidly. There's a
daughter, Pamela, quite pretty in a bovine sort of way.
We rowed which was dreadful and entirely my fault.
It is such a hopeless situation. I'm completely desperate
about the whole thing. I simply don't understand why

something that is so easy and straightforward for other people is so impossible for us.

By the way, Gloria is in the pig. Pinky has been in an alcoholic coma for the past three days. Dickey Fellowes finally located him under a table at 106 with a chorus boy from Drury Lane. I suppose you could say he's overjoyed.

Yours,

B xxx

Cate turned over in bed, trying to hide from the searing bright sunlight that filled the bedroom. Rachel's curtains were ancient, bleached Liberty prints, circa 1976; unlined and useless in the summertime. Groping for the alarm clock on the bedside table, Cate blinked at the time. It was after nine already. Rachel had gone early that morning, off to the country for a few days on another valuation job. Cate was alone in the house, alone in London. Rolling over onto her back, she shut her eyes again, longing for sleep to tug her back into oblivion. But it didn't. Consciousness, unwelcome as the blinding sunshine, left her wide awake.

Her first thought was of Jack, the revelations about his wife and their argument.

She understood his anger.

But her situation was different.

Wasn't it?

She shifted onto her side.

Was it?

Concentrating, she forced herself to think back. She'd known right from the start of the affair not to ask questions, that it would spoil the effect. Now that seemed absurd; irresponsible. But at the time she'd convinced herself that there was something more authentic about taking him only at face value. The world they inhabited together was an after-hours, night-time existence, separated from the harsh reality of day. He sent a car round to pick her up and take her home. Of course, there was a part of her that had known all the while what that meant. But she had never asked outright, instead deliberately choosing to occupy a smoky, grey moral area, where nothing was real if you didn't say it out loud.

The truth was that very quickly the balance shifted out of control. She didn't just want him; she needed him.

Whole undiscovered parts of herself came to the surface. All the rage she'd bottled for years seeped out into her sexuality, sharpening her, making her bold, demanding. It turned out that she had an appetite for intensity, for taunting, teasing interchanges; for graphic, even occasionally violent sex. And in his beautiful apartment, dimly lit, where the champagne and whiskey flowed freely, any inhibitions dissolved after a drink or two, melting like the ice in the bottom of the glass. It had been a relief, if she were honest, a liberation. In this new persona, everything was clear, uncensored, animal. No polite interchange of courtesies; no faltering attempts at conversation; no groping at half-intimated subtexts, trying to interpret what might have been said and what exactly it meant if it wasn't.

This was not the clean, icy blonde that she presented to most of the world. Not the girl who painted fat, pink-cheeked cherubs with golden curls on Ava Rottling's wall. No, for him there was a private view into the deepest, most unrestrained parts of her character.

When he began to pay her bills, it appeared to be only a natural extension of the one-upmanship that defined their time together; twisting, turning power plays of dominance and dependence that were merely foreplay. She affected nonchalance, as if it were her due. And when he offered her a credit card with her name on it, she hardly deigned to register it at all.

'Here,' he said, passing it across the table during their favourite post-coital Chinese.

They were sitting in a well-worn, red velvet booth, tucked into a far corner. The table was strewn with the remains of spare ribs, sweet-and-sour prawns, sizzling black beef and mountains of oily Singapore noodles. The bill had been brought long ago and sat, untouched, on its little black plastic tray. It was nearing midnight. They were the only customers left. The front door was locked. The kitchen staff were playing cards and drinking beer at another table; laughing and swearing in Chinese.

But they lingered.

In a hurry to meet. Reluctant to go. Only their conversation was cool and aloof.

She raised an eyebrow. 'Are you trying to buy me?' she asked, cracking open a fortune cookie.

'Do I have to?' he countered.

'No,' she smiled. 'For you, it's all free.'

She unravelled the message inside. 'Beware false friends,' it said. Crumpling it into a ball, she tossed it into the ashtray. 'I don't know why you bothered.'

'I like to know you're taken care of.'

'I'll never use it.'

He shrugged his shoulders. 'Whatever.'

But she did use it.

A few weeks after he'd given it to her, she found herself walking past Christian Dior, when a filmy chiffon shift dress in pale graphite caught her eye. That night, it too lay in a crumpled heap on his floor.

Twisting, turning, pushing, pulling, their relationship was a continuous tug of war.

That was love . . . wasn't it? Her intentions weren't like Julia's; she was innocent. Stupid, perhaps, very confused, but ultimately innocent of the same ruthless transgressions that had torn Jack's world apart. Wasn't she?

A telephone was ringing, interrupting her thoughts. Tossing off the covers, she headed into Rachel's room where there was an extension on the bedside table.

'Hello?'

'Miss Albion?' The voice was unfamiliar.

She hesitated. 'How may I help?'

'My name is Cyril Longmore.'

'Yes?'

'I'm ringing from the archives department of Tiffany's in Bond Street.'

'Oh yes!' Her shoulders relaxed. She'd written hoping for information about the bracelet. 'Thank you for getting back to me.'

'My pleasure. I wonder if you'd like to come in, Miss Albion, and have a chat. It's taken some digging, but I think I may have some information for you.'

'Certainly.'

'Half three?' he suggested.

'I'll see you then.'

She hung up and, standing, stretched her arms high. What could he have found? Suddenly her legs felt unsteady; her head dizzy. A wave of unexpected nausea hit.

Stumbling down the hallway to the bathroom, she only just made it in time to throw up in the toilet.

Crouched on the bathroom floor, sweating and shaking, she rested her head on the cool ceramic of the bath, waiting for the sickness to subside. How many times had she started the day like this when she was in New York? The excesses of the night before brought horrific hangovers, leaving her unable to function until early afternoon or sometimes not till the next day.

But she hadn't touched a drop last night. Not in weeks. Was it food poisoning? A virus?

Or . . .

It couldn't be.

It couldn't possibly be.

Desperately she tried to count back, fear rising. How many weeks had it been since her last period?

The restaurant was overlooking the harbour below. Seafood. They were having a late lunch. Perhaps not the slap-up one Rachel had proposed that morning, but fresh crab, soft sweet meat hidden beneath the brittle pink shell, chips and beer. They were sitting right by the edge of the sheltered veranda; below them families with small children played on the beach, hunting for their own tiny crabs among the rocky enclaves of the shore. But they seemed far away, like something on a movie screen, removed from them by more than just distance.

Jack leaned back in his chair, stretching out his legs.

Rachel lit another cigarette.

'I think that place is haunted,' she said, after a while.

'What makes you say that?'

'It has an odd energy. A kind of sadness.'

He snorted, took another swig of his beer. 'You don't think it's just us?'

'No.' She shook her head. 'After all, a widow and a widower cancel each other out,' she grinned wryly. 'No, that house has something all its own going on.'

'That's what Cate thought too. She was convinced there was some sort of mystery about it.'

Rachel looked at him hard. 'You like her, don't you?'

He shrugged his shoulders, averted his eyes. 'How did that come up?'

'You do, don't you?'

'Jesus, Rachel!' He struggled to frown, to look serious and uninterested, concentrating on his plate. 'Where's all this from?'

'I don't know.' She turned, looked out again over the beach. 'It just seems a shame, that's all.'

'What?'

'Honestly!' Her voice was sharp with frustration. 'Do you both think I'm blind?'

He looked up. 'What do you mean, both?'

'When you left the other day without staying for dinner she mooned about like a teenager.'

He tried unsuccessfully to suppress a smile. 'Really?'

She rolled her eyes. 'See!'

'Well, yes,' he admitted slowly, 'I do like her.'

'So what's the problem?'

'I don't trust her. And, I don't trust myself.'

Rachel leaned her chin in the hollow of her hand. 'It won't happen again, Paul.'

'What?'

'I said, it won't happen again.'

'You called me Paul.'

'Oh. Sorry.' She took another sip of beer. 'Freudian slip.'

'How do you know it won't?'

'Because you're different. You've changed. And Katie's not Julia. She's different too.'

He wavered. Should he tell her? That Cate had been a mistress? Perhaps she already knew. 'Maybe,' he sighed, deciding to leave it. Instead he confided something else. 'I went to see the grave. Last week. There was a bouquet of roses there. From him.'

'Good God!'

'That's why I didn't stay. I'd gone to, I don't know, to put it behind me, once and for all. To make my peace with it. But they were there instead.'

'How do you know they were from him?'

'I knew. There was a card.'

Rachel turned her eyes once again to a child in a sun hat, teetering on the uneven rocks, clutching its mother's hand with one chubby fist, a tiny net in the other. 'I'm sorry, Paul.'

Jack didn't bother to pull her up this time. He knew the tension that bound the two worlds, the seen and the unseen, sometimes bled into each other, especially at times like this.

He cracked open a crab leg instead, tearing at the soft white flesh. 'Paul used to tell me that we forgive not because we have to, but because we have a choice.' He popped the meat into his mouth. 'I didn't get it then and I still don't.' He looked up, smiled.

Rachel was staring at him, a strange expression on her face. 'What did you just say?'

Jack thought perhaps he'd offended her. He tried to explain. 'It's just, he used to talk about it sometimes. I'd get drunk and bore him half to death after work in the pub about it. How I was sure Julia had betrayed me, that I couldn't get beyond it. And he had some interesting thoughts on the whole thing.'

'Like what?' There was a quiet urgency in her voice; in the way she sat forward in her chair to listen.

'Like . . . well . . .' He was thrown by her sudden intensity. He tried to remember clearly. He could picture them, sitting at the far end of the bar in the pub round the corner from the office, the Wig and Gown. He could see Paul clearly, sleeves rolled up, pushing his thick grey hair back from his face, his intelligent dark eyes, filled with patience, and the compassion in his voice, tempered by an ironic, almost cockney directness. How many hours had he sat with Jack, listening to his litany of fears and resentments; keeping him company while he wrestled with their unseen meaning, twisting them round like a Rubik's cube he couldn't quite work out? Concentrating, he tried to be faithful to that memory and to Paul's words. 'Like he'd say to me, "You have no reason to forgive. No one would blame you if you never forgave her again in your life. And of course I could tell you that you would feel better if you did, that you might live longer, not be so angry, feel better physically and so on. But I know right now you don't care about that stuff."' He smiled. 'You know the way he talked.'

'Yes.' Her features were shadowed by some private memory. 'Go on.'

'His point was this. We forgive not because it's easy or the right thing to do, but that the choice to forgive is in itself powerful. It's an affirmation, a willingness to take life on life's terms. And a privilege that no one can take from you. It's one of the things that sets you apart from the rest of nature and connects you to the divine. Animals can't forgive; they're victims to what happens to them in life. They can't make a conscious decision to accept something offensive to them, something adverse and unfair. They can't decide to integrate it into who they are and move beyond their aversion to it. See, he talked a lot about that too. He kept saying, "You have to swallow it whole, Jack. The more you try to hold it at arm's length, to be rid of it, the more poisonous it becomes. And what you're really holding at arm's length is life – the realisation that this too is part of life. It's much easier just to swallow it, like an oyster. It becomes part of you, and if you don't resist it, it makes you stronger.'"

'It becomes part of you,' Rachel repeated quietly, to herself.

She turned her face away.

She thought she'd been alone in her guilt and regret. Paul could've walked away, certain that he was in the right. But in fact, the load was shared, carried between the two of them. He'd swallowed it. They, or rather the relationship, had digested it whole.

Her heart swelled with an almost unbearable tenderness, more painful even than her grief.

He'd stayed not out of convention or pity or shame. He'd chosen deliberately to love her.

Jack licked his fingers. 'He also said that in forgiving the other person, you were left with the most difficult bit of all: forgiving yourself. He said, "You're angry at yourself for being vulnerable. For not being able to protect yourself." That used to really cut me. I knew he was right about that bit. I didn't always agree with everything but I knew he'd got that right.' He took another drink, draining his bottle. 'He had a lot to say on the subject. Not all of which I understood at the time. I don't know where he got it all from.'

Rachel sat back in her chair. 'I do.'

Jack said nothing. He realised they were having a conversation that had greater implications and meanings, not all of which he was privy to. But it didn't bother him.

He hadn't thought of those conversations in a long time. Paul's words had fresh meaning for him now. He'd tried not to absorb his wife's betrayal; to distance himself from it through anger and control. But the effort was unsustainable. Life seeped in anyway. He thought of Cate, standing naked by the window; of the longing and desire that tugged at him to reach out and touch her; to dive into the dangerous, unpredictable waters once more.

'And you think he did?'

'What?' Jack looked up, shaking himself from his thoughts. 'I'm sorry . . . did what?'

Rachel seemed removed, oddly tentative. She kept her eyes firmly fixed on the view. 'Forgive this person he was speaking of?'

'Yeah,' he nodded slowly, half guessing at the reason she was asking. 'In fact, I have no doubt he did. The last thing he said to me about it was, "And then you'll know what freedom really is. You will have chosen your own life, even in the most difficult of circumstances."

'And he said it with a smile, like he really knew what he was talking about.'

The tension inside Rachel released, like a fist unclench-ing. Relaxing back in her chair again, her shoulders soft-ened and the distracted, vacant look in her eyes, deepened, gaining substance and depth. It was as if something in her that had been furiously spinning, day in and day out, was finally grounded. Again, she watched the children playing on the beach, but this time the weighty frown was gone.

'Of course, I didn't believe him,' Jack continued, speak-ing more for his own benefit than hers. 'I didn't want to know what that kind of love was. I wanted something without flaws. The kind of love that never went wrong because it was perfect in the first place.'

'Do you think that exists?'

'No. I don't. Actually,' he considered, 'I'm sure that isn't love at all. It's more like narcissism.'

'Wow. You don't say?'

He smiled.

Somehow he felt lighter, freer too. Being with her was easy. And he'd needed to talk. He'd forgotten that he could be with people that way. He signalled to the waiter. 'Do you want another beer?'

'Why not?'

The air around them softened; the searing heat of the day was gone. The families were packing up their buckets and spades, beach towels and picnic baskets, sandy and exhausted, heading back home for their tea.

Again, Jack thought of Cate. Was he capable of letting go of his disappointment, of accepting that she too could make mistakes and still be worth inviting into his life?

They sat, drinking, gazing out at the limitless horizon.

'Do you really think she likes me?' he asked, after a while.

Rachel picked around her plate, looking for a leg that hadn't been already ravaged. 'Why don't you ask and find out?' There was a teasing flash in her eyes. 'But first, dear heart, I'd have a shave.'

12 Birdcage Walk
London

3 March 1937

Darling Wren,
Oh . . . thank you, my darling! It will be the last time,
I promise, and I'm so terribly, terribly grateful! The
thing is, I went out with Anne and the next thing
I knew she was off and I was left alone at 106 with
Donny, Jock and Pinky. I dread to tell you exactly
how much money I lost but Jock said he'd cover me
and well . . . Oh, my darling! Of course, Jock never
gave me a penny. And without you I would've
been destitute.

   We went for a drink in Donny's room when really
I ought've gone home but we were all too far gone.

   You see, I blame it entirely on Pinky. He has the
most unnatural tastes.

   I made it clear to all of them it will never happen
again. And now I'm so full of self-loathing and feel so
wretched I can hardly move.

   Why do I do so many things I can't bear even to
remember? Why?

   D

The security guard of Tiffany's held the door open as Cate walked into its cool, art deco-designed show room.

'I have an appointment with Cyril Longmore,' she said.

He directed her up to the third floor where another assistant rang through and eventually Mr Longmore came down a narrow flight of steps. He was a slight man with glasses and thinning grey hair.

'Miss Albion.' He shook her hand. 'Would you like to follow me?'

She followed him back to the upper floor, which housed a warren of small offices. He directed her into one, taking his place behind the desk while she sat in the chair opposite.

'Thank you very much for your enquiry,' he began. 'I've gone into the archives and was able to find some information I think may be of interest to you.'

'Would you like to see the bracelet?' she asked.

'Oh yes! Very much so!'

She took the distinctive velvet Tiffany box out of her handbag and passed it to him.

'May I?' he asked.

She nodded and he opened it up.

'Oh yes! This really is something special, isn't it?' He held it up to the light. 'A very delicate piece. And in excellent condition. All it really needs is a clean, which –' he looked at her over the top of his glasses – 'can of course be scheduled at any time with our repairs department.'

Carefully, he arranged it back in its box.

Then he referred to some papers in a folder in front of him. 'I have to admit, it was something of a challenge tracking this particular piece down! When we got your enquiry through, at first I didn't think we'd be able to do anything for you. But luck was on our side.' He smiled, passing her a faded receipt. 'As you can see, it was made to order, as many pieces were in those days. And it cost really quite a considerable amount. Three hundred pounds.'

Cate stared at the receipt. 'Are you sure this is right?'

'Yes, especially now that I've seen the piece in question. See –' he pointed to the description – 'pearls, diamond and emerald bracelet. This is the one. There's no doubt.'

Cate frowned. 'Commissioned by Lady Avondale on 13 April 1941, paid by cash in full on the same day. Collected on 20 May 1941.'

'Yes. That's Irene Blythe, isn't it?' he said excitedly. 'This is a very special piece; a bracelet of real historical significance. With a copy of this receipt it would be worth a considerable amount as a collector's item.'

'And what's this?' Cate pointed to a childish scrawl in the bottom right-hand corner.

Mr Longmore looked it over. 'Oh, that's the signature of the person who collected it. Let's see.'

She handed it to him.

'Yes. It looks like . . .' He strained to see. 'Waites. A. Waites. If the bracelet was being collected by someone other than Lady Avondale, they would've required a signature and probably even a letter from Her Ladyship before releasing it.'

A. Waites. Who was that?

'And what about this?' She took out the small silver box with the diamond 'B' on the top. 'Did this by any chance come from Tiffany's too?'

Mr Longmore took his jeweller's glass out of the top drawer of his desk and examined it closely.

'Well, very interesting. But no.' He handed it back to her. 'This is paste.'

'Pardon me?'

'It's paste. Good-quality paste, but paste, nonetheless. Those are not real diamonds.'

'Paste,' she repeated, looking at the box again.

'But it's an excellent reproduction. To an untrained eye, it would've been utterly convincing. Many women used to keep their real jewels locked in a safe and wore reproductions instead. It was quite common practice. And I would have thought,' he added significantly, 'that, with an item like this, it would've been unwise to invest in real jewels.'

'What do you mean, unwise?'

He laughed uneasily. 'Do you know what it's for?'

She shook her head. 'Pills?' she guessed.

'I'm afraid it was more likely to be cocaine. You don't see many of them nowadays, but at the time, they were rather popular.'

'Really?' She stared at the silver box in her palm.

He nodded. 'See the little hook on the top? That's so that it could be worn on a chain round the neck. And –' he leaned forward, pointing to the side – 'it has quite a clever little latch to keep it closed.'

'I see.'

Cocaine. Of course it was rife during the twenties and thirties. Part of her felt stupid for being so surprised. It was yet another side to Baby Blythe she hadn't counted on. The reality of her was more disturbing; all too familiar in its vulnerability and capacity for paradox.

Mr Longmore was looking at her. 'I hope I haven't shocked you, Miss Albion.'

'No, you've been most helpful. I don't know why I should assume that everything about the past would be tea dances and roses.'

He smiled indulgently.

'Thank you. May I have a copy of that receipt?' she asked.

'I have taken the liberty of already photocopying one for you,' he said, passing it across the desk to her. 'Please let me know if there's anything more I can do to be of service to you and, if you don't mind, perhaps I could keep your contact details. Occasionally we launch various exhibits of our work. You might consider allowing us to display this piece.'

She stood up. 'Certainly.'

Mr Longmore shook her hand.

'Thank you for your time. You've been very helpful.'

'My pleasure.'

Cate walked down the narrow staircase, through the centre of the show room and out onto the street.

Irene bought the bracelet.

Just when she thought she might be on the verge of getting some answers, more questions arose.

She took the receipt out of her bag and had another look at it. The finished bracelet was collected on 20 May 1941. Wasn't Diana's birthday at the end of May – around the 30th? Could it have been a birthday gift? And who was this mysterious A. Waites?

None of it made sense.

Then again, so little about the Blythe girls made sense.

She strolled slowly up Bond Street, half window-shopping, her mind tugging at the knotted threads of Baby Blythe's story, trying to see it from a fresh angle. In the golden sunshine, everything and everyone looked polished, glamorous. When the sun shone on London, there was no more beautiful city in the world. She looked across the street to the window of the Richard Green Gallery.

Then stopped.

It couldn't be . . .

Crossing over, she stood in front of the window, a strange sense of horror slowly descending.

It was a painting. A nude.

A work she knew intimately.

It was as if someone had removed all her internal bearings; she felt queasy; unbalanced.

There was a little card in the bottom right-hand corner of the window. '*The Mistress* by C. Albion. On loan from the Private Collection of Mr and Mrs Alexander Munroe.'

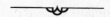

They were lying in bed, he was stroking her back, very gently. 'I want something original by you.'

'Here I am,' she smiled, stretching out lazily, like a cat.

'No. I mean a painting. I told you when we first met I had a commission for you.'

'Why?' she laughed. 'I'm already yours.'

'I want something I can look at. Something I can hang on my wall.'

'Like a trophy? Something along the lines of a moose head?'

'Yeah, paint me a moose head.' He pushed her hair back from her face. 'So long as it looks like you.'

'You have me.'

'I want more of you.'

'There is no more, this is it.' Her voice was tinged with frustration. What he called devotion felt like a demand.

He was quick to pick up on it. 'There's always more. If it matters to you.'

She closed her eyes. 'It's been so long. I probably can't even do it.'

'Probably not,' he sighed, rolling away. 'Who knows? Maybe you're all dried up. I was trying to do you a favour.'

She opened her eyes, looked across at him. Was he serious? But his face was hidden.

The tender moment was gone. He had a knack of building her up and then whipping the ground away beneath her feet. She was either soaring or falling; there was no in between. But once the doubts were planted, they took hold, rapidly. She moved away too, twisting over on to her side. Maybe she was dried up. But he wasn't going to get the better of her.

It began as a self-portrait, which wasn't like her at all. Cate had done a few in art school, as assignments. But she was hardly her favourite subject. They'd been rather terrified, conservative line drawings of her face and shoulders; just what she could see comfortably in the bathroom mirror. She'd found it excruciating to stare at herself so long, with complete objectivity; to note in ruthless detail each flaw, the unevenness of her features, the scar that still formed a shiny crescent-shaped mark on her forehead; the way her heavy eyelids lent her eyes an air of dull sadness. Her mouth turned naturally down in repose and at the time her hair had been darker and hung in thick, lank tendrils around her shoulders. There was a rigidness to the finished works that had baffled her instructors, who were used to more daring results. Her marks had been uncharacteristically low that term.

But this time she used the full-length mirror on her closet door, filling her little studio with candlelight. And she decided to paint herself nude, reclining on her fold-out bed.

After all those reproductions, that fastidious copying, the self-portrait became a turning point, even an obsession with Cate. At the end of her working day, she rushed home to finish it, often painting late into the night. She didn't like posing naked. But, oddly, that only made the painting more dynamic. It brought out tensions and contradictions; the bed became a dark, floating, slightly sinister mass. And she didn't so much rest on it as emerge from it.

It wasn't beautiful. Instead it was powerful, disturbing. And far and above the most accomplished work she'd ever produced.

When she finally presented it to him, he looked at it closely but said nothing. He was a man of constant snap responses, of quick, sharp quips. But he just stared at it, frowning.

'It seems you really are talented,' he said at last. It came out more like an accusation than a compliment.

'But do you like it?' She couldn't make him out; part of her felt frightened, rejected, and unsure why.

'Like I said, you're a world-class talent, Cate. What's it called anyway?'

She hadn't thought of that. 'I don't know. *Untitled*, I guess.'

His face softened. 'Well, I'll come up with a name, shall I?'

It wasn't the way it worked. And yet she'd conceded. It was as if he needed to own a part of everything she did.

He would love her, passionately, greedily. But she would pay for it with little pieces of herself.

Cate pushed open the heavy glass door of the Richard Green Gallery. There was a vacuum-like silence when it closed again, sealing her in.

She looked around, at the classic burgundy walls and illuminated paintings. There was a time when she had longed to be included in a gallery collection of fine art, but not like this. She felt exposed, as naked as she was in the painting. It was ridiculous to imagine that anyone would recognise her, but her heart thumped and her head pulsed nonetheless. She picked up a leaflet but had difficulty focusing. After a moment, an attractive young woman with dark hair came up to her. 'May I help?' she asked.

Cate shook her head. 'Oh, actually,' she reconsidered, 'I'm . . . I'm very interested in the painting in the window. The title . . . *The Mistress*?'

'Oh yes!' The young woman smiled. 'We've had a lot of interest in that one. I understand it's by an unknown artist. In fact, it's due to be sold later this month, although it's not been officially confirmed yet.'

The bottom of her stomach disappeared. 'Sold?' she repeated.

'Yes. The clients are liquidating some of their collection.'

'I see.' Cate nodded her head, tried to swallow.

'Are you all right?' the girl asked. 'You look a little pale.'

'I . . . It's just I knew them . . . well, one of them . . . slightly . . .'

'Oh, I see. Well, it's quite normal with people who collect on this scale.'

'It's just I had no idea that . . . that they were collectors.'

'Oh, yes. It's really quite a fascinating and informed selection of artworks. Very intelligently compiled and demonstrating a rather distinctive sensibility.' She stopped, frowned. 'Are you sure you're all right? Would you like a glass of water or something?'

'No, no, I'm fine.'

'You can have a seat if you like.'

'Thank you. I . . . I just need to go now.'

Her head was buzzing and her mouth was dry; a band of pain stretched across her abdomen. She made it out to the pavement, fumbled in her handbag for her mobile phone.

Yes, he was a collector.

She'd spent so much time and effort avoiding his calls, staying away from him. But now she had to reach him. She had to know.

Standing on the corner, she watched as passers-by stopped, staring at her self-portrait in the window. There she was – raw, stripped bare – for the entire world to see. And about to be liquidated.

There was the distant sound of the overseas connection being made and then . . .

'The number you are ringing has been disconnected. Please hang up. The number you are ringing has been disconnected. Please hang up. The number you are ringing has been disconnected . . .'

The last thing she remembered, someone was shouting and there was the strange sensation of the pavement rising to meet her.

And then the world went black.

When they returned to Endsleigh in the late afternoon, Jo's old car was in the driveway, its boot open, boxes stacked alongside.

They climbed out of Jack's Triumph.

'What's all this?' Rachel wanted to know.

Just then Jo appeared, struggling down the narrow pathway at the side of the house, carrying a particularly unwieldy box from the direction of the cottage.

'Here, let me.' Jack rushed forward to help, relieving her of the load.

'Thank you.' She smiled at them both, catching her breath. 'Nice to have a man around for a change!' She held out her hand to Rachel. 'Hi, I'm Jo Williams. I used to be the housekeeper here.'

Rachel took it. 'Rachel Deveraux. Having a clear-out?' she asked, looking round.

'Much against my will, I might add. Turns out I'd

forgotten about the loft space in the cottage. My mother got up this morning and was in a positive panic about it. Can you believe how much junk one old lady can hoard away?' She sighed. '"Josephine," she says to me, "there's something I need you to do. A few things that need to be collected from the loft." Well, will you look at it!' She shook her head. 'We've got nowhere to put anything! I don't know what she expects me to do with it all.'

Jack lugged the box over to the side of the car. 'I don't even know how you got this one down. It weighs a ton!'

'I can carry almost everything. Remember, for years I had a B & B with my ex-husband, which means I ran the damn thing by myself.'

Jack eased the box into the back of the boot. 'What is it? Books?'

'Oh, all sorts. Junk mostly.'

She opened the top and riffled through. It was filled with piles of old newspapers and magazines – some of them falling apart they were so fragile – a bolt of faded cream taffeta material, knotted balls of yarn and half-finished knitting, an old hot-water bottle, a couple of shapeless women's day dresses . . .

'Looks like personal effects,' Rachel said, lifting out a squashed misshapen pillbox hat with a torn black veil.

'Well,' Jo sighed heavily, hands on hips, 'what do you think? Is any of it worth anything?' She picked up a faded yellow ball of yarn and a half-finished baby blanket, the stitches clumsy and uneven. 'Jesus!' She poked her finger through one of the gaping holes before tossing it back in the box. 'Our house is filled to the brim as it is. I'm going to have to take this lot down to one of the charity shops in Lyme Regis.'

'Wait a minute.' Rachel unearthed a large wooden box buried at the bottom. 'This is nice,' she said, turning it over. It measured about twenty-two inches long and fourteen inches wide, fashioned from a rich, gleaming mahogany with an inlaid ivory Celtic knot design on the lid.

'What is it?'

'It's a writing case. Probably Victorian. Most likely used for travelling. See, ink, pens and paper can be kept inside and the top is large enough to write on.' She tried to open it, but it was locked. 'Only we need the key. Someone was careful enough to lock it.' Turning it over, she examined the bottom. A small label was fixed to the bottom, faded and brown with age. '"Benedict Blythe, Tír na nÓg, Ireland",' she read aloud. 'Who's that?'

Jo leaned forward to see it better. 'Oh, yeah. He was Irene's father. He was some sort of writer – an historian, I think.'

'Irene Blythe?' Rachel asked.

'Yes.'

'Well . . .' She turned it over again. 'If this belonged to him, it's quite valuable. For a collector, it would be worth a lot. Don't give that to the charity shop.'

Jo wrinkled her nose. 'Believe me, I'd like to sell it but Mum would kill me. Especially if it went to one of the nosy people who are always looking for memorabilia about Baby Blythe. She'd never forgive me.'

'I'll give you three hundred pounds for it,' Jack said suddenly.

Jo's eyes widened. 'Are you serious? As much as that?'

'It's a special piece. And I promise not to sell it on.' He looked at Rachel, who was staring at him in surprise.

'Wow.' Jo shrugged her shoulders. 'OK. Only I feel like I'm robbing you blind!'

'Believe me, you're not,' Rachel assured her.

'No,' Jack said. 'In fact, if you wanted to auction it, you could probably get a lot more.'

'Well, I'm not going to auction it.' Jo frowned. 'Seems like an awful lot for a wooden box.'

'You're meant to be bargaining the price up, not down!' Rachel hissed in a stage whisper.

Jo laughed. 'OK, OK! Done!'

Jack and Jo shook hands.

'Here.' He took out a pen and an old envelope from his jacket pocket. 'Write your address down on this and I'll bring a cheque over later.'

'Thank you.' Jo jotted the address down. 'Now –' she turned to Rachel, a gleam in her eye – 'what about you? Do you want some old dresses for a fiver? Or some dodgy knitting?'

A few minutes later, she headed back to the old cottage to lock up and Jack and Rachel stood in the drive on their own.

'So,' Rachel folded her arms across her chest, 'starting a collection of your own?'

'It's a good piece, don't you think?'

She clapped him on the shoulder. 'Well, your father would be proud of you. In there like a flash when you spotted it. And yes, it's unique, with valuable history. A smart buy.'

'The truth is I have no idea what I'm doing right now,' he sighed. 'Not a clue.'

A pair of magpies swooped down, landing on the lawn in front of them, bouncing after one another in the long grass.

'Look,' she pointed to the birds. 'One for sorrow, two for joy! It's a sign.'

'Do you believe in that sort of thing?'

'No,' she laughed, shaking her head. 'But we need all the help we can get in this world. And if a couple of birds can get us through the next five minutes, then so be it. I'm not above laying myself open to chance.'

## TELEGRAM

September 3, 1939, London

To: Lady Avondale, Endsleigh, Devon

Dear Lady ... stop ... War ... stop ...

Can you believe it ... stop ... What

shall we all wear ... Stop ... Love

Diana ... stop

Someone was pressing her forehead.

Cate's eyes flicked open.

It was the young woman from the gallery. She was looking very serious. And there was a crowd of people around them; she recognised the security guard from the gallery talking on his mobile phone. He too was looking at her anxiously. 'Yeah, she's conscious now,' she heard him say to whoever was on the other end of the line.

'Try and sit still,' the gallery girl commanded, pressing down again with a towel.

'Owww!' Cate winced, pulling away.

'Sit still,' the girl said again.

That's when Cate noticed the towel she was holding was red with blood.

'You fainted and hit your head on the pavement,' the girl explained. Her face was tense.

Cate closed her eyes. 'I don't feel very well,' she muttered. 'I think I might be sick.'

And the crowd moved back.

When the ambulance arrived, the girl from the gallery went with her, holding her handbag. There were bloodstains on her navy cotton shift dress.

At St Mary's Hospital in Paddington, she was taken into a cubicle. The girl came too, holding the clipboard the nurse at registration had given her, and, while Cate's head was cleaned up, she filled in the form with her name and address.

'Cate. Cate Albion.'

'Is that with a K?'

'No. A C'.

'Cate Albion,' she wrote, her brow wrinkling. Then she made the connection. 'You're the artist. You're C. Albion!'

Cate nodded very slightly. It hurt just to blink. 'What's your name?' she asked.

'Karen,' the girl said.

'Thank you, Karen. Thank you for helping me.' She closed her eyes again.

The nurse was back with a small plastic cup, some vials and a long needle. 'You've got quite a high fever. But if you can manage it, we need a urine and a blood sample. The doctor will be with you in a minute to see if you need stitches. Here,' she eased Cate up off the trolley, 'I'll help you to the loo.'

When she came back, Cate slipped in and out of sleep. The doctor decided stitches weren't necessary but a high dose of intravenous antibiotics were. They gave her a bed on a ward and Cate dozed until late evening. When she woke up, she was alone. Her mouth was dry and her head ached. She was still wearing her summer dress and cardigan, a tube dangling from her arm. She felt dirty and sticky. There were fans whirring away in each corner but otherwise the ward was as stifling as it was outside. Across from her someone was curled up on their side, their face hidden from view, and there was the sound of low moaning from another bed; she could hear them but couldn't see them. The light was dimming, lending the grey walls and tiles a soft blurriness.

Someone had left a copy of *OK!* magazine, a bottle of water and a KitKat by the side of the bed, presumably Karen.

Cate sat up, her head throbbing, and pressed the bell for the nurse. After what seemed like ages, a woman in her fifties, with close-cropped red hair, arrived.

'So you're up.' She had a thick Belfast accent. Holding Cate's wrist, she began taking her pulse. 'How do you feel?'

'Rough. When can I leave?'

The nurse finished counting the beats and let her wrist go, picking up the chart from the bottom of her bed. 'Maybe tonight, maybe tomorrow. The doctor will be through later and she'll give you a better idea. Is there someone you want us to contact for you?'

Cate shook her head. 'What's wrong with me?'

'You have a kidney infection. Quite a bad one. Those are antibiotics.'

'Oh. So, I'm not . . .' Cate hesitated, biting her lower lip. 'Am I pregnant?' she asked after a moment.

The nurse shook her head. 'No. But you have traces of blood in your urine.'

Cate relaxed back against the pillows. She hadn't realised how much it had weighed upon her; what a relief it was to know she wasn't. 'Good,' she murmured.

The nurse hooked the chart back on her bed and walked round, checking the readings on the dispensing machine. 'What happened anyway? The girl who brought you in said you'd just fainted.'

'What? Oh, yes. I guess that's right.'

She tapped the side of the machine. 'The doctor who admitted you wanted to know if you had been attacked.'

'Attacked? Why?'

The nurse looked at her closely. 'They did an examination on you. Don't you remember?'

Cate shook her head.

'There's a note on your chart. A query.'

'What kind of query?'

'There's some evidence, some scarring. That you've been sexually violated in the recent past.'

Cate was silent.

'Do you know what I'm talking about?' She touched her arm lightly.

Cate said nothing, moving her arm away.

'If you want to speak to someone,' the nurse's voice was low, confiding. 'to file a report –'

'No,' Cate cut her off. 'That's not necessary.'

'The police have a special unit – female officers . . . the whole thing's very private and very safe.'

Cate said nothing, concentrating instead on the folds of the hanging curtain opposite.

'I understand that it can be very difficult and upsetting, but if someone's hurt you . . .' the nurse persisted.

'It's not what it seems.'

'Yes, but . . . if you change your mind . . . if you need to talk to someone . . .'

'Thank you. I appreciate your concern. But it's not what it seems,' Cate said again, firmly.

The nurse sighed, shaking her head.

'I wonder if you would mind getting me a tea?' Cate asked. 'I feel a bit shaky.'

The nurse stared at her. 'Any sugar?' she asked finally, giving up.

'A couple. Thanks.'

After she left, Cate turned her face to the wall, trying to block out the low moaning of the person in the next bed.

She didn't understand; none of them would.

It wasn't what it seemed.

Especially not if you asked for it.

It was evening. Jack sat down on the bed in his room at the B & B. Across from him, on the chest of drawers, was the writing case he'd bought from Jo Williams. The one he'd promised not to sell.

He knew why he'd bought it; who he intended it for.

Was he being foolish? Would he even have the courage to give it to her? And would she understand what the gesture meant or how unique it really was?

Of course these things had to be learned, he reminded himself. There was a time when he would have dismissed a box like that out of hand as nothing special. A time when he wouldn't have been able to see it was worthwhile either.

He kicked off his shoes, stretching out on to his back. And thought of his father.

Henry Coates had a passion for the past. A respect bordering on reverence for it. Few things used to please him more than discovering an overlooked gem, then delving into its history, digging up every bit of its back story – who made it and when, what part of the country it was from, how it was passed from hand to hand until it finally came to be resting in his. 'It's a real-life history lesson,' he used to say. At the time, Jack had been interested in shaping whole cities, making his mark on the world with great constructions of glass and steel. His father's obsession seemed quaint and eccentric. Who cared what happened in the past or how some old chair happened to come into your possession? Sell it and move on. That was his feeling.

But now, looking at the mahogany writing case, he felt an uncomfortable affinity with his father. The past did deserve respect. Now that he was old enough to have one that baffled and confused him, he understood a little better.

He folded the pillow over, propping it underneath his head.

He'd been longing to change the world – his world. Move away from the piles of musty old furniture in his father's business. The truth was he'd been embarrassed by his dad when he was younger; certainly he'd been ashamed to work at the shop in Islington. There was a certain grandeur in saying, 'My father's an antique dealer' – with its implication of a refined eye and wealth of stylistic and aesthetic knowledge. It was different, however, sitting in a cold, draughty shop during the grey winter months, piled high with dingy old furniture, reading endless books and newspapers, drinking cups of tea, waiting for someone, anyone, to stop in out of the rain and buy something. He'd found it mind-numbingly boring. Henry had tried to persuade him to educate himself about the business, but at the time Jack was too cocky to care. If he could sell something relatively expensive early on in the day, then he could shut up shop early and get on with his own life. He had plans, ambitions. He didn't want to be stuck like his father, going from auction to auction, in search of some rare once-in-a-lifetime find.

And when Henry did find a piece worthy of all his years of acumen, it was Jack who allowed it to slip through his fingers.

The rare Georgian convex mirror had a filmy, dark glass and an ornate frame fashioned with twisting vines of ivy and delicate, detailed sparrows. Made around 1720, it had originally been a wedding gift, commissioned for the daughter of an earl in Wales, who had a particular fondness for the birds. Henry had found it in the sale of personal belongings from a house in Amersham. Wrapped in old blankets, it sat in the back of the shop for months while he lovingly did his research on it, which in those days involved trips to libraries and collection archives.

It was a misty April morning when the well-dressed man came into the shop, browsing lazily. Jack had been reading copies of *Interview* and *Rolling Stone* magazine in between dozing, sitting close to the space heater that provided the only warmth in the place. Henry was emphatic that no central heating be installed in case it dried out the delicate wood. The man was maybe ten years older than him and struck up a conversation. With his dapper appearance and lingering eye contact, Jack swiftly concluded that he was gay. But he was pleasant enough and easy to talk to; he seemed to understand how dull the business could be, especially if you'd been on your own all day. Soon Jack found himself confiding his own dreams and aspirations. The man admired his plans. Then he explained to Jack that he was on a buying trip from New York. He wondered if there was anything special that wasn't on the shop floor.

The instant Jack showed the mirror to the man, his eyes lit up and Jack could sense he had a real sale. In fact, when he asked Jack to name his price, he didn't even bother to barter. And Jack had doubled what he imagined it to be worth. The man had written him a cheque for it then and there, even going so far as to have Jack ring a local cab company to come and take it and him away immediately.

At the time Jack had been euphoric, swollen with a feeling of accomplishment, closing the shop early and heading over to the pub to celebrate. It was only later that his father explained to him that he'd undersold it by thousands. Henry had tried to contact the dealer, tried to get the mirror back by appealing to the man's better nature. But it was useless. It was clear he'd spotted that Jack was a novice, someone who had no respect for what he was doing. 'We're not junk dealers!' his father had shouted at him in exasperation. 'These things have real value when you bother to understand them!'

It had formed a rift between them. Full of arrogant, self-centred youth, Jack had spent years silently judging his father, finding him wanting, even vaguely effeminate. And the truth was that Henry was a simple, gentle, unremarkable man. Under Henry's anger that day was the sudden realisation that his son found him ridiculous.

Now, years later, Jack was still paying penance; trying to prove, by following in his father's footsteps, that it wasn't true. Only his father wasn't paying attention; he was lost in a world all his own, drifting in and out of the slow, creeping dementia of Parkinson's.

Jack stared at the writing box, its smooth mahogany gleaming in the warm evening light.

It was humbling, so many years later, to see that his entire career to date had been little more than an extended pantomime performance of a 'good man'. And even more humbling because it was all for his own benefit. No one else was watching or even noticed.

How much of his persona was wrapped up in that idea of himself? That he was 'good'? And that somehow people could see that, indeed were observing and quietly commenting on the superiority of his actions and judgement? It was a false front – an elusive, circuitous front, readily endorsed by society, but false just the same. He liked to pretend there was some value in sacrificing his own desires. But in fact it was simply a version of himself that gave him comfort at night, when, alone, he lay awake in the dark, wondering who he was or what he was doing. A mental security blanket to cling to when the terror rose inside him, twisting it round and round, well . . . at least I'm good.

Hadn't his marriage been based on that idea too? Again, he'd abdicated his vision of becoming an architect as too time-consuming and expensive when there was money to be made, a life to build together, property to buy. He'd taken up increasingly less space in the relationship, imagining that she would see this as proof of his devotion. But in reality, he'd just withdrawn, disappearing into the idea of himself as a lover in the same way an actor loses himself in a part, hoping that if he never made demands on her then she would love him more. In the end, he was so vague, so hidden, she couldn't even see him.

Perhaps that's why she strayed. Looking for someone who would risk being seen for who he truly was.

Outside, Jack could hear seagulls screeching, calling to one another mid-flight. Getting up, he went to the window and opened it. The wind was brisk, smelling of sea and wind. The oppressive humidity of the past few weeks was gone.

And as he looked out over the view, vast and unfamiliar, it occurred to him that he was at a turning point. And as at most crossroads, there was something to be paid, given up, in order to move on. Perhaps it was time he let go of the idea of being good and its childish promise of sleek moral perfection. It didn't work any more; he'd outgrown it. Maybe now he needed to make peace with the idea that he was closer to those he liked to judge; that he couldn't separate himself off from the more unsavoury, less palatable parts of his own character.

And in that way, perhaps for the first time in his life, Jack finally became free.

*12 Birdcage Walk*
*London*

*23 March 1940*

*My dear one,*
*You are, as always, so very kind. And I will come*
*if you want me to. It is horrid in London but oddly*
*thrilling at the same time. Everywhere there is a sense*
*of real purpose. Anne is training for the Red Cross.*
*She has the sweetest uniform and has shown me how*
*we can stack our beds up on soup cans and sleep*
*underneath them on the mattresses on the floor. That*
*way if the windows get blown in we'll be perfectly safe.*
*She is so clever.*

　*D xxxx*

After getting dressed and having breakfast, Jack spent the next morning in the local library, looking up material on the owner of the writing case, Benedict Blythe. The librarian pointed out a recently published biography, yet another book about the Blythe sisters, packed with photographs, which had come out only a few weeks ago. As he leafed through the early chapters, Jack discovered that their father, Benedict Blythe, had been an obscure academic and historian, whose work in Celtic myth (most notably *Into the Mists – A History of Irish Imagination*) had been in fashion briefly at the end of the Victorian era. An old photograph showed him to be a handsome, rather flamboyant figure, with wild, pale blue eyes and delicate, almost feminine features. According to the author, he'd pursued and married the young society beauty Gwenevere Healy with frightening speed and determination when she was still only seventeen. They settled in a house on one of the less fashionable streets of Dublin.

Among his peers Benedict was known to be romantic and impulsive; loved for his witty sense of humour and boundless generosity. However, it seemed he also had a taste for reckless, self-destructive encounters, which were neither understood nor countenanced by his young, devout bride. So he indulged in a secret life, taking frequent trips to the Continent, particularly to Paris where his increasingly voracious sexual appetites were only satisfied in the company of cheap, common prostitutes, most famously La Galoue, who was known for accepting clientele from even the lowest of the low. These episodes undoubtedly led to him contracting syphilis, which later killed him, aged forty, and contributed to an increasing dependence on opium, compromising both his family's financial future and isolating them from all polite society. Ashamed and terrified of anyone discovering the true nature of her husband's illness, his wife led a secluded life, educating her daughters at home herself and relying heavily on her religious beliefs for solace and guidance. As children, the young Blythe girls had free rein of the old house, which they believed to be haunted by ghosts and goblins, playing wild lonely games, with only each other for companionship. Torn between their mother's strict Catholic beliefs and their father's heightened, fanciful stories, they developed into bold, extreme characters in their own right, veering between periods of almost pathological disregard for conventional moral standards and intense religiosity.

Upon his early death, the young widow sold the house, and, leaving her two daughters with her parents in Dublin, used the money to accept an invitation from a married cousin in Belgrave Square, setting out to establish herself in London society. Her efforts were a resounding success, charming many of London's most eligible bachelors and finally accepting a marriage proposal from Lord Warburton, whose own wife had died three years previously from tuberculosis. Gwenevere Blythe, then just thirty-five years of age, became Lady Warburton. Putting Ireland and her disastrous first marriage firmly behind her, she collected her two adolescent daughters and never returned to Dublin. The Beautiful Blythe Sisters became famous debutantes and socialites and, in time, their mother developed into a rather outspoken pillar of Catholic society in London, especially during the Second World War when her dedication to helping Catholic foreign refugees created an ever widening gulf between her and her husband.

Jack leafed through the pictures. There were formal groupings, taken at a photographer's studio, of Gwenevere and the girls. The force of her beauty struck Jack; full lips, wide-set eyes and a bold, challenging stare. The girls had inherited both their mother's strong features and their father's delicate blue eyes. Then he came upon a photograph of a modest, quite unremarkable Victorian house on a quiet street. 'Tír na nÓg,' the caption read, 'named after the mythical fairy afterworld which translates roughly as "the land of the forever young". It was meant to be a haven that mere mortals could only dream of, where the fairy folk spent eternity gaming, feasting, lovemaking and listening to beautiful music.'

There it was, Benedict's Land of the Forever Young – an everyday, red-brick suburban home.

Jack leaned back in his chair.

Benedict Blythe had only written three books; had died around the age he was now. For all his talent and initial success, the true legacy of his life had been a series of kamikaze emotional missions, throwing himself blindly into the fray of his own childish romantic determinations, only to emerge bloodied and baffled, and ultimately dead.

Jack closed the book, looking up at the clock on the wall. Two hours had flown past. He photocopied the relevant pages, then left the library, strolling out onto the seafront; feeling the bracing wind, cool and refreshing on his face.

The sad thing was, he could identify with Blythe. How seductive simply to sidestep reality and slip into another world. But also how tragic and pathetic the consequences. The shabby little house, the debts, and a young wife, betrayed and destitute, forced to find another husband in order to support her two young daughters.

What had he written on the writing case? Chapters about the mysterious, dark, dissolving divides between the seen and unseen worlds of mythology? Or vague, dishonest letters to his wife and children, composed from third-rate brothels in the cold, stinking backstreets of Pigalle? Had the case been a gift, from his bride who had believed in the ascendancy of his academic career and their budding life together? Or had he bought it himself, armed, yet again, with resolve and the intention of starting afresh a new life marked by solid effort and achievement?

To the naked eye, the writing case was little more than a wooden box. But in truth, it was the last remaining evidence of a dream, an aspiration. And a life gone terribly, terribly wrong.

It was very early in the morning when Cate took a cab back to Upper Wimpole Street, unlocking the door and letting herself in. The flat was empty. Without turning on the lights, she threw her bag down in the hallway and sat down on the stairs. A window banged in an upstairs room from where it had become loose in the night. The rooms were dark. It seemed shabby and dreary; not a haven at all but a sad, second-rate existence. She pressed her hands over her face, tears filling her eyes. She had nothing. Nothing to show for her years in New York. Nothing but an infection and an outstanding debt.

He had betrayed her.

Her nose was running; she wiped it on the back of her wrist.

She had always known. What she'd said to Jack was a lie. Of course, she'd never asked outright, but in her heart she'd known not to ask, which was the same thing.

She'd been at the hairdresser's, leafing through a copy of the *New York Times*, when she'd come across a photograph. There he was, his arm wrapped easily around her slender waist. 'Mr and Mrs Alexander Munroe'. He was escorting her to some event at the Met. Tall and elegant, with shiny dark hair down to her waist, she possessed a dancer's bearing and poise. She was dressed in understated flowing silk, in chic, muted colours that set off her dark skin. Anne Marie, that was her name. She was French. She existed. And they looked good together. It wasn't so much a shock as an affront to her childish fantasy.

She'd put the paper down. And then, of course, picked it up again. She was unable to stop herself from turning back to the page; staring hard, for a long time. There was something that was both painful and perversely liberating about seeing the truth.

When she'd left the hairdresser's, she didn't go home. She went across the street, to a bar. She'd had a drink. And then another.

Late afternoon turned to evening. Her phone rang. It was him. He was sending his car to get her.

She remembered being in the back of the limousine. She remembered the doorman and the ride in the elevator.

But what happened in the apartment was fuzzy, unclear.

She'd shouted and she remembered crying. It seemed to her that he'd tried to comfort her; tried to reassure her that he loved her. But she hadn't believed him. She'd told him he was a coward and a cheat. That he wasn't even a real man. She'd thrown the credit card at him. He was revolting. She was never going to see him again.

That's when he'd grabbed her; hit her hard across the mouth. Her lip split, her mouth filling with blood. And he pulled her to the floor.

Had she wanted him to? Wasn't any response from him better than none at all? He'd torn at her clothes, hiking her dress up, pinning her to the ground. Even while she'd fought against him, punching him and kicking, there had been another part of her that seemed to be watching from a distance, like a stranger watching TV. Yet the more it had hurt, the more unreal it had felt, as if she'd been acting out a part, a predestined role. And hadn't she been wet as he thrust himself inside her? The lines were blurred between pain and passion; she couldn't tell the difference any more. There had been a part of her that had responded, against her will; pushing her hips up to meet his, pulling at his hair, biting his lips as she'd pulled his mouth closer. She remembered him whispering, hissing in her ear, 'You belong to me.' And that was true too. She was lost. In the absence of love anything, even violence, would do.

When it was over he'd got up, left her there. After a few minutes she'd heard the shower running.

Then, she'd crawled onto her hands and knees and, shaking, got up off the floor. She'd found her coat and her bag.

There had been no car to take her home. She'd wandered, dazed, until she'd finally had the presence of mind to hail a cab.

The next day she had flown to London.

And now she sat on the stairs of Rachel's flat, broken and unreal.

*The Mistress.*

Everything about it was a slap in the face – the title, the fact that he was selling it, that it was part of an official collection he shared with his wife. She'd been devalued in every way possible, and yet instead of feeling angry, she was crushed – as if it were the culmination of a prevailing emotional truth in her life. She would never truly matter to anyone. She was disposable and always had been.

Could you even betray a mistress? she wondered, reaching into her pocket for a tissue. Not really. No more than they already betrayed themselves.

He wasn't searching for her on the streets of London. She was alone, with a life that didn't work. It was as if she'd been asleep, reeling from event to event in an extended nightmare. Now it was over. And all she longed for was to slip back into that dreamy half-world again and stay there, this time forever.

There was the little bag from the pharmacy, jammed into her pocket. The pills the doctor had given her. Some were antibiotics, others painkillers.

She stared at them. Rachel wasn't back for days.

Reaching over, she took the bottle out and tilting it on its side, counted the little white pills.

Her heartbeat slowed, she felt calmer, almost serene.

How many would it take? Maybe there were some more upstairs.

It took her a while to hear the phone ringing. She waited for the answering machine to pick it up.

But still it rang. Again, and again and again . . . She stumbled in the half-light of the living room, feeling for the receiver. 'Hello?'

The line was fuzzy, far away. 'Hello? Hello, Katie? Is that you?'

'Mum?'

'What's going on? Why are you in London?'

Cate sank down into the chair next to Rachel's desk. 'Mum . . .'

'Katie?'

She began to cry. 'Mum . . . why are you calling?'

'Calm down, Katie.'

'Why? Why are you calling?'

'Katie . . .'

'Why, Mum?' Jagged sobs tore at her chest; pulling her apart. 'Why?'

Her mother's voice was firm, solid; terra firma in a world spinning wildly out of control. 'I just am. Stay with me. I'm here now. I'm not going anywhere. I'm here.'

# Part Three

*Endsleigh*
*Devon*

*7 October 1940*

*My darling,*
*What news? You cannot pretend that London is*
*dull; dangerous yes but never dull! And please don't*
*say that you've been drafted on some top-secret mission*
*and are forbidden all correspondence. You know that*
*I'm languishing here and therefore it's your civic duty,*
*on behalf of the war effort, to send me as much gossip*
*as possible. The titbits I've heard won't last long. For*
*example, apparently Wooton Lodge has been taken*
*over as some sort of hospital for dotty servicemen, which*
*makes us laugh, as that sums up the place perfectly,*
*especially the weekends I was there – people who*
*couldn't remember their names walking into walls,*
*falling down stairs and babbling like idiots. Irene said*
*Baba Metcalf wrote to tell her. Too funny! And Irene*
*is studying nursing and is being very grand and humble*
*at the same time, which is quite a trick. Crisis seems to*
*suit her. We live now in only a handful of rooms. The*
*rest are blacked out. We've been sent a couple of*
*evacuees from Shoreditch of all places – a boy and a*

girl, though the girl is really only a baby, just coming up to three, or so the boy tells us. His name is John and she, dear thing, is Jess. They are terribly sweet, though Irene hates to have them in the house as she says they have nits and has confined them to the cottage with Alice until she can get them properly deloused. And little John has some chesty cough she thinks may be contagious so she keeps me far from him, which is too bad as he has the most killing accent and says things like, 'Cor! That ain't 'alf a 'igh roof!' when going into the hall with the great dome. I long to keep him with me just to hear him speak! But Irene is quite odd with them really. I suppose I expected she'd be thrilled to have children around and yet it's as if she can't bear them anywhere near her. She does stare at the little girl, whom Alice has adopted quite as her own. But it's more like a dread than a fascination. She says Malcolm shouldn't like them in the main house anyway and I suppose she's right. She is forever deferring to him, even when he's not around. Still, she is so kind to me . . . in her own way. Do write, darling. Do write soon.

Baby xxxx

It was a very different journey to Endsleigh the second time. Cate travelled down with Rachel for the auction in her battered blue Volkswagen; the sky clouding over, dull and grey, heat rising from the road.

The conversation she'd had with her mother ran round in her brain. She'd told her pretty much everything, which was strange, because she was normally quite distant with her mother. Part of her, an unfair, cruel childish part, had always blamed her mother for leaving her father; never quite believing that things had been as bad as they were. Perhaps if she'd tried harder or been more loving, he would've changed; things would've been different. And when he'd died the wedge between them had grown into a yawning gap. Cate knew that most of her resentment came from the fact that her mother had always been there, doing all the things parents should do, like making her finish her homework or go to bed on time. In her childish mind, she couldn't be angry with her father; couldn't risk him moving even further away from her. So she had punished her mother instead – the person who had shown up for her. Keeping her at arm's length, she'd determined only to share fragments of her life with her, especially her New York existence.

But when she'd confided in her, there was none of the judgement Cate was expecting. Her mother wanted to know if she would like to visit her in Spain; she'd gladly buy her a ticket. But Cate explained that she was doing some work for Rachel, promising to come when it was all over.

She didn't tell her about the shoebox or her obsessive interest in solving the mystery of Baby Blythe. She knew there was something compulsive about it; it had blossomed from a diversion into a real need to untangle the knotted web of personalities that went beyond mere curiosity or interest.

They checked into a small hotel in Lyme Regis, near the offices of the solicitors. Cate and Rachel shared a double room. Jack had made arrangements elsewhere. Cate tried not to think of it as significant, and yet it seemed so. She couldn't help but compare this second journey with the first. And part of her missed the hours she'd spent alone with him, in the old house.

When she and Rachel arrived at Endsleigh the day before the auction, the drive was backed up with cars and the house was full of people wandering around viewing the sale objects, catalogues in hand. The event was being overseen by Mr Syms, just as grim as ever in the same dark suit and humourless temper. Security guards patrolled up and down the hallways while removal men hauled various pieces from the floors above; all the furniture in the library had been taken out in order to create a makeshift auction room. But Jack was nowhere to be seen.

While Rachel discussed the details of the proceedings with Mr Syms and issued instructions, Cate wandered through the house once more on her own. But it was a very different place now; gutted and bare. There were marks on the walls, sun-bleached patches on the floor, indicating where things had been. The rooms themselves looked naked, and oddly vulnerable by comparison.

Cate walked up the wide staircase, to the landing, heading to Irene's room. It was as lifeless and impersonal as a hotel suite now. The bed was stripped bare; the carpet was rolled up in the centre of the floor. She turned, checking the bedside table. The stack of books was gone.

She'd hoped she'd be able to look at everything with a fresh eye; maybe discover something that would fit the pieces of the puzzle in place. But nothing was left.

Walking past the main landing, she went down the long corridor to the west side of the house. There was one more room she was longing to see. The door was closed, she turned the handle and, just as before, the golden light hit her, almost blinding after the darkness of the hallway.

Only she wasn't alone. Jack was there, piling books into boxes. He turned.

'Close the door,' he commanded.

She pushed it shut.

'And hello,' he added, shoving another stack of books in. 'Don't even ask what I'm doing unless you want to be party to a crime.'

'OK.' She leaned against the frame. 'So, what are you doing?'

'Do you remember Mrs Williams? How upset she was about this room, these books? Well –' he stood up, brushing the dust from his hands – 'I thought it might be a nice gesture if we gave them to her. And I'm afraid, as this room wasn't formally even acknowledged before, that I took the liberty of not including its contents in the catalogue. So now I'm reduced to sneaking these boxes down the back stairway.'

He smiled, a lopsided, sardonic sort of grin. He seemed different; more relaxed and easy-going than she remembered.

'Let me help you,' she said, bending down to fill up an empty box with the final row of books.

She concentrated on stacking; he on sealing the other two boxes.

'Did you have a good trip down?' he asked, tearing off a strip of packing tape.

'Yes, and you?'

'Fine.' He folded the flaps inside one another. 'And, you're well?'

'Yes. Fine.' She slotted the last books in place. 'And you?'

'Yes. Yes . . .' His voice trailed off.

He took a step back, watching her. Her hair was longer, softer, less rigidly cut, her face more open. There was something unstructured about her, or rather, deconstructed, though he couldn't put his finger on exactly what had changed.

She looked up at him. Her eyes the same disarming clear green, translucent in the morning light. 'All done, boss.'

Together they took the boxes down the back staircase that led into the kitchen and piled them on the table, gasping from the effort.

'Can you drive?' Jack asked.

'Yes.'

He pulled a set of car keys out of his pocket. 'Listen, I've got to see Rachel about a few things. Would you mind taking these over to Jo? She moved out of the cottage a few weeks ago and is staying with her mother. I've got an address here. If you don't want to, we can just put them in the boot of the car and I'll take them down later.'

'No, that's fine. That is, of course, if you trust me with your car,' she smiled.

'Actually, I don't trust you.' He took out a slip of paper from his breast pocket. 'But I've always wanted to see it driven by a beautiful blonde, so I'm willing to trade my peace of mind for a glimpse of the fantasy.'

'Perv.'

'Yup.'

They put the boxes on the back seat and Cate climbed in. 'Have you got a map?'

'Here.' He stretched across her, popped open the glove compartment and took out an atlas. 'This is the page,' he said, flicking the book open, resting it against the steering wheel. He leaned in close, tracing his finger along the page. 'You need to turn right, go all the way down past the dairy and then left at this junction. Wait, let me see that address again.'

She handed it back to him. He lingered, drawing out the chance to be close to her. And she let him.

'Yeah, just follow along here and it should be some-where along this road.' He turned, his face close to hers. 'Does that make sense?'

'Sure.' She put the book onto the seat next to her; turned on the ignition. 'Take one last look at your pride and joy, pal.'

'Don't make me hunt you down!'

She revved the engine. 'I'll leave a trail of breadcrumbs, shall I?' And she pulled away, speeding down the long winding drive and into the distance.

Jack shoved his hands in his pockets.

He'd wondered what it would be like to see her again. But his imaginings never prepared him for the reality of her.

She looked good behind the wheel. He'd never let anyone else drive that car, not even his wife.

Why was he so quick to hand her the keys?

Cate downshifted, speeding up a steep hill to the next corner. It had been a long time since she'd driven, maybe two years. And this car was exposed, raw, visceral. The engine rumbled, a deep throaty growl beneath her; the wind tossing her hair. It was a sexy animal despite its age. And there was something intimate about driving it; a feeling of connectedness to a part of Jack that was wild too; unpredictable and yet sophisticated.

She accelerated over the crest of the hill, whipping round the corner past a field of stunned sheep. Here was the road. Slowing down, she checked the house numbers. Number twenty-seven. This was it. She pulled up outside. It was a detached William and Mary-style cottage, of considerable charm, with a view overlooking the sea below. It had a large, romantic front garden, filled with hollyhocks, rambling rose bushes, bluebells and daisies. Cate climbed out and, hauling one of the boxes off the back seat, pushed open the garden gate. The scent from the flowers was as refined as any blend by Creed or Guerlain. Putting down the box, she pressed the doorbell, excited to think of how pleased Jo would be with her unexpected gift.

The door opened. But instead of Jo, a tiny, very elderly woman with bright black eyes looked up at her. 'Yes?'

'I'm looking for Jo, I mean, Mrs Williams. I wondered if she was here.'

'That's my daughter. She's gone out shopping. Can I help?'

'Yes, my name's Cate. I met her over at Endsleigh. I'm with Deveraux and Diplock, the valuers. I have something for her, a gift. I wanted to drop it off.'

'Oh, she will be pleased!' The woman smiled. 'You know she was very upset to have to move. The whole thing's been a bit of an adjustment for her. Would you like to come in and have a cup of tea?'

'That's very kind, but I don't want you to go to any trouble.'

'It's no trouble. You're in the country now – tea is our national sport!'

Cate carried in the box, placing it on the floor by the door.

'Milk?'

'Yes, please,' Cate called.

It was a lovely home, opening onto a light-filled conservatory at the back; filled with comfortable chairs, a profusion of doilies and what appeared to be vast collections of small china figurines. While Jo's mother put the kettle on, Cate examined the photographs lined up on the mantelpiece. There were faded black-and-white photographs of various family groupings, children and grandchildren, a couple of very old baby photos of startled infants in long white christening gowns, a picture of Jo and a man in a wheelchair, presumably her husband, in front of a beachfront property next to sign reading 'The White House'.

'I hope this isn't too strong. I do like strong tea.'

Cate turned. 'I'm sure it's fine,' she said, taking the steaming mug. 'I was just admiring the pictures of your family.'

'Thank you. I've been very blessed.' She settled into one of the armchairs. 'And now Jo and I are off to see the world!'

'Really?'

'Hasn't she told you? She's booked us into one of those fancy cruises. We leave for London in a week's time, spend a few days at a posh hotel and then we're off – for three months! We go to South Africa, the Middle East, Egypt, Russia, Spain, Marrakech . . .'

'That sounds amazing!'

'I've never even been out of England. But I've always wanted to travel only I'm too old to be getting on and off planes. Jo says we can see everything and at night we come back to our little cabin and eat our tea. She says we don't even have to get off the ship if we don't want to. Normally I'd never consider anything so extravagant but we've both come into a little money, so I suppose it's fair enough.'

'You must let us know when you're in London and we'll come and meet you.'

'Oh, yes. We're staying somewhere right in the centre of town . . . the Belleview or something like that. I have to look it up.' She smiled. 'So, I'm not very good at keeping secrets,' she confessed. 'What have you brought her?'

'Well.' Cate put her tea down and tore off the packing tape on the box. 'While we were there valuing the contents, we came across a room in the west wing of the house. I'm sure you're familiar with it. Really quite beautiful, painted the most brilliant gold. Do you know the one I mean?'

'That room has been locked a long time.'

'Well, in there, we discovered these old books. See.' She handed her one. 'Many of them are first editions. Your daughter was particularly taken with them,' Cate continued. 'We thought she might like to have them.'

'I see.'

It wasn't quite the flurry of excitement that Cate was expecting. Perhaps she didn't understand.

'Most of them have never even been read. They're really quite valuable,' she explained. 'And in wonderful condition. For example, this *Wind in the Willows* is extremely rare.'

'You're too kind.' She held the book, unopened, in her lap.

'I mean, of course . . .' Cate faltered, 'if you don't want them . . . it doesn't matter. We only thought . . .'

'Forgive me. It's just that we have so many things, my dear,' she said quietly. 'And with my daughter moving in we have even less space than ever. Neither one of us is very clever that way.' She handed the book back to Cate. 'I don't mean to sound ungrateful but I think perhaps it's best if you gave them to someone else, or perhaps kept them for yourself.'

Something had shifted. The woman who'd appeared lively and enthusiastic only a minute ago was suddenly subdued and withdrawn. 'I'm sorry.' Cate put it back inside, folded the lid of the box down again. 'I . . . I mean, we thought it might be a good idea.'

'No harm done. I'm sorry you took the time to bring them all this way.' She took another sip of tea.

Cate stood awkwardly, picked up her tea too. 'Endsleigh is lovely,' she said, trying to start again on more neutral footing.

'Yes. Certainly very beautiful to look at.'

'Your daughter was telling me all about how you came there when Irene Blythe was first married.'

'Yes, as a lady's maid. That was a long time ago.'

Cate looked around the room again, desperate for a fresh topic of conversation.

'It must've been exciting working for such a famous person.'

'Well,' Jo's mother frowned, brushing a bit of lint from her skirt. 'it wasn't quite the same in those days.'

There was something unyielding between them now; an invisible door she couldn't budge. It had something to do with the house, the books . . .

'That room upstairs,' Cate persisted, 'I thought it was the most beautiful in the house. Do you know why it was locked?

'They didn't need it,' the woman answered briskly. 'Most of the house was shut down during the war to conserve energy. That wing was never properly used again.

Besides –' she put down her teacup decisively – 'how many rooms does a person need?'

Suddenly it was obvious – they were all children's books. Cate wondered why she hadn't seen it before. 'It was a nursery, wasn't it?'

'I don't know what it was for. It was always locked.' The old woman stood up. 'I'm sorry you had a wasted trip. I'll let my daughter know you were here. She was thinking of stopping by the auction so you may see her then.'

Cate put down her unfinished tea. Her visit was clearly over now. Picking up the box, she followed Jo's mother to the door. 'Did you know Diana Blythe?'

'I met her.'

'What do you think happened to her?'

'I have no idea.'

Cate laughed, trying to charm her. 'I suppose you must get asked questions about her all the time!'

The woman said nothing.

'It's just odd, isn't it, that there's no grave?'

'Grave?'

'I know her body wasn't found but, I mean, it's unusual not to mark the loss of a loved one in some way, with a grave or a monument.'

Jo's Mother seemed to consider this. 'Not everyone wants to remember the past,' she said at last.

'Yes. Yes, you're right. I'm sorry to have disturbed you.'

She opened the door. 'It was good of you to stop by.'

(Cate got the feeling this wasn't entirely true.)

Walking back to the car, she put the box back with the others. Her mission was a spectacular failure, that was certain.

Turning back to the cottage, she raised her hand goodbye.

But the old lady had already shut the door firmly behind her.

Endsleigh
Devon

17 November 1940

My dearest,
What news, my love? A few lines are all that I
require. I do hope you got my last letter. Life here in
Arcadia continues to be more of a paradise lost than
regained. Not least because Alice keeps looking at me
in Horror. Of course it's obvious I'm in the pig. Last
night I finally braved it. 'Alice, I'm going to have a
baby.' Again, that Horror face and then Complete
Silence. So I said, 'I may need some help.' To which
she replied. 'Yes, ma'am, most women do.' And left the
room. I simply howled. But now at least she's a little
less open-mouthed, which is a blessing. Little John has
developed quite an infection in his lungs and the
doctor came round to see him. Irene has spent two days
praying with him by his bedside and he seems to have
turned a corner. She's quite triumphant. Still, she's
asked Alice to find them somewhere else to stay. I
know it's all on my account which makes me feel
dreadful.

Irene makes me keep myself only to the house and gardens. I am so bored I could scream but she's right I suppose; even if I don't care two beans what anyone thinks, she does very much. And yet there's always masses to do – paper drives, scrap-metal collections; Irene is forever out giving stirring speeches about physical and moral hygiene: 'A clean heart and a clean body cannot fail to bring us closer to victory!' (How killing!) She brings me piles of bandages to roll from the hospital – it seems the one domestic talent I do possess. I do thousands in a day and still there are always more. That old gardener of Irene's (I so long to call him Toad for no good reason other than I'm aching to call someone Toad) has ploughed up the whole of the side garden and planted the most incredible lot of vegetables. He used to be quite slow but now whips round the place in a positive tornado of activity. But Irene has done something terribly sweet, which is to give me a little project. All her restoration of course has had to wait and the gilding she was going to use for the library she's given to me to paint the nursery. She's terribly excited, says it will be beautiful and we shall decorate it in such a lovely way. It's so extravagant but I started the other day and the effect is quite striking. Cannot help the feeling she thinks that I will stay here forever. Already she's had the most extensive collection of children's books sent from

*Hatchards and every day she has some new plan. We paint together; I do the low-down bits and she is quite good at dealing with heights and being up on top of the ladder. It reminds me of when we were children; it is so much easier between us when we are painting in silence.*

*Your own, very own,*

*Baby xxx*

The next day and a half were a flurry of organisation and activity. It wasn't until early evening, when the auction was over and most of the crowds had dispersed, that the pace relaxed again. Rachel was seeing to the final paperwork with Mr Syms; removal vans were loading up the last of the furniture, now headed for various destinations throughout the UK and even the world. Cate wandered through the house looking for Jack. Eventually she found him lying on his back, eyes closed, stretched out under the horse-chestnut tree in the garden.

'Hey,' she called and he looked up, shielding his eyes from the sun.

'Hey! I never got to ask you what happened with the books. You managed not to get lost?'

'I got there all right. But Jo's mother didn't want them. She turned me away.'

'Really?' He laughed, shaking his head. 'So ends my life of crime. And public service.' And he closed his eyes again, inhaling deeply. She looked down at his face, peaceful in repose. Rachel was right; he *was* handsome and there was something incredibly appealing about the way he didn't seem to notice it or care.

She sat down next to him on the grass. 'You're pretty fierce with that gavel.'

'Ah, the power and the glory! My favourite bit is slamming it down.'

'Very impressive.' Cate turned over onto her side, plucking at a bit of grass. 'Are you heading home tonight?'

'No. I'm going to drive up to Melton Mowbray. My mum has a cottage there and I'd like to visit my dad. He's just gone into a nursing home nearby and it's been a while since I've seen him.'

'And then what? Any more big houses on the horizon?'

'Actually –' he opened his eyes, staring up at the canopy of thick green boughs above him – 'this may be my last one.'

'Really? What do you mean?'

He paused a moment. 'I think it's time I moved on.'

'What? Leave Deveraux and Diplock?'

'Yeah.'

'Does Rachel know?'

'Not yet. I haven't been thinking about it for very long.'

'I see. And . . . you think she'll be all right without you?' Her tone was strangely accusatory.

He looked across at her. 'She'll be fine. She has you now.'

'I'm not here to replace you,' she pointed out, suddenly irritated. 'There's no need for you to leave. I don't even know what I'm doing!'

He sat up, propping himself on his elbows. 'I didn't mean it that way. It's just it's time. I've been there far too long.'

She frowned, knotting the long green leaves together. 'But what are you going to do?'

'I'm not sure. I have some money set aside. Enough to keep me going, at any rate. What about you?'

'What about me?' For no real reason, she felt as if she were being attacked. It came out far too sharp.

He laughed, which was even more disconcerting. 'Well, aren't you going back to New York?'

'I don't know.' She stared at the clump of grass balled up in her fist. 'I'm really not sure any more.'

'So, you're thinking of staying here?'

'I don't know,' she said again.

They were quiet a moment.

She was being unreasonable and was afraid to look at him. Her reaction confused him.

'You know . . .' He hesitated. It probably wasn't the right moment but if he didn't say it now, he might never. 'I wanted to talk to you about the conversation we had –' he smiled – 'if you can call it a conversation. At Rachel's. Do you remember? You were angry with me.'

She nodded.

'You accused me of wanting to think well of you, and of finding it difficult.'

'Yes.'

He shifted, leaning in a bit. 'You were right to be angry. It was none of my business.'

She stared at him. His frankness frightened her. It felt as if he were letting her go. Yet his transparency touched her too.

'I was angry at myself,' she said at last, deciding that his honesty deserved to be reciprocated in kind. 'I was angry that I'd been such a . . . that I'd done any of it. I regret it. My time in New York.' Her eyes met his. 'All of it.'

She didn't shy away from his gaze, but looked squarely at him.

'Why did you tell me?'

'Why shouldn't I? Why shouldn't you know who I am?'

'But that's not who you are.'

'How can you be so sure?'

'It's not who you are,' he insisted.

'It's some of it. Think of it as a service. At least now, you always have an excuse.'

'An excuse for what?'

She seemed small and vulnerable, with light grey circles under her eyes and pale, translucent skin. 'To walk away.'

The wind blew her hair. It fell across her mouth. Reaching over, he brushed it away, his fingers lingering against the warm curve of her cheek. 'Do you want me to walk away?'

She closed her eyes, leaning into the pressure of his hand against her face. 'I don't know. What would happen, Mr Coates, if you . . . lingered?'

'I don't know, Katie.' He opened his palm, his voice was soft. 'I don't know.'

'Hey, Jack! Jack?' Rachel was calling from the terrace. 'I've been looking for you! Do you have the other set of keys?'

Cate opened her eyes. 'Good luck with your father.'

Rachel started across the lawn. 'Mr Syms is about to leave and we need to sort this out. Also, do you know where I put those transport receipts? I can't find them anywhere.'

Cate stood up.

He took her hand. 'Katie . . .'

She smiled and pressed his fingers to her lips, softly, before letting go. 'Good luck with everything, Jack.'

And turning, she walked away.

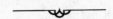

The next day, back in London, Rachel was leafing through the post. 'These are for you,' she said, handing Cate a couple of envelopes.

The first one was official-looking. It was from the records department at HMS Drake Barracks.

She sat down and opened it.

*Dear Miss Albion,*

*Thank you for your letter requesting any information on an officer under the name of Nicholas Warburton stationed at HMS Vivid, now HMS Drake, any time before or during the First World War. We do have a record of a young officer who was, for a brief time, on tour as part of the HMS Mercy, engaged in landmine sweeping during the period of 1917–18 in the Scottish Sea. I regret to inform you that unfortunately our records show that he was disgracefully discharged after being 'found engaging in actions unbecoming to an officer'. Although facts are vague on this matter, it appears that only the intervention of his family, most notably of his father, Lord Warburton, prevented the case from reaching a full trial. The other midshipman involved was also dismissed and was later sentenced for his conduct, serving time in Portsmouth Prison. It is a sad legacy that the navy operated on these terms, as did the rest of the country at the time, and I am pleased to point out that this is no longer the case and, in addition to the rest of the armed services, we are now fully dedicated to eliminating sexual discrimination and to protecting the private rights of our servicemen and women.*

*I hope this has been helpful to you.*

*Sincerely,*

*Captain A. S. Hamler*

Cate reread the letter, frowning.

Was Nicholas Warburton gay? That was the gist of it. A photograph of a handsome stepbrother, a cocaine vial, a secret fascist badge, an expensive bracelet . . . what did it all mean? She sighed. The objects in the shoebox seemed more disjointed now than ever.

The second letter was from the Richard Green Gallery. She tore it open.

It was a postcard, advertising the Private Auction of the Munroe Collection.

Across the back was written,

*Meet me at the gallery, Friday, 7 p.m. A. Munroe*

Suddenly she felt unbalanced, as if her legs were about to give way. Heart thundering, she tore it up, tossing it quickly into the kitchen bin.

Rachel caught her eye. 'Is everything all right?'

'It's nothing,' Cate lied. 'A circular, that's all.'

'For you?'

'Some cosmetic offer,' she said, flashing a rather unconvincing smile. 'You know how these department store make-up women are. You pause for one second . . .'

'True.' Rachel agreed, taking her reading glasses out of handbag and settling down at the kitchen table to go through her own post. 'They're very persistent.'

'Yes. That's it exactly. Very persistent.'

*Endsleigh*
*Devon*

*February 18 1941*

*Darling,*
*I do so ache to hear from you, my love! One word is all*
*I require. Do not forget me. I can assure you that I do*
*not forget you. Have been fighting off a terrible Black.*
*Spent all yesterday in bed. It is so cold in this house.*
*Oh I do so regret my actions! Please believe me. And*
*every day I don't hear from you, I regret them more. I*
*don't know what I shall do or how to fix it. I want to go*
*back, to before this all began. The burden of my own*
*consciousness is more than I can bear.*

*B*

Cate looked at her watch and then back at her reflection in the mirror. It was 6.23 on Friday evening. She was wearing a dress, hair curled softly back from her face, lipstick, perfume. This was not a woman about to end an affair. This was a woman wavering, one foot in, one foot out; waiting to see if maybe this time things would be different. She thought of her mother, the trip to the hospital, and yet here she was, curling her eyelashes, putting on blusher. Rinsing her mouth out with Listerine.

She shouldn't go. She should ignore the whole thing. Put it behind her. Then she thought of Jack, of his hand on her cheek, and felt stupid and confused.

She had nothing. Nothing to lose and nothing to gain. Nothing.

She took off the dress. Put on jeans and flat sandals.

She wasn't going. She would stay in with Rachel. Watch TV.

There was no point going. Nothing to say.

Rachel was reading the newspaper in the living room when she came downstairs. 'Where are you off to?'

'Nowhere. I just need . . .' She twisted her watch round her wrist, agitated. What was the time, anyway? 'I just need some cigarettes, actually.'

Rachel took off her glasses. 'Why don't I come with you?' She folded the paper up. 'I could do with a walk.'

'No.' Cate shook her head adamantly, her hand already reaching for the doorknob. 'I'll only be a minute. I just need to clear my head.'

It was inevitable, heading down the steps, onto the street. There wasn't even an internal debate any more. She knew where she was going. She'd always known.

When she arrived, the gallery was closed. She pressed the bell. A man's voice came out of the video intercom.

'Cate Albion?' he asked.

'Yes.'

The door buzzed open. 'Please come through.'

For a moment she thought she was going to laugh out loud from excitement, the sheer release of seeing him again. Would he look the same? He'd come all this way. What would they say to one another?

She walked into the main gallery, with its wooden floor and dim lights. So dim, in fact, that at first she didn't see her.

In the far corner, next to a small table, sat a woman of very upright bearing. Her face was turned away towards the window, but her long dark hair spilled over her slim shoulders.

Behind her stood a tall man in a dark suit with sandy hair and glasses, his hand resting lightly, protectively, on the back of her chair.

It was Anne Marie.

'Please forgive me if I don't get up,' she said, without bothering to turn round.

Cate tried to speak, but no words would come out. It was meant to be him, not her. After all this time, it was meant to be him. And yet, the fascinating details of Anne Marie came flooding in, the tawny thinness of her arms, her long fingers, with short, tapered nails and the large opal ring she wore, the way the light fell across her face, and the lines, deep around her eyes, which nonetheless didn't diminish the effect of her features. She was smaller, more beautiful, older and far more real.

'You must think it strange that I contacted you,' Anne Marie continued, her voice steady, measured; devoid of any emotion. 'But I noticed a grave oversight of my husband's. I wanted to make sure that I rectified it as soon as possible. My lawyer here, Mr Trask –' she inclined her head slightly, indicating the tall man with the glasses – 'was unfortunately unable to elicit a response from you. So I thought a more informal invitation might persuade you to join us. You really are quite a recluse,' she said, turning, meeting Cate's eyes for the first time. The sureness of her gaze was chilling and at the same time mesmerising. Cate found she couldn't match it, and yet still couldn't quite bring herself to look away. Never in her life had anyone regarded her with such unguarded hatred.

She opened her mouth but again, nothing came out.

In the silence that followed, Mr Trask stepped forward. 'It seems that Mr Munroe has failed to pay you for the painting he commissioned.' Reaching into his breast pocket, he produced a cheque. 'Mrs Munroe hopes that you find this amount sufficient.'

He put it down on the table between them.

'My husband really is the most avid collector. He's surprised me so many times with his new acquisitions. Sadly, though, we'll have to auction some of them later this month. One cannot always keep what one's picked up. And of course, others . . .' she paused, giving a little shrug of her shoulders, 'others one just becomes bored of.'

It was as if Cate were made of lead, unable to move or even think clearly. It was beyond her comprehension. It was meant to be him. She thought it would be him.

'I'm told it's the going rate,' Anne Marie said.

Cate stared at the cheque. It was for £50,000.

'For services rendered,' Anne Marie added.

The gallery was so dark and close, the very air itself felt as if it were pressing in against her skin.

'It's . . . it's . . .' Cate stumbled, her throat tightening around the words.

'Pardon me?'

She swallowed hard. 'It's not for sale,' she managed at last.

'I'm sorry?' Anne Marie gave an incredulous little laugh. 'What did you say?'

Cate forced herself to meet her gaze. 'The painting is not for sale.'

'Are you trying to bargain with me?'

'No. I'm telling you it can't be bought. It's not for sale.'

Anne Marie's eyes narrowed.

'I am at a loss then, Miss Albion, to understand exactly how it came to be in my husband's possession.'

Cate weighed up her words carefully. 'It was a mistake,' she said quietly. 'A serious mistake.'

Anne Marie's face hardened.

'Would you be so good as to have the gallery return the painting to me?' Cate asked, turning to Mr Trask. 'I believe you have my address.'

He frowned, pursed his lips.

'Or shall I speak to them myself?' she suggested.

'No, no,' he conceded, glancing sideways at Anne Marie, who ignored him. 'I'm sure I can make the necessary arrangements.'

'Thank you.' She looked back at Anne Marie. 'I'm truly sorry, Mrs Munroe.'

Anne Marie's dark eyes widened in rage. She turned her face away, stared out of the window again. 'You're mistaken if you imagine the matter to be of any importance to me at all.'

Somehow Cate made her way out and on to the street.

It was only when she reached Brook Street that she began to breathe properly again. And Oxford Street before her head stopped pounding and her hands stopped shaking. She'd had a very narrow escape.

The only thing worse than being a mistress to a man like that was being his wife.

*Endsleigh*
*Devon*

*17 March 1941*

*Oh darling!*
*Irene has gone to London and I am so jealous I could*
*scream! Of course I can't as I am the size of a bus.*
*She's to have lunch with Pippa Marks and do some*
*shopping. Have begged her for a pair of shoes as my*
*feet are so swollen now. Last time she was there she*
*had to spend the night due to bombs, tucked in the*
*basement of the Dorchester along with Lord R,*
*Nicki Monckton and Baba Metcalf. Came back*
*looking tense and old. Wouldn't tell me anything*
*and went upstairs to lie down. I do hope she brings*
*me shoes.*

*I have successfully knitted the most misshapen little*
*jumper for my son and heir. Really quite revolting and*
*in a ducky yellow. Alice just shakes her head while I*
*knit and then spends half an hour pulling it apart. If it*
*fits it will only be because he's completely deformed.*
*With all the disruption I can only conclude that you*
*don't receive my letters but I will still try. I cannot do*

*without you, you see. Even when you don't write, I*
*need to know that you are there — that you exist in the*
*world. One cannot carry on otherwise. What would be*
*the point?*

  *Your only,*

  *B xx*

Jack pulled up on the long wooded lane to Wooton Lodge Nursing Home. The drive wound around for almost a half a mile before the house finally became visible, behind a thick clump of trees. Tucked miles away from even the smallest village, it had been difficult to find. His mother had admitted his father about two weeks previously, after years of struggling with him on her own. As he climbed out of the car, he noted the grandeur of the place, the extensive parkland and the profound sense of solitude that pervaded. This wasn't so bad. Neat manicured lawns and flower beds bordered the main building, which was neo-Gothic in design, with high cathedral-style leaded glass windows and arched flying buttresses. A little further in the distance, a man-made lake was visible and what looked to be converted stables, now presumably a state-of-the-art medical facility. His father might be comfortable here.

Reaching into the back seat of the car, he pulled out a bag containing the old writing case as well as a copy of Benedict Blythe's *Myth and Irish Imagination* which he'd managed to find in a second-hand bookshop in Malvern. It was a surprising book, what he'd read of it. Lyrically written and much more entertaining than he'd expected from an academic work. Clearly part of Blythe's popularity had been his ability to translate the ancient tales into fresh, highly romantic adventures, lavish in their sensual detail and innuendo. The author's sexuality seeped through the descriptive passages of a land and a people taut with physical longing and passions, which undoubtedly mirrored the paradoxes of his own torn psyche.

Jack walked up to the main entrance and smiled at the woman at the reception desk.

'Hi. I'm here to see my father, Henry Coates.'

'Is he expecting you?'

'Ah, not really.'

'And your name?'

'Jack. Jack Coates.'

'Coates . . .' She entered the name, checking the details on her computer. 'Here we are. He's in the east wing. Let me ring through to the nurses' station and see if I can get someone to take you down. Do you want to take a seat?' She indicated a long, leather bench.

'Thanks.'

Jack wandered, loitering near the doorway, suddenly nervous and filled with dread. From the outside it had seemed like a posh hotel. But now he could see the security guards and locked doors, it felt properly like an institution. Was his father really that bad? What if he hated it and wanted Jack to take him out? Or would this be one of the days when he had trouble placing Jack at all?

'Someone will be up shortly,' the woman said, putting down the phone.

'Great.' He picked up one of the nursing home's glossy brochures and sat down, leafing through.

Originally belonging to Rothermere Estate, Wooton Lodge was built as a private hunting lodge in 1873, its architecture modelled after that of Notre Dame in Paris. During the Second World War it was taken over as a psychiatric hospital and rest home for soldiers recovering from the traumas of active service. Its secluded location and wooded surroundings were thought to be highly therapeutic. After the war it remained a psychiatric hospital, bequeathed to the nation by Lord Rothermere, until the Alpha Group purchased it from the state in 1983. It then shifted its focus to geriatric care, particularly assisted living for people suffering from Parkinson's, Alzheimer's and dementia, providing the most comprehensive, up-to-date facilities possible.

A nurse was walking towards him. 'Mr Coates?'

Jack dropped the brochure on the bench and stood up.

'Annabel,' she introduced herself, and they shook hands. 'Do you want to follow me?' She led him down a hallway. 'Have you been here before?'

'No, this is my first time.'

'Allow me to show you around.' She swiped a pass key and they went through a door and down another hallway. 'This is the common room,' she pointed out. 'It must've been the main drawing room. And as you can see, it gets quite a lot of use.'

It was a cavernous space, with huge oversized features and an enormous fireplace. Whoever had designed it had obviously pictured it as a kind of latter-day Camelot; there were stained-glass windows with vaguely Masonic, medieval imagery, arched doorways and a flagstone floor, now covered with crimson deep-pile area rugs. Jack looked around at the clusters of elderly patients, some playing bridge, others dozing in front of a television. A few drinking tea and looking out of the front bay window. They seemed daunted, diminished by the sheer grandiosity of the place. There was a feeling of waiting, as if they were being held in a rather comfortable airport lounge. It disturbed Jack to think of his father sitting here, staring forlornly out of the window with all the other patients, unsure of where he was or why. 'Great. Very nice,' he said.

They continued on. 'And the dining room.'

He poked his head into the narrow room with its vaulted ceiling. Long tables were arranged with plastic-covered chairs; easy to wipe down and well spaced from each other. 'Very nice,' he said again, his apprehension growing. Who did his father sit with? Was it like school? Were there little cliques?

She took him round to the left and through a set of large double doors. They were obviously out of the main public spaces and in the wing with the private rooms now. It looked more like a hospital and less like a cathedral. The ceilings were lower, the floors beneath him wooden, creaking from use. The nurse paused before a room on the right.

'I think he's asleep,' she said, softly.

Jack peered in. His father was sitting upright in a cushioned armchair; his head lolled to one side. 'Dad?'

Henry's chest rose and fell, a quiet, soothing rhythm.

'It's the medication,' she explained. 'Can I get you anything? A cup of tea?'

'No. No, I'm fine.'

She left and Jack sat down on the bed, holding the bag on his lap, looking at his father. He seemed to have shrunk since he last saw him; his hands and feet appeared exaggerated, much too big for his slender limbs, and his face was like a soft rubbery mask, mouth open, snoring softly. He was sitting in a warm patch of sunlight.

'Dad? Dad?'

His father stirred slightly, his eyes flicking open. 'Hello? Yes?'

'It's me, Jack.'

The old man shifted. 'Yes. I'll be with you in a moment.' His head rolled to the other side and his eyes shut again.

Jack sighed and looked around. It wasn't a bad room, after all. The bed was a hospital model, but the rest of the furniture he recognised as coming from his parents' home, along with pictures, paintings and books that helped give the room the familiar understated style he associated with his father's tastes. Jack got up, looking at the spines of the books his father was reading, picking up and examining the photographs he'd chosen to keep with him, paying attention, for perhaps the first time in his life, to the finer details of who his father was. There was a certain type of fountain pen he liked to do the crossword with. A vein of rather sensationalist historical fiction that caught his imagination. A positive devotion to his mother, whose face smiled back at him from no less than four of the photographs that were crowded on top of his chest of drawers. Jack ran his finger across a shiny silver frame; there were large thumbprints from where his father had picked it up, looking at her.

It brought to mind his own flat; ordered, spare; devoid of any tokens or memories.

He turned away from the chest of drawers, checked his watch. Taking the writing case out of the bag, he arranged it, along with the book and the pages he'd photocopied at the library, where he knew his father would see it, on the side table next to his chair.

Taking off his jacket, he folded it, sat back down on the bed and waited. There was the faint ticking sound of his father's alarm clock.

It hadn't been that long ago that his father had owned his own business. Now he was visiting him in a nursing home. The physical ache of loneliness filled his chest.

Jack thought of Cate. Of her hand in his, the smooth silkiness of her cheek; of her standing, naked, by the window.

Then he imagined his thumbprint on the picture frame of the woman he loved.

He wanted the picture on his chest of drawers to be of her.

'So, what are we having tonight?' Cate asked, wandering into the kitchen.

Rachel was chopping an onion. She nodded to a cookbook on the worktop. 'I thought we'd try something different. A fish pie.'

'Wow!' Cate laughed. 'How retro is that!'

'I thought it might be fun.' Rachel smiled.

Cate watched as she flitted between the oven and the worktop, humming a bit of a Burt Bacharach song softly under her breath. There was something different about her today. She had an energy and an ease Cate hadn't seen in her before. Then she noticed something else.

'You haven't got your red shoes on! You look so different without them.'

Rachel looked down on her feet, adorned by a pair of simple flat summer sandals. 'No. I think my red period is finally over.'

'That was a long phase.'

'Too long. Do me a favour and have a look in that book.' She nodded to the page that was propped open. 'Does it say one or two carrots?'

Cate read the recipe on the faded yellowing pages. 'Two. Finely chopped. God, this is really ancient! Where did you get it? From Grandma?'

'I bid on it. Cost me two pounds!' She opened the fridge to get some carrots from the vegetable bin. 'I always like to have a little something from the auctions we do. And this book is such a scream.'

'You mean it came from Endsleigh?'

'That's right. It belonged to the housekeeper, Jo's mother. Jo was telling me some hilarious stories about her during the war. Apparently she didn't know anything about cooking. Put some of the family silver into the oven to warm and when she went to take it out it had all melted! Can you imagine?'

'Yeah, she told me that one too.' Cate turned the cook-book over to see the cover. It was faded cream with a red title, *An Introduction into the Basic Culinary Arts*. Great!' she chuckled. 'The culinary arts, no less. So this must be from just before the war, right?'

'You're getting good at this stuff.' Rachel gave her a smile. 'I'll make a dealer out of you yet. How do you like "Deveraux and Daughter"?'

'Right! And what would Mum say?' Cate flicked through the pages to see the publication date.

'It sounds better than "Deveraux and Niece". Besides, I'm sure she wouldn't care. As long as we kept it in the family.' She saw Cate's expression. 'Hey, I was only kidding!'

Cate was staring at the flyleaf.

'You say this belonged to Jo's mother?' she asked, without looking up.

'Yes. Why? What's going on?'

'Alice Waites' was scribbled across the right-hand corner of the page, in childish, uneven handwriting.

Jo's mother was the same A. Waites who collected the bracelet from Tiffany's.

And the one person alive who probably knew anything about what really happened at Endsleigh when Baby Blythe disappeared.

*Endsleigh,*
*Devon*

*19 April, 1941*

*No news. None. Not a single letter or a telegram.*
*I pray every day, all day, that you are still alive. I cannot*
*move and cry for hours. I am huge. Vast. Rotund.*
*What if you should see me now? Would you still love*
*me? But God, this awful house is so dreadful and dank!*
*I used to think of it as a haven, a palace by the sea.*
*But now it's like a prison to me. I want to leave so*
*badly. I want to find you, somehow. We listen to the*
*radio. And of course the news is all so desperate. What*
*if you are alive and you simply don't love me any more?*
*Irene says fresh air is what I need. Sea walks. If she*
*only knew how I'm longing to drown myself! If I stand*
*on the cliffs and stare down, the water below seems like*
*the churning black in my head. It's a sin to kill myself.*
*It's a greater sin to kill a child. So I make myself walk*
*back. But what difference is it if I live in hell now or*
*in the afterlife? My only hope is that you will come*
*and take me away.*
   *B*

After a while, Jack decided to stretch his legs. It had been a long drive. On the left-hand side of the nurses' station, a door led outside. There was a breeze in the air, the sky had brightened and it was a comfortable temperature. A few patients were dotted along the lawns, a couple of men playing boules and a woman being pushed in a wheelchair by a nurse. Jack strode up the hill a way; it felt good to move. Near the back of the house, he came upon a walled-in garden. Here slender birch and eucalyptus trees filtered out the sunlight; the plantings thick, wild and lush, smelling of moist black earth and moss. As he walked closer he could hear the gentle, lulling sound of a fountain. It was built in a far corner, a gargoyle's head, emerging from the undergrowth with a comical, grotesquely leering face, emptying water into a round marble pool below, filled with flowering water lilies, their blooms a luminous other-worldly white.

He came closer. Along the edge of the pool was an inscription, carved into the stone. *'The dawning of morn, the daylight's sinking, The night's long hours still find me thinking, Of thee, thee, only thee.'* Huge golden and red Koi darted, sleek and fast, just beneath the surface of the dark water. Leaning over, he dipped his fingers into the cool depths.

'They're dangerous, you know,' said a voice behind him.

He turned round.

The elderly woman sitting on the bench behind him was so tiny, that from a distance she almost looked like a child. In fact, there was something youthful and disarming about the way she tilted her head to one side, surveying him with a pair of startling blue eyes. 'They like nothing better, you see, than biting the hand that feeds them.'

The Belmont Hotel was located on Queen Street in Mayfair. It was a narrow boutique establishment, so discreet and like every other town house on the street that it was possible to walk right by it without noticing that it was a hotel at all. Only the presence of a uniformed doorman stationed at the front entrance set it apart.

He opened the door as Cate walked in, the foyer opening graciously into an elegant drawing room on one side and a formal dining room on the other. She went up to the concierge at the reception desk. 'I'm meeting someone in the library,' she explained. 'Can you point me in the right direction, please?'

'I can do better than that.' He escorted her through the drawing room, where tea was being served, and down a narrow hallway into a smaller, oak-panelled room.

Alice was sitting near the unlit fireplace, staring into the charred recess, lost in her own thoughts.

She looked up as Cate walked in.

'Would you like any tea?' the conceriege asked, looking from one to the other.

Alice straightened. 'I don't think that's necessary.'

He gave a little bow and left.

'I can't bear to be waited on. I would never tell Jo, but these places make me feel quite uneasy.'

Cate sat down opposite her on one of the wing arm-chairs. 'Where is Jo?'

'My daughter's out for the day. Sightseeing. London's too crowded for me. And I don't want to go shopping – I have everything I need. So,' she said, folding her hands across her lap. 'You're back.'

'You knew I would come back?'

She nodded. 'I knew someone would, eventually. I just wondered how long it would take. What is it you want to know?'

'Your maiden name is Waites, isn't that correct? Alice Waites?'

'Why are you asking?'

Cate took the copy of the old Tiffany receipt out of her handbag and placed it on the table between them.

Alice picked it up, frowning, straining to make it out. Then she looked up. 'How did you get this?'

Cate ignored the question. 'You collected the bracelet. That's your signature, isn't it?'

Alice's eyes widened. 'How do you know about that?'

'I found it. In an old shoebox.'

'But where? How?'

'It was in the locked room. Behind the books.'

'Books?' Alice ran her hand across her eyes, trying to place them.

Cate took a deep breath, tried again. 'Why did Irene buy her sister such an expensive gift?'

'She had her reasons.'

'Why?'

'You wouldn't understand.'

'Wouldn't understand what?'

'We did what we had to do,' she snapped, suddenly furious.

'Alice –' Cate's voice was quiet – 'what exactly did you do?'

The old lady stared at Cate a long time. It was as if something inside her let go, visibly. Her expression softened; she looked overwhelmed, lost. 'You remind me of her. The blonde hair, the shape of your face. The first time I saw you, it was like seeing a ghost. Which is really saying something. People look at the photographs and think she was beautiful, but there was the way she moved also, the sound of her voice and, well, just the way she was. It took your breath away. If she was in the room, you didn't notice anyone else.'

Cate was silent.

'You see, it wasn't always easy having a sister who was that beautiful. That famous.' She handed the receipt back to Cate, unable to look at it any longer. 'I'm not defending her. But I've tried to understand.'

'Who?'

Alice sighed deeply. 'She hated her so much. In the end, I thought she'd kill her.'

Cate's blood ran cold. 'Kill who?'

'She didn't, of course.' Alice turned again, staring into the empty grate. 'But she might as well have.'

Sitting on a bench in the far corner, propped up against a mass of cushions, he hadn't seen her at first. Quite elegantly dressed in a pale blue skirt and matching jacket, she had a copy of *Le Figaro*, folded across her lap. Her features were soft yet distinctive with very high cheekbones and a halo of white hair framing her face. And there was something about the tone of her voice, her clipped, slightly affected pronunciation, which belonged to another age. Next to her on the bench was a small canister of oxygen and a mask, presumably for emphysema or asthma.

'I'm sorry,' Jack said. 'I didn't mean to disturb you.'

'I've known those fish a long time. They're beautiful to look at but really they're quite vicious characters.'

'Thanks for the warning.'

'You wouldn't happen to have a cigarette, by any chance?'

'Are you supposed to be smoking?' he asked, nodding to the oxygen.

'I'm supposed to be dead,' she shot back. 'Besides,' she smiled, 'I've been smoking since I was sixteen and I dread to tell you how long ago that was. It hasn't killed me yet.'

'Well . . .' he hesitated, feeling for the pack he kept in his jacket pocket, 'when you put it that way . . .'

He took them out and handed her one, then fumbled in his other pockets, looking for a match. She leaned forward, waiting patiently. Finally he found some and, striking one, held it out to her.

Inhaling deeply, she leaned back. 'Thank you,' she said, savouring it. 'Fresh air is overrated. Who are you here to visit? Or perhaps you're a lunatic, come to join our merry little band.'

He laughed. 'I'm sure I am a lunatic but on this occasion I'm here to see my father. Henry Coates. Anyway, I thought it was a nursing home.'

'That's what they call it now. And Henry's adorable!' She nodded. 'Such an intelligent man!'

'Well, right now he's asleep. I see you read French.'

'Of course.' She raised an eyebrow. 'Don't you?'

'Well, not as well as all that,' he admitted. 'Anything interesting?'

She shrugged, sighing. '*Plus ça change* . . . The world is always on the brink of disaster. And of course the French are still quite excited about this money thing.'

'The euro?'

'Quite. A united Europe. To read about it, you'd think this was the first time it had ever been proposed.'

'It's a terrible idea.'

'Life is a series of terrible ideas.' She took another drag. 'One catastrophe after another.'

He crossed his legs. 'Britain will remain independent.'

'We have no choice – we don't even get on with one

another, let alone a bunch of foreigners. But enough. I abhor politics and especially the stale second-rate conversation it produces. Religion isn't the opium of the masses, rhetoric is.' Suddenly she began to cough, a deep, painful rasping which shook her frail frame. Reaching for the oxygen, she covered her mouth and inhaled.

Jack looked around anxiously for help. 'Should I call someone?'

She shook her head and, after a moment, her breathing eased. She took off the mask. 'Tell me, where are you from?'

'London.'

'Really?' She sat forward. 'What's it like these days?'

'Busy. Dusty. Hot.'

'Who's cooking at the Mirabelle?'

'Pardon?'

'The head chef.'

'I must admit, I have no idea.'

'You do dine out, don't you?'

'Occasionally.'

'And dancing . . . do you go out dancing afterwards?'

'Well, not really.'

'Where do you go?'

'Like I said, I'm not the dancing type.'

'How extraordinary!' She sighed. 'You know, you remind me of someone.'

'Who's that?'

'A man I adored about a thousand years ago. Handsome, charming, witty!'

'Thank you.' Jack smiled.

'Of course he was queer.'

He laughed. 'I'm not sure how to take that!'

'As a compliment. He was the most tremendous company and the only man I really loved.'

'That must've been complicated.'

'When isn't life complicated? We had an arrangement. I was his beard. Of course, in those days it used to be more of a stage one passed through rather than a way of life.'

'His beard?'

'A rather quaint term. Your father will understand.'

'What became of him?'

'I really can't say. People lose touch.' She stubbed the cigarette out and sat back, closing her eyes wearily. 'You haven't by any chance got the latest copy of *Hello!*?'

'Sorry. No.'

'Of course not. It's utter rubbish. But I do love gossip. Don't you think Queen Elizabeth has got fat?' She opened her eyes, looked at him sideways. 'I don't suppose you could get a copy, could you?'

*Endsleigh*
*Devon*

*25 May 1941*

*My darling Nick,*
*Just when I had given up all hope! My love, it's too,*
*too beautiful! And so gorgeous! Of course I can barely*
*get it round my wrist, as they are so fat now, but I*
*cannot tell you how I wept when I opened it! It's simply*
*the most extravagant gift in the world and when I had*
*given up all hope of ever hearing from you again! You*
*cannot imagine what I've been thinking — that you*
*were dead under the rubble of London or that you'd*
*been shipped far away . . . You have not forgotten me*
*and my heart is positively singing with joy! I can't*
*imagine where you got the money or even care. Thank*
*you, my love! Thank you a thousand times! Please*
*come and see me — I beg of you! And till then I shall*
*stare at my swollen wrist for courage! Oh my darling!*
*Oh my sweetest, truest love! We shall begin again.*
*Anything is possible, you see, anything!*
   *Yours forever,*
   *Baby xxxxx*

'There were two sides to her, Irene. She could be incredibly charming, really, the nicest woman you ever met. And as long as you did exactly as she wanted, she adored you. But if you put a foot wrong . . .' Alice looked up. 'I once made a mistake in the kitchen, with some silver. I put a platter in the oven to warm and it melted.'

'Jo told me that story.'

'Stupid, really. Irene used to laugh about it – it was one of her favourite stories at a dinner party. Only she never told it except when I was in the room, serving. To everyone else it made her look like the most wonderful, forgiving hostess in the world. She'd pretend to shrug it off and everyone else at the table would look at me for a reaction and laugh. But it used to mortify me. I could hardly wait to leave the room. And then one evening, while she was doing it again, I happened to look up and catch her eye. And I could see, she didn't even bother to hide it. She understood exactly how humiliated I was. She was making me pay for getting it wrong, only she did it in such a way that no one would ever know that but me.'

'Why didn't you leave?'

'I was very young at the time, I didn't have a lot of experience. I thought she was doing me a favour by hiring me. And like I said, she wasn't always that way. She could be very charming. And I was in awe of her. She had great plans for Endsleigh. It was all going to be restored and updated; it was meant to be a showplace. But then again, she had great plans for everyone, for her husband, herself. I think for a while she really thought he was going to be prime minister. But there was always one fly in the ointment. Baby. Baby was always doing something impossible, something that put her ambitions at risk. And then of course the thing about Baby was that everyone was fascinated by her, men especially. Even Irene's husband was charmed. Baby used to say right to his face that if she had to listen to him bore on another second about politics, she was going to strangle him with his tie, and all he'd do was laugh. But Irene wouldn't have dared to speak to him that way, not in a million years. She worshipped him and he knew it. But Baby could get away with anything and no one would bat an eyelid. It infuriated Irene. She was too proud to admit that her little sister had that much power. And in public, she treated her the same way you would treat a naughty pet. But alone, in private, I think it ate her up. None of the rules she lived by applied to Baby – she was as fast as a racing car and no one seemed to mind. That's the way it is with the truly beautiful. It was as if God had given her a special dispensation.'

'I thought Irene was very religious.'

'Yes. But to Irene, even God was meant to follow her rules. And she hated to lose. Then the war came. All the men went away. That's when she really came into her own. She headed all sorts of charities, trained as a nurse, and went around giving speeches and talking on the wireless about the importance of making sacrifices for the war effort and living by Christian values. Then London was bombed and Baby came to stay. But she was pregnant. Again, Baby was flouting decorum, getting what Irene wanted and couldn't have. Only this time, Irene had an advantage. Baby couldn't go anywhere, couldn't even leave the house for fear of being seen.'

Alice paused. 'Irene really wanted that child. She never said anything. But I knew. She started doing up the nursery, filling it with toys and books. Painting it so that it looked like a perfect, golden dream world. But Baby wasn't very well. Being locked up didn't help. She got worse rather than better. And although she used to write long letters, presumably to her lover, he never wrote back. Irene took them to be posted herself. Every day she'd ask if there was anything for her. There never was. Irene tried to keep Baby's spirits up but some days she wouldn't even get out of bed, she was so bad. See, Baby had done things before. Hurt herself. Irene got scared. Told me I had to watch her. That's why she bought her the bracelet.

'She ordered it special and then there was an air raid over the coast and she was put on extra shifts at the hospital. So she had me collect it. I'd never even been to London before. I was terrified I was going to get bombed or mugged. And the shop! I'd never seen anything like it. Irene was insistent that I had to post it from London with a little note she gave me. That was very important, she said. It must have a London postmark. I guess she wanted Baby to believe that the man, whoever he was, still loved her.

'And it worked. For a while she was over the moon. And then suddenly, without any warning at all, she turned. We were collecting old newspapers. I was tying them in bundles and Baby was so big then she could only help with simple things. Her job was to go round the house, gathering up any leftover bits we'd missed. And then she was gone for a very long time. I got worried. And I went to find her.

Alice stopped.

'She had one of the Colonel's razors. I'd never seen so much blood.'

Cate felt a chill through her whole body. 'Did she die?'

Alice shook her head. 'No.'

'What happened to the baby?'

'You see –' Alice looked down, concentrating hard on the space between her hands – 'everything was meant to be perfect. Endsleigh was meant to be a showplace . . . not just to their friends but to the whole nation . . .'

Cate leaned forward. 'I don't understand . . .'

'The child was . . . all across his little face, a terrible red stain.'

'You mean a birthmark?'

Alice nodded. 'It seems it ran in the family.'

'The family?' Cate frowned. But Baby was so beautiful, so flawless. And Nick so classically handsome.

Then suddenly she remembered the old black-and-white photograph on Irene's dressing table. Irene and her husband standing side by side at some veterans' function, not touching. She was holding the plaque and he was smiling proudly, hat off, wincing into the bright sunlight . . . and the unexplained shadow that crept across the right side of his skull, just visible beneath his thinning hair.

Only it wasn't a shadow.

It too was a stain.

Cate sat back.

The child had never been Nick's.

Down the corridor in the drawing room a harpist had begun to play; there were people chatting and laughing. But here, the only sound came from a large grandfather clock ticking dully in the corner.

'What happened to him?' Cate asked quietly.

'There was an argument. A terrible argument. The Colonel took him somewhere, I don't know where. Baby never even saw him. And then a few nights later, a car came with a man . . . a big, tall man. In the morning she was gone.'

Cate had only one more question. 'Alice, is . . . is Baby still alive?'

'I honestly don't know. It was my job to watch her. I'll never know what made her turn like that. I'll never know.'

The old woman seemed visibly weighted down by the effort of telling her. Her shoulders slumped forward and the light in her eyes dimmed, as if she'd retreated somewhere deep within herself.

'So what are you going to do now?'

'What do you mean?'

She looked up. 'I've never told anyone, not even my daughter what I've just told you. Are you going to sell it? Are you a journalist?'

'No. No, of course not.'

'Then why?'

'I'm sorry?'

'Why go to all this trouble, digging up the past of someone you don't even know?'

'I'm sorry, I . . .' Cate stopped.

Alice was staring at her, her dark eyes filled with confusion and loss.

'I don't know,' Cate admitted finally. 'She didn't feel like a stranger. In fact, for a while, she felt like the person I wanted to be.'

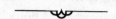

An African male nurse came round the corner, pushing a wheelchair. 'Sorry to interrupt.' He flashed a wide gleaming smile. 'It's time for your lunch, Duchess.' Then he stopped, eyeing her sternly. 'I think you've been smoking again, haven't you?'

'Oh honestly!' She pouted, reaching out to take his arm. 'Don't be such a Nazi, Samuel! Besides, it wasn't me this time. It was him!'

Samuel looked at Jack.

'All I can do is apologise, I'm afraid,' he said, struggling to conceal a smile.

'She's seduced you, hasn't she?' Samuel saw through them both, shaking his head. 'Don't think you've fooled me, Duchess. Besides –' he eased her gently into the wheelchair, placing the oxygen canister on her lap – 'I thought I was the only one covering up for you.'

'Well, you're my favourite, Sammy.' She smiled up at him. 'But I never promised to be faithful. What time is it anyway?'

He checked his watch. 'Almost one thirty.'

'Come on. We can row later.'

'OK,' he said softly.

Her brow wrinkled and there was urgency in her voice. 'I don't want to be late.'

'We have plenty of time.'

Jack stood up. 'It's been a pleasure.'

She took his hand. 'You have to forgive me. I must go. I'm expecting someone.'

'Yes, yes, of course.'

Jack watched as Samuel pushed her up the wheelchair ramp at the side of the building and in through the double doors. She was such a strange creature, not at all what he'd imagined the residents would be like.

He felt in his pockets for his cigarettes; he searched the table, the bench. They were gone.

Strolling back inside he was about to go back to his father's room when he stopped suddenly at the nurses' station. He felt in his pockets again, this time for change. 'Excuse me, I don't suppose there's a payphone I could use?'

The Underground train swayed from side to side, windows open. Rush hour was over. Cate sat alone in the front carriage, her bag on her lap. Crumpled newspapers blew through the empty car like urban tumbleweeds. More news of Brussels and the repeal of Section 28 filled the headlines.

Cate looked out into the darkness of the tunnel. Her conversation with Alice had left her feeling hollowed out with frustration and hopelessness. She'd wanted so badly to know the truth. Now she knew and instead of making her feel calmer or resolved, it left her drained and disillusioned. Despite all her glamour and beauty, Baby was disposable.

The train rattled round a bend. Another newspaper floated down the aisle, caught in the wind. It landed in front of her. The sales had started early again this year. And that red-headed actress from *EastEnders* was getting married. Was that the first or second time for her?

Cate stared hard at the picture of the smiling, young actress. It reminded her of something; something she was so sure she'd seen somewhere but hadn't quite registered. Opening her bag, she lifted out the shoebox. She'd had a feeling that she should take it with her, just in case. But in the end she hadn't shown it to anyone, least of all Alice.

Taking the lid off, she unwrapped the shoes. Only this time, instead of focusing on the objects, she smoothed out the crumpled old newspaper. On one side were some advertisements – fur storage, slimming girdles and health elixirs. She turned it over.

Like a camera lens readjusting, suddenly what was vague and formless came into view.

Of course. Alice and Baby had been collecting paper that day. Until Baby didn't come back . . .

How many times had she held it in her hands yet never made the connection?

The train pulled into a station.

It was a copy of *The Times*, Births and Marriages from 3 June 1941.

Midway down was a six-line entry.

'Mr Nicholas Warburton and his new bride, the Canadian oil heiress, Pamela Van Outen, were married in a small civil ceremony in St James's yesterday afternoon. They were joined by the bride's parents afterwards for a luncheon at Claridge's before flying via New York to Ontario where they will live.

The doors closed. The train sped off into the tunnel. thick and black.

It didn't take much to change the course of a person's life. Just a few lines in a newspaper.

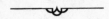

Walking back to his father's room, Jack found him awake, reading glasses on, looking through the photocopied pages. The writing case was on his lap. He looked up when Jack came in.

'Dad.'

'Hello,' his father grinned, looking at him over the top of his glasses. 'It's been a while, son.'

'Yes, too long, too long.' Jack reached out, took his father's hand. 'I've missed you.'

'Have you now?' Henry gave it a squeeze. 'So, here you are. At last.'

'Nice place you've got here. Do you like it?'

'It'll do. And thank you. I can see you've brought me a little something to keep me entertained.'

'Yes, well –' Jack settled himself back on the corner of the bed – 'I was doing a job in Devon and came across it. Endsleigh. Do you know it?'

'No, but I can see from this material that it has connections to the Blythe girls.'

'That's right.'

'It's a nice piece. Good-quality wood and inlay. What is it? Victorian?'

'Yes.'

'And you bought it for me?'

'Actually –' Jack felt himself blushing – 'I bought it for someone else.'

'A woman?' his father deduced.

'Yes. A woman. She has a particular interest in the Blythe sisters.'

'And you're trying to impress her.'

Jack nodded. 'Of course.'

'You've done this before. I seem to recall a mirror some years back.'

'Yes, well, this girl's different.'

'They're all different. We're the ones who stay the same.'

'Trouble is, the damn thing's locked.'

His father put down the pages and turned the box over. 'Let's see what we can do about that.' He concentrated, feeling along the bottom of the box. 'Sometimes these things have a hidden panel . . . How long have you been here, anyway?'

'Not too long. I was out in the garden. Chatting to a little old woman.'

'You'll have to be more specific. This place is full of little old women.'

'That's true.' Jack smiled. He'd obviously caught his father on a good day. 'But this one was . . . I don't know how to describe it . . . very unusual. She had very blue eyes and the most extraordinary way of speaking. Like someone in a Noël Coward play.'

'Ah! Mrs Healy.'

'Is that her name?'

Henry turned the box over on its side. 'Was she reading a French newspaper?'

'Yeah, that's the one!'

'She charms everyone. Hand me that letter opener, will you? The one on the desk.'

Jack got the letter opener and handed it to him. 'Where is she from?'

'No one's really sure. She's been here forever, it seems.' He slipped the edge of the opener into a tiny gap in one corner. 'Was sent here during the war as a suspected typhoid carrier; locked in solitary confinement for years. That was before antibiotics, when people used to be quarantined. I believe she's been diagnosed as delusional, possibly schizophrenic. Though to be honest she's always struck me as quite lucid, if a bit affected.'

'Are you telling me she's been here for over fifty years? Doesn't she have any family?'

He shook his head. 'If she does, they don't want to know.'

'That's shocking!'

'She's from another age, Jack. And another class. Out of sight, out of mind.'

'But she said she was expecting someone?' Jack got up and held the top of the case steady for him.

'Yes, they all say that. Mrs Healy is always expecting someone. She has been for years.'

Jack watched as he jimmied the opener along, easing it gently towards the central hinge at the back. The case began to creak, then suddenly the back hinge snapped, falling away in a single piece, leaving the box unharmed.

'How did you learn how to do that?' he asked.

'Old trade secret.' Henry opened it up. 'Hello! What's this?'

When Cate arrived home, she put her bag down in the hallway. It slid off her shoulder, landing on the faded green carpet with a thud. She'd taken such care with the box; the objects inside. But now she simply wanted to walk away from it; to forget the whole thing.

'Hello! Hello?'

She'd hoped Rachel would be there but she was out. The flat was empty. And not for the first time, it struck her as overcrowded, its interior too dark and and frozen in time. When she first came back from New York it had comforted her. Now it seemed too big and even faintly ridiculous for one person.

She wandered into the kitchen, opening the fridge, digging around among the leftovers, even though she wasn't hungry. Closing it, she filled the kettle instead, moving mechanically, numbly; switching it on, though the last thing she wanted was a cup of tea. She didn't know what she wanted, only that it wasn't here. She couldn't find it. And she didn't know where to look any more.

There was a note on the kitchen table.

*'Jack rang while you were out. Left a message, on the machine, which I don't understand – a private joke, perhaps? He just says, No more excuses, Katie.'*

She stared at it.

Read it again.

The kettle boiled.

She sat down.

*No more excuses.*

It was written on the back of a telephone bill, two months over due.

Closing her eyes, she pressed the moment into her memory, feeling her whole body warm.

Fate could rebuild a heart as quickly as it destroyed it.

Henry took out several stacks of tightly bound letters, wrapped together with string. The paper was brittle and yellow with age, the handwriting bold and distinctive, despite the faded ink. He handed a sheaf to Jack. Some were opened, clustered in groups, and others were still sealed, as if they'd never even been posted.

Jack pushed the string back to see the addresses on the stack that remained sealed, flicking through. Every single one was addressed, to 'Hon. Nicholas Warburton, Belmont, Mayfair, London'.

'Good God, Dad!'

'Yes.' Henry stroked his chin thoughtfully. 'Yes. Exactly.'

'This is private correspondence. From the Blythe sisters.'

'All except this one.' He passed an unopened letter to Jack. 'This one's got very different handwriting.'

Jack took it, blinking in disbelief. 'Do you realise what we've got here?'

'Yes, I think I do.' He looked at his son, his eyes alive with a gleam of excitement Jack hadn't seen in years. 'Question is, will that new girlfriend of yours be impressed?'

*The Great House*
*Ontario, Can.*

*15 September 1941*

*My dearest girl,*
*I have not heard from you for so long and this is my final attempt*
*to contact you. I am sending this to your sister because I have tried*
*every other address I can think of and no one, no one I know, will*
*tell me where you are.*

   *I well understand that you're disappointed in me, perhaps*
*you hate me too much to reply and this letter is in vain, and*
*yet I must try one more time. I never thought I'd have to write*
*this. Please, believe me when I say it has broken me, utterly,*
*to embark upon the actions that I have taken. If there had been*
*any other way, I wouldn't have done it. But they found me,*
*my dear one, in an act I won't pain you to describe. And the*
*penalty this time would not have been avoided. I had to leave*
*the country, my love, or go to prison. And the only way was*
*to make an arrangement with the only other woman I knew*
*who would understand and who could take me out of the*
*country in time.*

   *I do not love her. There's only one woman I've ever loved and*
*that's you. But I could not go to jail. It's no good – I haven't the*
*courage for it.*

*I am a man not worthy of you. I know this. I have always known it. From the very first time I saw you, weeping in that hotel in Paris, I have felt bound to you. I have never told you how I stood a little, watching you, before I approached. In all truth, I had never seen anyone so beautiful or so completely, so charmingly unaware of it. And when you began to speak and your thoughts came tumbling out in that disarming way they do, I knew without doubt that I had found my soul's equal; my finer, more perfect self. Even though you were only a child then, it took every ounce of self-control to leave you. As it takes every ounce of self-control to leave you now.*

*My love for you has always been so hugely, so terribly flawed, through my own foulness of being, that part I wish I could tear out of me and thrash into conformity. What sort of creature am I that I cause harm to the one person I love above all else? I know for all my fine words that you are better off without me. Mine is a compromising, soiling obsession that rots everything it comes in contact with. I cannot bear to have it defile you.*

*And yet, could it be that you could forgive me?*

*I have no right to ask you, but if you do, please send word. I will come back for you. I will find you. I will get a divorce and we will start again in some other corner of this wide, wounded world. You see, it is as you have always said, life is one long series of catastrophes. Especially, when like me, you have very large, very determined feet of clay. But I would give anything to spend my days stumbling alongside you.*

*There is not one part of me that won't shrink and die without you. There is not one moment when I will not regret the very air*

*I breathe. I am inadequate, a complete failure in the very task of loving and yet I love you. I love you. Badly. Stupidly. As clumsily and as greedily and as hopelessly as a child. And I would not, for all the world, have you believe otherwise.*

   *I am broken.*

   *Nick*

The air was cooler now; heavy with the promise of rain. It had been a glorious summer so far, the hottest in history. And yet it was a relief when the sheer unbearable brilliance and heat of the sun softened. There's a nostalgic tenderness, a delicacy about a true English summer. It's a fragile, fleeting thing; more of an apparition than an actual event. The grass was damply fragrant and the first fallen leaves crunched beneath the feet of the people who passed by the bench on Primrose Hill. Cate pulled her cardigan more tightly around her shoulders.

It was evening. The sunset was gradual, a fading out of the light, leaving the sky streaked by pink and lavender, melting into strips of deepest navy blue. New York was gone now. London spread out before her, older, convoluted, defined by paradoxes and a series of familiar historical landmarks, their outlines vague in the distance.

Suddenly a pair of white Labradors cut across the hill, almost glowing against the darkening horizon, chasing each other. She couldn't help but smile at them; couldn't help but admire their boundless enthusiasm; their cheerful ignorance of anything beyond the present moment.

And behind them was Jack, walking up the hill towards her.

Some people disappoint when you see them again after a while. The imagination constructs an impossible image that the reality can't begin to approach. But as Cate watched him making his way towards her, she felt a physical certainty and exhilaration that far exceeded any expectation.

He stood before her, catching his breath a little from the climb, a messenger bag slung across his shoulder.

She inclined her head. 'Mr Coates.'

'Katie.' He sat down next to her, placing the bag carefully at his feet and turned, looking at her with a wide, knowing smile.

'What is it?' she laughed, suddenly self-conscious.

'Kiss me.'

'What?' Her heart pounded; instantly she felt about twelve years old. 'Just like that? Kiss me?'

But before she could go on, he pulled her towards him, his mouth over hers.

He kissed her softly, slowly, her eyelids, cheeks, the slender arc of her neck. She kissed the bridge of his nose, his chin, pulling him closer, relaxing into his embrace, until the kisses grew harder, longer, more urgent, and they had to pull apart from one another.

The dogs had settled now, exhausted in the grass, curled round one another in an easy, lolling heap.

'Are you hungry?' he asked, gathering himself.

'OK.' She nodded, pulling her cardigan back up. 'Sure.'

'The usual, my love?'

She smiled. 'Yes, darling.'

They got up.

'Have I missed something, Mr Coates?' she asked softly, leaning her head on his shoulder.

He turned to face her. 'No more excuses.' His face was serious, his gaze sure, direct. 'No excuses any more.'

'All right then,' she agreed, knowing herself to be stepping off an inner precipice. Only this time it wasn't into a void. It was solid, real. And more terrifying for it. 'No excuses.'

'Oh, and I have something for you.' He tapped the bag. There was that smile again. 'I think you'll like it.'

'Do you now?'

'Oh, my little mistress of innuendo!'

They were heading down, towards the Greek restaurant on the Regents Park Road.

She stopped. 'Of course, we could always get a take away . . . later.'

'I make world class eggs.'

'Prove it.'

He held out his hand. 'Linger with me, Katie.'

'Yes.' She took it. 'Yes, I'd like that.'

They didn't look remarkable; not in the least. Just a couple, like half a dozen other couples that evening, walking through the park on their way home. Yet no one would guess what it cost them, to be there, speaking tenderly, teasingly.

For to love.

Again.

Will always be the most daring, dangerous thing of all.

# Author's Note

There have been several key influences that have inspired the writing of this book that I'd like to acknowledge and share with the reader. The first one is the most important to me, namely because it concerns a dear friend of mine.

About a year ago, I had the idea of writing a novel in which a wayward heroine in present day London, stumbles across a mystery concerning a glamorous young debutante from the late 1920s and, as the book develops, their lives and choices began to parallel one another. I was also intrigued by the notion that the story should take place in the Victoria and Albert Museum, mainly because I found it such a fascinating and evocative building.

In my grand scheme, my main character should be called in to help inventory its contents and discover a letter (or some such useful device) that sets her off, uncovering this other woman's life and that all the "clues" for the mystery should be out in the open – displayed in the vast collection of the V&A. For example, the designer dress the debutante wore on a significant evening would be on show in the fashion department, a custom-made bracelet hidden in the jewellery department, a provocative portrait in the archives of the photography department and so on. I was thrilled by my seemingly brilliant concept.

Only, once I began to write, I became rapidly overwhelmed with the scale of the V&A, the scope of researching so many different departments and disciplines, and the task of orchestrating the increasing number of characters which came with writing about a national institution of that size. I wanted the book to be a fast-paced, lean mystery. Instead I was trudging through lumbering explanations and unintentional crowd scenes.

One evening I was moaning to my friend, fellow writer Annabel Giles, on the phone. 'I just can't seem to get them all under control,' I complained. 'What you need,' she suggested, 'is to narrow the whole thing down. You don't need a museum – you need something more manageable, like a shoebox.' She paused. 'In fact, I have a shoebox.' Then she began to laugh. "How would you like a real challenge?"

A week later, she met me in London and handed me a fragile shoebox she'd come across years ago. It was from the 1930s and contained a pair of tiny, silver mesh dancing shoes. I was to discover later that, packed underneath the newspaper, she'd thoughtfully hidden a selection of unrelated objects, including a photograph of a handsome sailor, a beautiful Tiffany bracelet, and an old badge from her girls boarding school. (There was also a spoon, some lace, a brooch in the shape of a butterfly and other objects

I wasn't able to incorporate into my tale. I really tried to write about the spoon but it, in particular, proved quite tricky.) 'Now,' she instructed me, in her best head girl voice, 'you can use a few or all of the objects in any way you choose. But they must add up to the resolution of your mystery. Oh, and you're not allowed to even look at the objects in the box until you've written up to the point in the story where your main character finds it. Then it will really be a surprise!'

And it was.

That's how the book really began. Annabel was right, of course. I didn't need an entire collection of rare treasures on display in one of the world's largest museums. The shoebox was more real and far more human. One of her many gifts as a friend is her ability to slice right through my grandiosity and get to the nub of the thing.

The inspiration for the characters of Irene and Diana "Baby" Blythe was culled from many well known sources – the Mitford sisters, Zita Jungman, the Curzon sisters, Thelma Furness, Viscountess Furness and Gloria Morgan Vanderbilt. These woman have inspired many with their beauty and paradoxical natures and I'm not the first to be intrigued by them. However, the closing revelations of the book were influenced by two remarkable true stories in the national press.

The first one came out just after the Queen Mother died, in April, 2002, when it was discovered that two of her first cousins, Katherine and Nerissa Bowes-Lyon, daughters of the Hon. John Herbert Bowes-Lyon (the second son of the 14th Earl of Strathmore and Kinghorn and brother of the Queen Mother) and the Hon. Fenella Hepburn-Stuart-Forbes-Trefusis, had been locked away in the Royal Earlswood Hospital at Redhill, Surrey for some sixty years. They arrived at the mental institution, aged fifteen and twenty-two, in 1941. Both were said to be severely mentally-handicapped. Such was the shame of the family at having handicapped children that Nerissa was listed in Burke's Peerage as having died in 1940 and Katherine was listed as having died in 1961. In this way, they simply ceased to exist anymore. The family rarely visited them and the royal household never acknowledged them.

They were later joined by three of their first cousins who had all been certified as mentally disturbed. Daughters of the Hon. Harriet Hepburn-Stuart-Forbes-Trefusis and Major Henry Nevile Fane – Indonea Fane (known by staff as "Baby"), Etheldreda Flavia Fane and Rosemary Jean Fane – were admitted to The Royal Earlswood Hospital, all on the same day. When Nerissa died in the mid-1980s, she was buried at Redhill Cemetery (at first there was only a plastic tag with a serial number on it to mark her grave, though there is a headstone now). Katherine (called "Lady" by staff) was then moved to Ketwin House – a care home for the mentally disabled where she was joined by Indonea.

Ketwin House was eventually closed in 2001 amidst allegations of sexual, physical and financial abuse of its patients. The fees to keep Katherine Bowes-Lyon at Ketwin House were paid for by the NHS, despite her family's wealth.

Katherine is apparently still alive and a resident of an unidentified nursing home in Surrey.

The second story is more recent. In July 2008 it was revealed that more than forty women suffering from typhoid had been locked up for life in a large red brick Victorian mental asylum in Long Grove in Epsom, Surrey between 1907 and 1992. It was reported that, although they were sane when admitted, many went mad as a result of their incarceration, though painfully, some remained completely compos mentis despite the hardship they endured. Many had families, jobs and children, yet were forgotten by everyone and detained in prison-like conditions, some for up to sixty years. Despite the advent of antibiotic treatments in the 1950s, the women continued to be detained for the rest of their lives on the grounds that their mental health was compromised. The information only came to light when researchers found two volumes of records in the derelict building, long after its closure.

I hope these postscripts have been helpful. As you can see, the writing process for me is a series of elaborate plans, predictable failures, and occasional divine interventions. If I've made an error regarding my historical facts, I apologize in advance and assure you it wasn't intentional. I'm extremely grateful for my readership and for the privilege of being a published author. I can hardly wait to see what fresh follies the next book will bring, so, if anyone had any interesting shoeboxes lying around, feel free to fill them up and send them my way!

KATHLEEN TESSARO